Do What Matters

DIANN SHOPE

DEDICATION

This novel is dedicated to the main guys in my life:

Steve, Russ, Ed, Scott, Michael, Carter, and Owen.

CONTENTS

ACKNOWLEDGEMENTS

I would like to thank three of my neighbors for being "beta readers" for me. Leslie Herlich is a high school English and drama teacher, and parent of two now-grown teens; her input on high schoolers was very helpful. Libby Hill and Sarah Beshlian, also parents of teens, were kind enough to read the manuscript and give me feedback.

Also, thanks to Michael Shope and Mary Howland for advising me on aspects of teenage slang.

Carrie Wicks did a fine job of copy editing. I learned a lot from her, and she not only caught mistakes, but also pointed out places where I could make improvements. Any remaining mistakes are entirely my own.

Bob Lanphear turned out another zowie cover for me. Since covers are key to getting people to look at a book, I really appreciate Bob's creativity and attention to detail.

And many, many thanks to my friends and family, who have offered ongoing encouragement and tireless support.

1 THE BEACH

Scanning the crowded beach and swimming area at Madrona Park from the high lifeguard's chair, Paul Emory pushed his sunglasses back up on his nose, slippery with sunscreen and sweat. Most of the time he could keep his focus on the job, but occasionally his mind wandered. A year from now he'd be leaving for college. Meanwhile, what would his senior year bring? The fall play and spring musical, the Outdoor Program, some heavy-duty classes, maybe a girlfriend. He dragged his mind back to his job.

It seemed as though everyone had come to enjoy the treat of swimming in Lake Washington in the hot—for Seattle—late summer weather. The park was long and narrow, wedged between the shore and Lake Washington Boulevard, with trees, lawn, and picnic tables to the north of the elegant old brick bathhouse and the sandy swimming beach to the south. It was filled with sunbathers, swimmers, children playing in the shallows, picnickers, dog walkers, boaters: they were all there. The lifeguards were on full alert.

Paul's light-brown hair was bleached by a summer in the sun, his lean six-foot body very tan. On his way to tell an elderly dog owner he couldn't have the dog on the beach, Paul picked his way through the crowd of sunbathers, trying not to be too distracted by the girls in skimpy swimsuits who were doing everything they could to get his attention. As he approached, a group of four girls leaped up from their towels and ran down to the water, shrieking and splashing each other. He smiled to himself and pretended not to notice.

However, he couldn't help noticing his ex-girlfriend, Jennifer, and her boyfriend, Raj, as they arranged their blanket on the sandy beach. Paul didn't have any regrets about splitting with Jennifer, but he still wondered why it took him so long to figure out what an airhead she was. He'd been blinded by her good looks, and she had definitely come on to him. They'd been together for about three months of their junior year when she dumped him for Raj and his BMW convertible.

He watched her look around to see whom she knew, and who was watching her. When she saw him, she wiggled her fingers in a little wave and immediately turned to Raj, assuming a provocative pose that showed off her very hot body and minimal bikini.

*****

"Bicycle Built for Two" blared, annoying and repetitious, as the ice-cream truck pulled into the Madrona Beach parking lot. For Georgina, the driver, this was the most—the only—exciting time of the day, since she might see Paul Emory. She'd had a crush on him since they were both freshmen.

Strands escaped from the cap covering her dark-blonde hair, curling around her face and neck in the heat. Her uniform was smudged with ice cream. Georgina had beautiful hazel eyes in an otherwise unremarkable face. But when she smiled, an openness came through that was generally hidden behind her shy demeanor.

She was immediately surrounded by customers. Though she was busy, she couldn't help noticing Stan, standing patiently on the outskirts of the crowd. He was hard to miss—very tall and about seventy-five pounds overweight, with his almost pretty face, his black curly hair and complexion any girl would die for. She sighed inwardly, hoping she could make a quick escape. She and Stan had been partners in chemistry lab last year, and he seemed to think she was the only girl in the world, just because she had talked to him like he was a real person. Off-the-charts smart, he had jumped ahead two grades, though he acted more like a sophomore than a senior. He'd asked her out a couple of times, but she'd managed face-saving excuses not to go. Why couldn't he get the hint and ask someone else?

All her customers were gone but Stan, who smiled happily and said, "Hi, George, how's it going?"

"Hi, Stan, it's fine. Only another hour and I'm done for the day, and only two more days till I'm done for the summer."

"Two fudgesicles, please. And, uh, would you like to go to a movie tonight?"

Before she could think of an excuse, Paul appeared. "Hey, Stan, George. My break is just about over—I've just got time to get a fudgesicle, if you've got any left."

"Can you wait a minute, Stan?" she asked, hoping Paul would be gone before she had to answer Stan.

"Sure, I've got plenty of time." He smiled genially and told Paul, "I just asked her to the movies tonight."

Georgina flushed bright red as she took Paul's money and gave him change and his fudgesicle.

She thought she caught some sympathy in his easy smile as he left, saying, "Well, have fun. See ya. I gotta get back to work."

"So, would you like to see a movie with me tonight?" Stan asked again.

Georgina was pretty sure he wouldn't get the hint, even if she turned him down again with another excuse. She'd have to figure out a way to tell him directly, and try not to hurt his feelings. "OK, how about *Midnight in Paris* at the Crest?"

He looked like he'd won the lottery. "Great! I'll check the time and call you about when I'll be by to pick you up." He lumbered off down the beach with his fudgesicles.

Georgina turned on the recording and began the last loop of the day. She was mortified at what Stan had said to Paul. What would Paul think of her, going on a date with someone like Stan? Well, what did it matter? Paul would never have any interest in her anyway. And she wanted to believe he was too nice a guy to make fun of her or Stan. So she'd just pretend it never happened and daydream about what it would be like to go out with Paul, as she'd been daydreaming for three years.

*****

As Paul walked back to his post, his ex, Jennifer, came up behind him and splashed him. "Hey, Paul, how's your summer going?" she asked, giving him a big smile.

"Just fine. Only two weeks of work to go. How's yours?"

"Oh, just great! I've been sailing in the San Juans, and our family went to Spain for a month. It's going to be a real bore going back to school. So I'm planning a back-to-school party on Labor Day. Why don't you come? Bring friends, your brother, whoever you want."

"I have to work that day, but I'll think about it. Thanks for the invitation. See ya—got to get back to work." He walked back down the beach, wondering what that was all about. In the bathhouse storage room he rummaged through his pack, looking for a towel to wipe off his sticky face. Keisha and Sunny, his coworkers, were about to exchange places. They stood talking for a moment outside the storage room door before taking up their new posts, unaware that Paul could hear them.

"Did you see that slut, Jennifer, coming on to Paul?" said Sunny. "You'd think she'd leave him alone after she dumped him for that rich guy from Lakeside."

"Well, she isn't exactly the 'Do unto others' type is she? More like the 'Screw others to get what I want' type." Keisha looked disdainfully down the beach at Jennifer and her boyfriend. "Paul's such a nice guy, you wonder what he saw in her."

"Well, I doubt he'll make the same mistake again—he's too smart for that. Do you know his brother, Drew? What a hunk—an Armani face and a Jockey body."

"I've never had any classes with him," said Keisha, "but I know who you mean—he's pretty hard to miss. They call him Abercrombie, don't they?"

"Yeah, and he just laughs it off. I can't believe a guy that hot isn't conceited, but he's just as nice as Paul." Sunny's gaze swept the beach as she talked. "Well, what do you know—there he is, talking with that bunch of girls on the blue blanket. OK, back to work, girl."

*****

From the lifeguard's chair Paul watched his brother strolling down the beach, stopping to chat and joke with friends and acquaintances.

Drew must have come straight from his landscaping job to have a swim before dinner. No doubt about it, his brother was attractive to girls. Thinking about the conversation he'd just overheard, Paul couldn't help feeling complimented, but it was disconcerting to know that his classmates were speculating and talking about his recent relationship. Did they talk about him and his first girlfriend too? Did they talk about everybody's relationships? Was it just a girl thing?

Paul was a typical firstborn—a leader, with a strong sense of accountability and responsibility, serious about doing well in whatever he did. With his blue eyes and light-colored hair, he resembled his father. Drew, a year younger and a little taller than Paul, had his mother's dark hair and eyes; he was more easygoing and unconventional than his brother, always happy to have a good time, liked being a little on the edge. Both brothers were heavily into aikido and outdoor activities—hiking, climbing, camping, kayaking. Paul had joined the school's drama program as a freshman, and Drew played trumpet in the jazz band.

"Hey, dude, s'up?" It was Paul's friend Ron and his girlfriend Polly. They talked for a few minutes about what classes they'd be taking and soccer practice starting, and Ron invited Paul to join them for pizza and a movie after he got off work. Ron and Polly dropped their stuff nearby and went down to the water for a swim.

His mind back on his job, Paul noticed a young couple with a toddler walking along the beach. The couple spread out a blanket away from the main swimming area while the child played in the sand at the water's edge. He had a little rubber toy he'd throw into the water—again and again—and then watch it float in. Each time he picked it up, he'd venture a little farther into the water. A few minutes later, as Paul scanned the beach, he noticed the couple with the baby were into some heavy-duty making out, not paying much attention to the toddler, who was still playing with his toy.

Sunny came up from the water's edge, where she'd been patrolling, and stood beside him. They watched a big cabin cruiser approach, going too fast near the float and swimming area. She said, "He thinks he's doing us a favor, making surfing waves, the idiot!" They watched the float rock wildly back and forth and the boat's wake crash on the shore. Paul looked down the beach just in time to see one of the big waves knock over the toddler, who was facedown in the water in an instant. Paul jumped down from his chair and ran down the beach, dodging couples, coolers, picnic baskets, and water toys, and grabbed the child, thrashing and sputtering, out of the water. The baby began to cry, finding himself in the arms of a stranger and his nose full of water. Since the child had wandered farther and farther from them, the couple didn't even hear him.

"Hey, little guy, it's OK—you're going to be fine," Paul tried to reassure him, as he carried the child toward the couple, who were still acting as if they were in their bedroom.

"Excuse me, this is your baby, isn't it? I just pulled him out of the water. He got knocked down by a wave." Paul was trying to keep the anger out of his voice.

"Hey, Frankie, where you been?" the guy drawled to the baby. He turned to Paul. "Dude, thanks. I'm sure he's fine. He's real independent. No problem." The guy sounded drunk.

The toddler was really crying now. "He doesn't sound fine to me, and if I hadn't fished him out, he could have drowned. You need to pay more attention."

"I don't need advice from a fuckin' lifeguard, dude. Get the hell out of here!"

The woman got up and took the child from Paul's arms, saying, "Come on, Johnny, don't pick a fight. He's just trying to help." To Paul, she said, "Thanks, I'll take him."

Johnny chose to be insulted, rather than chastened. He stood up and said belligerently, "You trying to tell me how to take care of my own son, man? Who the hell do you think you are?"

The woman said, "Johnny, leave it. All he did was tell you Frankie fell in the water. It's time to go get some dinner."

"No, he's out of line—I want an apology!"

"You want an apology because I kept your kid from drowning while you weren't watching him? No way!" Paul turned to leave, but Johnny grabbed his arm and jerked him back around. "I want an apology, dude!"

Paul pulled his arm away and the woman stepped between them. "Johnny, come on. Let's go get some dinner. Me and Frankie are hungry. Let's go."

"Oh, all right! He's a fuckin' jerk! Let's get out of here." He began picking up the baby's clothes and the blanket.

People who knew him well would have noticed the slight frown and clenched jaw that meant Paul Emory was angry as he returned to the guard's chair.

*****

Sunny was on the float, having traded places with Keisha, who now stood a few feet away from Paul, surveying the beach. Their shift was almost over. The sun was low in the sky and people were beginning to leave. The crowd was thinning out. "Hey, Paul, Keisha, how's it goin'?" called a girl as she and a friend trudged through the sand on their way to the refreshment stand. It was Shaunee Brown, one of his brother's jazz band friends. He waved and tried to get his mind back on the job. This beach was packed with nothing but gorgeous girls!

He felt a poke in the ribs. "Hey, Bro. You almost through? I thought we could go out to eat—Mom and Dad are going out with Grams and Will for dinner, so we're on our own." Drew leaned against the lifeguard stand and took a long drink from a water bottle.

"Yeah, fifteen minutes and we're done. Ron and Polly invited me for pizza and a movie. Want to come?"

Just then their attention was drawn to the refreshment stand about fifty yards away, from which they heard yelling and laughing and angry voices. Shaunee was gesticulating and shouting at a short but well-muscled young man in green basketball shorts, who was shouting back at her. Three other young African American men lounged against a car with cans of beer in their hands, egging on the arguing pair. Then things began to escalate: he poked her shoulder with his finger, she slapped his face, he grabbed her wrist.

"I'm callin' the cops," said Keisha, who pulled her cell out of her shorts pocket and punched in 911. Paul shouted through the megaphone, "Hey, you in the green shorts! Let go of her and get out of here! We've called the police." The beers were tossed into a garbage can as the young men jumped into the car, except for Green Pants, who finally let go of Shaunee, giving her a little shove.

"Come on, James, get in the car!" urged one of his friends.

Keisha charged up the hill toward the altercation, Paul and Drew right beside her. She was about five feet ten, and a competitive swimmer. No one messed with Keisha.

James nonchalantly gave them the finger and got in the car, as the sound of a siren grew louder. They drove off down Lake Washington Boulevard.

"You OK, Shaunee?" asked Drew when they reached her. "He didn't hurt you, did he?"

Tears were running down her face, and she was rubbing her wrist. "Fucking bastard! I'm gonna kill that guy one of these days!" But she minimized the incident with them and the police, said she was fine, and it was just a personal feud that would blow over. She didn't want to talk about it.

It was time for the lifeguards to go off duty. Drew offered to help and the four of them put out the "No Lifeguard on Duty" signs, picked up trash, carried in the dinghy and paddleboard, and got ready to leave. Paul was silent and scowling as they worked, thinking about what he'd like to have said to the negligent father and to James, whoever he was. "We got some real sweethearts today, didn't we?" he said as they left the bathhouse and he locked the door behind them.

"Yeah," Sunny said. "I feel sorry for that little kid. Looks like he's in for a life of neglect—if not worse."

"He won't exactly have a great role model."

"Well, I'm glad the guy didn't start a fight, anyway. Forget about him, Paul—go do something fun. See you tomorrow."

"Yeah, Paul," Keisha added, "don't waste your time thinkin' about that trash."

Paul and Drew walked down the nearly empty beach, speculating about who James was and the cause of the argument between him and Shaunee. Ron and Polly met them at the parking lot, carrying their blankets and cooler. "Shall we check out the pizza place in Madison Park?" she asked.

"Sounds good to me. We'll meet you there. I'll go with Drew," said Paul. "I'm glad you guys are here—I could use some distraction." He told them about the toddler episode and the altercation Shaunee was involved in. They loaded Paul's bike into the back end of the brothers' old pickup truck and talked about their movie options.

At dinner Paul was unusually quiet. Ron said, "Hey, dude, life's too short to spend it thinking about some asshole. Think about what matters—we've got a great year coming up!"

2 THE PAPER ROUTE

Two thousand teenagers brought their hormones and boredom and rebellion and high spirits to the halls of Eisenhower High as school began. It had been as crisp and colorful a September as Seattle could offer, but rainy and colder than normal for October as Paul took Drew through the route for the *Capitol Hill Times* weekly bulk delivery, which he was turning over to Drew. Each Wednesday night for two years Paul had picked up about twenty-five hundred copies of the neighborhood-oriented paper at the printer on the east side of Lake Washington, then delivered them in bound stacks to cafes, barber shops, coffeehouses, hospitals, and apartments on Capitol Hill, finishing about one in the morning. The Emory brothers were eating hamburgers at Dick's Drive-In on Broadway, having interrupted their route for some sustenance. They were discussing the neighborhood paper route they'd walked as little boys, first Paul and then Drew.

"There was that lady on Galer who always had the window shades pulled," said Paul, punching his straw into the plastic cover of his milk shake. "As long as I can remember, every shade in the house has been down. When I first started delivering the paper—I think I was about ten—I was a little scared to go to that house to collect. But the old lady was nice enough. She always paid me. Why do you think she always had the shades pulled?" Paul asked his brother before biting into his burger.

"I don't know. I wondered about that too when I went with you on your route, but after a while, I just didn't think about it anymore." Drew dipped a french fry in ketchup.

"This paper route is a really sweet deal," Paul told his brother. "I wouldn't give it up, if I didn't have so much going on this year—I don't even think I'll have time to be in the fall play. I'll just have to dig into my savings for spending money."

"Yeah, well, your loss is my gain, Bro. I'm looking forward to having some regular income. You can't buy much mountaineering gear on the summer pay from shoveling dirt for a landscaper."

They finished their burgers and then the route, as Paul pointed out the peculiarities of each delivery stop. He had honed the route to perfection, to spend as little time and gas as possible.

*****

The next Wednesday evening, Drew was on his own. He thought he'd pick up the papers early in order to finish earlier, so he left Seattle about five thirty, heading east across the floating bridge. The lake was gray with a strong southwesterly wind blowing spray across the traffic. Big mistake. Peak rush-hour traffic, going slower than usual due to the weather. By the time he arrived at the printer, frazzled from the stop-and-go driving in the twenty-year-old stick shift, it had taken an hour longer than it would have taken had he left at eight, as Paul had instructed. He got out of the truck and slammed the door, walking toward the loading ramp. No papers. He walked around to the office. Closed. He finally found a door into the noisy pressroom, where one of the guys reminded him that his load of papers wouldn't be ready until about eight thirty—which Paul had also written on the instructions. So he had ninety minutes to kill.

The printer directed him to the Totem Lake Mall, where he got some pad thai and iced tea, did some girl-watching, and then wandered around a sporting goods shop until the time came to pick up his papers. He reread his instructions before leaving the printer and got home, tired and sleepy, about two in the morning.

Each week it was easier and faster. He began to recognize people and get into conversations. The security guy at Harborview Medical Center, an off-duty policeman, found out Drew did aikido and liked to chat about martial arts—the guard had a black belt in karate. The bartender, Sebastian, at the gay bar always offered him a good-natured proposition. The fussy proprietor of the Shantung Tea House watched like a hawk to make sure Drew took away the remaining papers from the previous week.

This evening was going well; he drove down Broadway about one in the morning with only a few more stops before he could go home. He noticed a couple of young women laughing and weaving down the sidewalk in their high-high heels and short-short skirts. One of them looked like Shaunee Brown. Her jazz band nickname was Ella, after the famous jazz singer. Couldn't be—she wouldn't be out here at this hour on a school night, dressed like that. He'd known her since they were freshmen from all the band practices and competitions they'd been in. She was very talented—and very hot.

The next day at band practice he made a point of chatting with her. She looked tired, and was less outgoing than usual. She sang her numbers competently, but without the flair and energy she usually had.

The following Wednesday night he had just about completed his route when he saw Shaunee at the corner of Twelfth and Pike talking to a guy who looked quite a bit older. The guy took her elbow, and she jerked away, moving down the street. The guy followed her, saying something, but she just walked faster. Drew pulled over to the curb and ran across the street. "Hey, Ella, want a ride home? It's on my way." He put his arm around her shoulder and steered her across the street, leaving the guy standing on the sidewalk. She looked panicked, but didn't resist. He opened the truck door for her, and she got in.

"Would you mind sticking with me for another twenty minutes or so, until I finish my deliveries? Then I really will drive you home," he said, as he buckled his seat belt.

"Look, Drew, you don't have to take me home. I appreciate the rescue—that guy was a drag, but you don't have to do this. I . . . was just . . . on my way to meet a friend." She gave him a quick, sidelong glance and began adjusting the strap on her shoulder bag.

"Well, I don't want to interfere—even if I just did—but, uh, I could take your friend home too, if you want," he finished lamely, fiddling with the car keys.

"No, that's OK. I'd appreciate a ride home and it's fine for you to finish your deliveries. I'll call my friend and tell her I've got a ride."

They didn't say much as Drew concentrated on his route, jumping in and out of the truck, dropping and picking up papers at the remaining stops. "OK, all done. Where do you live?" She gave him the address, and they headed down Madison to Twenty-Third, and then south. To ease the awkwardness, he asked, "So, how did you get interested in jazz?"

"My grandfather played the trumpet, like you, and he was in a lot of bands. He wasn't home much—always working—but he and my grandmother raised me, so I grew up with jazz."

"You're really good, Shaunee. You know that, don't you?" He glanced over at her.

"No, I don't really think I've got what it takes," she answered, eyes downcast. She looked over at him. "But thanks for saying that."

"You're kidding! You almost won first place at State last year—as a sophomore. You'll win for sure this year and next year. It's so cool, watching you onstage—you're so . . . *there*, and into the music, and having a good time. How can you say you haven't got what it takes?" He smiled at her and said, "You're just fishing for compliments, girl."

Her face was glum in the dim streetlight. "No, no, I wouldn't do that—I've just been lucky, that's all." She was uncharacteristically quiet; usually she was very outgoing, talkative, joking with everyone in the halls and in band class.

They drove on for a few minutes in silence, then Drew said, "This, uh, whatever it is, will just be between us, OK?"

"What's the matter? Is the white boy afraid people will know he's been with a black girl?" she shot back.

He was startled, first by the sudden change in demeanor, second by the accusation.

"No. I just wanted you to know I wasn't going to be blabbing around school about picking you up at one a.m. on Broadway dressed like a . . ." He stopped. "Wouldn't do much for your reputation, if I did."

Her only response was "Left at the next corner; it's the second house on the right." He pulled up in front of a shabby little house with a bare light bulb hanging from the porch roof and bars on the windows and door. There was a young man sitting on the porch steps.

"Who's that?" Drew asked.

"Oh, that's . . . uh, my . . . cousin. He kind of acts like a big brother. Maybe Grandma called him when I didn't come home on time. Thanks for the ride, Drew. See you at school," she said, her voice flat. She got out of the car quickly.

"Sure you're all right?"

"Yeah, fine, thanks. See you tomorrow," she said, closing the door. He left, wondering if the guy sitting on the steps really was her cousin, and if not, who he was. He looked vaguely familiar.

*****

In the next few weeks, Shaunee missed jazz band practice more and more frequently. He didn't see her as much in the halls between classes as he used to. One day he was standing behind one of her friends at a vending machine, so he said, "Hey, Charlene, you know what's up with Shaunee? I haven't seen her around lately."

"Oh, she's cool, no problem," came the answer, as the girl hurried off with her purchase.

The next night Drew was delivering papers. On his way home, he made his customary stop at Dick's for a quick burger and shake. About to get out of the car, he noticed Shaunee standing at the curb, talking to someone in a black Mercedes. She was bare-legged, wearing very high-heeled shoes, a skirt so short it barely covered her butt, and an unbuttoned, short fuzzy jacket over a skin-tight top that revealed considerable cleavage and a strip of midriff. He considered the situation, trying to decide what to do. He was shocked and angry—she didn't have to do this shit—what the hell was she thinking? She'd seemed embarrassed the night he drove her home. Well, she ought to be, given what she was apparently doing. But being embarrassed meant she wasn't exactly proud of what she was doing, so maybe he could talk her out of it.

He got out of the car and walked up to her. "Hey, girl," he said, putting his arm around her shoulder and pulling her away from the car, "sorry I'm late. Let's get a burger first." She resisted a little, but then went along, his arm around her shoulder not giving her much choice, unless she wanted to make a scene. They walked up to the window and he ordered two burgers, fries, and two shakes.

"You're not going to run away, are you?"

She shook her head.

He let go of her long enough to get his wallet out. Looking back, he saw that the Mercedes was still there. He paid for their food and then made a show of taking all the rest of the cash out of his wallet and stuffing it into her coat pocket. He was relieved there was no one else around besides the Mercedes, and he'd just cashed his monthly paper route check. He put his arm around her shoulders again, and they walked back to his car. The Mercedes took off. Drew opened the door for her, then got in himself, locking the doors.

"Here, this is for you," he said, handing her a foil-wrapped package and a little sack of fries. She unwrapped the burger mechanically and started eating.

"What the hell's going on, Shaunee? You don't have to do this."

"How do you know what I have to do, Abercrombie?" she hissed. "You live in the fancy part of town, you got parents, a job, play the trumpet like Chet Baker. You can have any girl you want— for free. You got it made! You don't know anything about me!"

"I know you're gorgeous and talented and people like you. You could do anything you want!"

"Yeah, right! My mom's a doped-up hooker, my grandma's a part-time secretary at her church and she's got cancer and no medical insurance. Sure, I can do anything I want. Sure, I can go to college— dream on, Drew!" She pulled his money out of her pocket and threw it on the dashboard. "Thanks, but no thanks." She began eating her fries.

He was at a loss. "Jesus, Shaunee, I had no idea. I'm sorry about your family." He paused, and then went on. "I don't mean to say your situation isn't tough, but other people have tough situations and they don't . . ."

"Turn into hookers?" she finished for him. "Well, a lot of them do. Got any solutions for me, Drew?" she asked, taunting him. "And what makes you think you can just walk up and put your arm around me, and stuff me in your car, and tell me what I can and can't do? Fucking males think women are just made for them to order around!" She threw her wadded-up burger bag at the windshield. "Nice of you to at least buy me some food."

There was a long awkward silence in the aged pickup. Drew knew he'd stepped over the line, even though he meant well. Finally he said, "I'm sorry, Shaunee. I guess I shouldn't have butted in. I didn't mean to push you around; it just didn't occur to me you'd take it that way, and I was trying to make it look like we had . . . an appointment . . . or something. But I'd like to help. If I came up with some ideas, would you consider them? Have you made up your mind you haven't got any other choices?"

Her defensive anger evaporated, and tears filled her eyes. She brushed them away with her coat sleeve, glancing at him and then back out the window. "It's not that I've made up my mind, Drew; it's not that I *want* to do this, I just don't see what else I *can* do."

He asked her, between bites, "Who have you talked to about the situation? What does your grandmother think? Don't you have any uncles or aunts? What about the people at your grandma's church? Can they help out?"

"I told my grandma I got a job at McDonald's, so she thinks that's where the money comes from. She'd freak out if she knew what I was doing. She's already lost her daughter, and it would kill her to know what's going on." She brushed the tears away again. They finished their food in silence.

"Shaunee, would you let me try to help? At the very least, couldn't we just brainstorm some possibilities? It sounds like you haven't talked to anyone about this, and maybe there're things you haven't thought about. I just can't take you home and . . ." He paused and then continued, "And drop you off, like nothing's happened."

She stared out the window, twisting a gaudy ring on her middle finger. "OK, Drew. I know you're just trying to be helpful. When shall we talk?"

"Friday night," he answered immediately. "That'll give me time to think about things. I'll pick you up."

"OK, pick me up at seven thirty." He drove her back to her grandmother's house.

Drew couldn't go to sleep. He lay in bed, wide-awake, thinking about Shaunee's situation. He liked her. What was it like for a girl to think this was the only thing she could do—and to actually do it? What would it be like to have to suck someone's cock—a total stranger—or have it rammed up inside you, because you needed money to survive? Not many guys would put up with that. You had to have guts to do this shit! Or be really screwed up. Or both.

It made him sick. And who could help? Should he tell his parents? Should he talk to the school counselor? He needed to protect her privacy; he knew she'd never speak to him again if she felt he was talking about her behind her back.

*****

"Hi, Mom; bye, Mom," Paul said as he came into the kitchen and grabbed one of Drew's three pieces of peanut butter and jam toast and a couple of bananas. "Let's go little brother—we're late."

"Hey, you two," their mother said, looking up from the morning newspaper over her reading glasses, "the dirty laundry in your rooms is starting to rival Mount Rainier and Mount Baker. And the aroma leaves something to be desired."

"This weekend, Mom. Got to be this weekend because I'm out of clean clothes. Drew took my last clean shirt this morning. We're out of here." And they were gone.

On the way to school, Drew gave Paul a two-minute overview of Shaunee's situation. "I decided not to tell Mom and Dad about it—at least not yet. You know how they get when they hear about bad situations with kids. If I can't come up with some ideas, I'll talk to them. This is between you and me, OK?"

"Right, just between us, no problem. What're you going to do?"

"I'm going to do some Googling during my lunch break. I'll start with that and see what I can find. We're getting together Friday night, so I've got to have some good ideas by then, or she'll just write me off. I have a bunch of questions to ask her, to see what she has and hasn't thought about, but I don't have anything concrete yet. One thing I thought about is maybe someone from her grandma's church could help. It's a big church—one of our jazz ensembles played there one Sunday—it was really cool."

He thought while Paul drove. "You know, she's not stupid. She's not into studying and grades, kind of an average student, I think, but I can't understand why she didn't think about trying to find stuff on-line."

"Maybe her friends aren't into online research—her grandmother probably isn't. Maybe she doesn't have her own laptop or smartphone, and didn't know where to go to get online for free and have privacy, like a library. Maybe she tried, but got frustrated— couldn't find what she was looking for. There could be lots of reasons. But I think you should take your laptop when you get together with her, and show her how to find help. Maybe you could walk her through it. Do you think she'll go for it?" They waited at an intersection to make a left-hand turn.

"I don't know. She sounded really down. I don't think she has a lot of confidence," said Drew, rummaging around in his pack for a leftover banana. "I'm afraid she'll tell herself she can't do it. She already said she didn't have what it takes—but she was talking about her singing then. Maybe if I pitch it as a way to help her grandma, and save her grandma from having a hooker granddaughter, maybe she'll really try." Drew waved at a classmate crossing the street in front of them.

"Something else I was thinking, maybe if she thought she could go to college, she'd stop this shit." Drew zipped up his pack. "She's so talented, she could probably get a scholarship to Cornish or the U. They'd be falling all over themselves to give a scholarship to a really talented African American woman, wouldn't they? She could probably sing in clubs for extra money, or waitress, or do whatever other college students do. There're all kinds of possibilities."

"Drew, think about the differences between her and us," said his brother, pulling into the school parking lot. "We've got parents and grandparents with a ton of education. They have lots of experience in the world, lots of connections, they know how to get things done. What would it be like not to have any of that? It's good for you to be encouraging and give her ideas, but don't assume she'll be all hopeful and positive, like you are."

Drew was psyched to help; he could hardly wait for lunch so he could start his research. He booted up his laptop and Googled "medical help for elderly." Too general, but he noticed states are all supposed to have some kind of help for low-income elderly. He tried again and added "Washington State." There he found the Department of Social and Health Services, which looked like the mother lode. He searched the site for another twenty minutes and took some notes. Good stuff. He was pleased.

3 THE PRESIDENT

Both boys were home for dinner and then back at school for a seven thirty meeting of the school's Outdoor Program. They had been active in the program since they were freshmen, but Drew especially had been tireless in behind-the-scenes activities: planning, organizing, and publicizing trips; buying groceries; teaching classes; renting gear; picking up kids who needed rides; and so on. Gene Lockhart, the president, called the meeting to order. "OK, we've got three things on the agenda tonight: final prep for Survival School, status report on the Mount Baker climb, and getting organized for Desert School. Delia, are we all set for Survival School next weekend?"

Delia, a sophomore, had been through survival training, but didn't really know what she was getting into when she volunteered to be in charge of the planning arrangements. Usually these jobs were given to seniors who had been involved in planning at least two, preferably three, years of the program. Gene had only been involved in the planning for Survival School once, and gave her the job because she was cute and wanted it. Delia stammered through her report, sounding more and more desperate as she talked.

"Uh-oh," said Paul quietly, looking at Drew. Some of the other upperclassmen were exchanging concerned looks as well.

"Well, let's see how our fearless leader handles this," Drew whispered back.

Drew had expected to be elected president at the start of the year. It was unusual, but not unprecedented for a junior to get the post. But Gene, a senior, had campaigned hard, even though he had less experience and had won mainly on the argument that Drew would have another chance as a senior. It was hard for Drew not to feel a little bitter. Gene was not doing a good job, which could jeopardize the experience of the participants, and worse, the whole program. Drew had deserved the recognition, and it was his first experience with losing unfairly. To make matters worse, REI, the gigantic outdoor outfitter whose headquarters was in Seattle, had volunteered to pay the way of the representative of their school organization to a national youth conference on outdoor education programs—and Gene got to go.

Gene knew he had to get help for Delia, but he didn't want to ask either of the Emory brothers to bail him out. So he asked Cathy Walther, an experienced senior, if she would help Delia. She flashed Drew a smile and told Gene she would help if Drew would help also. Drew nodded that he would and grinned at Cathy, who didn't like Gene.

After the meeting, while he was waiting for Cathy and Drew to talk to Delia, Paul sat on a table, bullshitting with Pete, a classmate who was also in the drama program. They were discussing the possibilities for the spring musical. Gene joined them. "So, who's going to get the lead in the musical this year?"

Paul and Pete looked at each other. "Well, it's hard to say, since we don't know which musical we're going to do," Paul answered, wondering why Gene would ask such a dumb question.

"But it's probably going to be you, isn't it, Paul? Aren't you the *numero uno* actor around here?"

"I don't think there's a *numero uno* actor, Gene. A lot of us have been doing this since we were freshmen. There's plenty of talent to go around."

"So you don't care who gets the lead?" asked Gene, with a sly look. "I was thinking I'd audition. I did a lot of acting at UPA my freshman and sophomore years, before I transferred over here. It's fun—and it'll look good on my college application."

"Think it'll look as good as being president of the Outdoor Program?" asked Paul with a challenging look. "Besides, it's too late for college applications, so I guess you missed your chance."

"Yeah, well, got to run. Later, guys." He walked over to where Cathy, Drew, and Delia were just finishing up a list of things left to do and who would do what.

"Can you believe that jerk?" said Pete. "Does he really think he can come in and get the lead in the biggest production of the year when he hasn't even been in the program?"

"I don't think he was serious, dude. Just showing off. I think he's got a thing about Drew and me—why I don't know, but he's always coming up with these little jabs. He's a pain in the butt, but at the same time, I kind of feel sorry for him. It's like he has to be at the top of the pile, no matter what."

"This is a freakin' mess!" Cathy said to Drew and Paul, as they all walked back to the parking lot. "He's lucky we're willing to step in."

"Yeah, at least we've got time to get it together," Drew said. "But what about the next thing. I don't have much confidence in him—he's all show and no go, and if he makes a bad mistake, a lot of people would suffer."

"Maybe we should have a regime change," Cathy said, not entirely joking. "I'm going to give that some thought and talk to a few people."

On the way home, Paul asked, "Did it bother you much when Gene won the election, Drew?"

"Yeah, a little. I thought I deserved it and he didn't, but it also made me think that maybe some people didn't like me. I started to think about how I looked to other people; maybe they think I'm a jerk or something."

"You're not a jerk, Bro—you know I'd be the first to tell you if you were," Paul said, laughing. "If somebody doesn't like you, it's probably because he's jealous."

*****

In his calculus class the next day, Paul was trying to follow Dr. Chen's explanation, a constant challenge since English was not the teacher's native language. Suddenly a book flew through the air, narrowly missing the teacher's head. "You idiot! I could teach this better than you!" someone shouted. "And the rest of you, just sitting here, taking it, like it doesn't matter that you can't understand a word he's saying and you're all going to flunk calculus and mess up your GPAs!" It was Greg, whose last name Paul didn't know. Thin, of medium height, with nondescript hair and clothes, he was always quiet and didn't seem to hang out with anyone. His usually furtive expression had been replaced by one of fury. He stood up, grabbed a book off the desk of the girl behind him, and threw it at the window.

"Hey, Greg, this isn't a real good way to solve your problem. Why don't you sit down and—" began Gene, who was sitting next to him.

"What do you know about my problems, slacker?" interrupted Greg.

"It's pretty clear you're worried about your grades, dude."

"I'm not worried about my grades!" shouted Greg. "I'm not goin' to college like most of you guys. I just can't stand people getting away with stuff. I learned calculus when I was twelve, this is an easy A for me, but this guy is making it hard for everyone, and I'm sick of it!" He swept an overhead projector beside him off the table with his arm, sending it crashing to the floor, glass scattering. Two girls screamed, and Dr. Chen ran out the door, presumably to find help. Gene and the other students sitting close to Greg quickly moved away from him.

Paul moved toward Greg, sitting down on a desk a couple of rows over from him. "I hear you, dude. I admit I'm having some trouble learning calculus from Dr. Chen. But you're not helping. How can I learn calculus when you're throwing books and breaking stuff?" His voice was very matter-of-fact. "Maybe you'd be willing to spend some time with me after school, you know, like tutoring or something. Maybe some others would be interested in coming too. I'll meet you at the library right after sixth period. What do you think?"

Greg was flummoxed. No one ever talked to him. Now one of the most popular guys in the school was asking him for help with calculus.

"I could use some help too. Mind if I come?" asked a girl with a long dark-blonde ponytail.

"Uh, sure, yeah sure. It's really not hard, if you come at it the right way. I'll come to the library after sixth period. Anybody who wants to can come." Greg's furious demeanor was rapidly disappearing.

Just then two security guards rushed into the room, followed by the principal. "What's going on here? Is everybody all right?" asked the principal, out of breath.

"Yeah, everybody's fine," said Paul. "We've just got a little mess to clean up. Greg and I'll get a broom and dustpan and just get rid of this glass. OK, Greg?"

By now, Greg had resumed his invisible persona. "Yeah, sure. Guess I made the mess, so I gotta clean it up." The two guards stepped aside and he walked out of the classroom, followed by Paul and the "authorities."

Everyone started talking at once. "Dude, I thought he was going postal!"

"What a relief! He's like Jekyll and Hyde. First he's foaming at the mouth, then he's all mousy again."

"Paul was really brave to talk to him like that. It seemed to calm him down."

"Yeah, he seemed to know just what to do. Did you notice Paul walked toward him while the rest of us were trying to get as far away as we could?"

"Well, I didn't think he was dangerous," said Gene. "He's just pissed off and not as polite as the rest of us. Paul was just showing off."

"Paul's not a show-off and you know it, Gene," said Georgina, she of the ponytail. "I noticed you moved over a row to an empty desk."

The bell rang as several people laughed at Gene, who hurriedly gathered up his books and left the room.

When Paul and Georgina showed up at the library after their last class, Greg wasn't there, but Principal Henderson was. "I wanted you to know that Greg's been suspended for a couple of days while we talk with his parents about what happened. I think he'll need some psychological evaluation before he can come back. Thanks for helping out, Paul. No telling what he might have done."

"No problem. I just basically agreed with why he was angry, and tried to get to, uh, something more . . . positive. A long time ago my dad told Drew and me that's what you should do with someone who's really pissed off. So I try to remember—seems like people are pissed off a lot. Anyway, can you let him know that we came?"

"Sure. I'll be talking to his mom tomorrow, and I'll ask her to tell him."

Georgina turned and started down the hall. "Got to catch my bus. See you." And she was gone. He was sorry to see her go—he'd wanted to discuss the Dr. Chen problem with her.

As he walked down the hall with the principal, Paul said, "Greg had a point, you know, Mr. Henderson. It's pretty embarrassing, but Dr. Chen really isn't cutting it. It's not fair that we're not learning anything because he can't speak English very well, or doesn't know how to teach math, or whatever."

"Yes, I hear you, Paul. The dean of faculty and I will be taking up this incident. It's a difficult situation, and I don't know if we can fix it before the end of the term. But we'll try."

4 TURF

Shaunee was standing on her front porch Friday night, waiting for Drew. She'd been going over and over what had happened and what she should do. It was a freakin' mess having this really nice guy— who was also really hot—know all about her. She was embarrassed that he knew what she was doing, maybe more embarrassed than ashamed. That was lame. She should be ashamed; she *was* ashamed. But she couldn't see any way out. Maybe he'd have some ideas, but she didn't want to get her hopes up. It had taken all her nerve to get started, and she didn't want him to talk her into quitting with no alternative. Then where would she and Grandma be? Broke.

*****

He saw her grandmother peeking out from behind the curtain to see who was picking up her granddaughter. Shaunee got in hurriedly, before he could even get out of the car. "Where we going?" she asked, glancing at him and then out the window as she adjusted her scarf and fluffed her hair nervously.

"I was thinking we could go to the Bellevue Mall. Have you been there?" She shook her head.

"Besides the shops, they have theaters and restaurants and stuff. Does that sound OK?" He chose this location because he thought it would be anonymous enough; they wouldn't be likely to see anyone they knew. He didn't mind people seeing them together, but he wasn't sure she felt that way.

She nodded. "Sounds fine." While they didn't see anyone they knew, the pair certainly was noticed as they walked through the upscale mall and found a table outside a Starbucks. Even in old jeans, a plaid flannel shirt, and down vest, he was strikingly handsome. Shaunee looked like a model in her high-heeled boots, tights, thigh-length faux fur vest, and stylish scarf. Her long hair, highlighted with caramel streaks, flowed down her back in loose curls. After buying them coffee, Drew turned on his laptop and showed Shaunee the DSHS website. They both leaned over the screen. "Have you seen this?" he asked. She shook her head. He spent about an hour showing her how to look up various kinds of programs, so she could check into whether she and her grandmother were eligible.

"You could go to the public library and use a computer for free, if you didn't want to research this stuff in the school computer lab," he told her. "Or you could use my laptop. Looks like you can apply online for a lot of these programs. What do you think?"

She looked up from the screen at him, her eyes shining. "I think this is awesome! If we had access to some of these programs, Grandma could get help with her cancer and we might even get a little extra income. But do you think I could do this, like, by myself? She won't be any help at all—she thinks she can't understand computers. And she's all proud, you know; she thinks she should be able to make it on her own."

"Well, from what you've told me, she can't make it on her own. You'll probably have to be pretty blunt. If she won't get help, she may just die and leave you by yourself—or in foster care until you're eighteen. Or does she want you to end up on the street? I think if she knew that was a possibility, she'd get over the pride thing." Leaning back in his chair, he said, "I'll bet her church is into helping people. That's the Christian thing to do, isn't it? Does *she* look down on people who need help? She doesn't, does she?" Drew drank the last of his coffee.

"Another thing, Shaunee. That's a really big church, and there's got to be someone in the congregation who could help out, maybe a social worker, or someone who knows a social worker, someone who could help you get through the bureaucracy. I think you could do a lot of this yourself, but if you're not very confident, you should get some help. Would you be willing to ask for help?"

She sighed and turned her coffee cup around and around. "It's kind of scary, but going down the road I'm going down now is pretty scary too. It's such a relief to think . . . there's maybe a way out. I'll talk to Grandma tonight. I know she's really worried about what's going to happen to us. But she thinks talking about it will worry me. Really, *not* talking about it is what worries me. We're both afraid to talk, and we're, like, getting nowhere."

Drew closed his laptop and put it back in the case. "Hey, want to go to a movie? There're lots to choose from right here."

She looked surprised, but pleased, so he bought tickets to a romantic comedy. They came out laughing and compared notes on the way to the car.

When they arrived at her house, the same guy was sitting on the front steps. It came to Drew where he'd seen the guy—arguing with Shaunee at Madrona Beach last summer. James got up and sauntered toward the car as Drew and Shaunee got out. "Where you been, ho?" he said dismissively. "Hangin' with the honkies?"

"Drop it, James," Shaunee said hotly. "He's a friend."

"The question is: Is he a *paying* friend?" James smirked.

Drew tried not to lose it. But not very hard. "You must be the scumbag pimp, right, dude? Well, forget it—you just lost yourself a meal ticket. This woman doesn't need you, you sorry-ass slacker." Drew was so angry he could hardly control his voice. "Why don't you get yourself a job instead of living off girls? Shaunee, maybe you'd be safer inside. How about just going in now? I can deal with James." Shaunee ran up the steps and let herself into the house.

"Listen, dude, if Shaunee doesn't come to school regularly, or if she looks roughed up, you're going to pay. Leave. Her. Alone."

James feigned nonchalance, his smirk glued to his face, pretending not to be cowed by this very angry guy who was a foot taller than he was.

Drew got in the car, slammed the door, and peeled out. He was home in ten minutes, but sat in the car for a while, waiting for the anger to fade.

*****

Monday afternoon Drew was thinking about his Advanced Placement literature class as he left the building and walked toward the parking lot. They were reading Joseph Campbell on myths. It was all very interesting, but he was having trouble figuring out how myths related to girls and trumpet playing and mountain climbing and grades.

Reaching the pickup, he leaned against the shotgun door and waited for Paul to walk across the parking lot with Pam, who was on a mission to capture Paul. "Jeez, Drew, look at the tires—they're all flat!"

Drew walked quickly around the truck, mystified. Sure enough, all the tires were flat. And on closer inspection, they could see the tires had been slashed.

"What the hell?" Paul said.

"James! Fucking James!" exclaimed Drew, hitting the hood with his fist.

"See you guys later," said Pam, who scurried off to her carpool.

"Who's James?" asked Paul, something tugging at his memory.

Drew reminded Paul of Shaunee's altercation at the park and told his brother the story of his ultimatum to James the previous Friday night. "I'll bet that's what this is all about."

"Well, now what?" said his brother. "I think we're going to have to tell Dad what's been going on. Probably the car insurance will cover vandalism, but he's going to want to know if it isn't just random." He bent over to inspect one of the front tires. "We've got to get this fixed before your Wednesday night delivery. Probably have to have the car towed to a tire store. Shall I go ahead and call Dad?"

"Yeah, might as well. I'm going to the office to see if they have any security cameras around, and if they've had any other incidents of tire slashings. Maybe it isn't fucking James, but I think it is." Drew left for the office while Paul called their dad, Alex. They conferred and agreed that Alex would call a tow truck and have the car towed to the closest tire store to have the tires replaced. Paul was taking photos of the car and tires with his cell phone when Drew came back.

"No cameras in the parking lot, and no similar incidents," he reported.

By the time they waited for the tow truck, arranged for the tires to be replaced, and got home, it was time for dinner.

"Paul told me you had an idea who might have slashed the tires, Drew. What's going on?" asked his father, passing him the meatloaf.

"Well, it's kind of a long story, and I gotta ask you to keep it confidential, as much as possible." His father and mother, Sylvianne, looked at each other and then back to Drew, who summarized what had happened with Shaunee.

"So I'm guessing that James is getting back at me for dissing him and trying to make me stop helping her. It's going to take more than slashed tires! I mean, I'm sorry you have to go through the bother of the insurance claim, and all that, Dad. But I'm not going to stop helping her because of that jerk!"

"I'm kind of worried about what he might try next," said Sylvianne, "if it was who you think it was, Drew."

"Me too," said Alex. "We have no evidence, but I think you need to talk to Shaunee about this, Drew. She could tell you something about him, whether she thinks he might have done it, whether he might try something else. We don't know—he might be dangerous. If he really is a pimp, those guys can be pretty nasty. I'm not saying you shouldn't be trying to help Shaunee, Drew, just that we need to think through the implications."

Drew called Shaunee that evening. She was furious when he told her what had happened, and his suspicions. "James is a wannabe; he's trying to get girls to work for him, build up a business. He might have some trafficker connections, but I've never met any of them, if he does. I told him I won't have anything to do with him, but he keeps hanging around, offering me drugs, acting all big-time. He's just a punk! I'll tell him to lay off."

"Have you got any leverage, any way to get rid of him?" asked Drew.

"No, I don't, really." She was more subdued now. "But I can threaten him. I'll tell him I have some big friends who'll come after him if he doesn't leave me alone."

"Do you know where he lives or how to find him?"

"No, but I know some people he knows, and I could find out."

"Well, be careful, Shaunee. Hey, did you talk with your grandma?"

"Yeah, I did, on Saturday—we had the best talk ever! I feel a lot better now. She's OK with asking for help. Charlene brought her laptop over, and I sat down with Grandma and showed her all the programs, and how we could apply, and she was just amazed. We're doing stuff online, and today I made an appointment to see a state social worker. So it's happening! They told me it can take a while before everything kicks in, so I'm still worried about money, but I think we can make it. I owe you, Drew—big-time!"

He was really feeling good when their conversation ended.

*****

Wednesday evening about midnight, Drew had two stops to go on his route before he could go home. He pulled up on a residential street in front of a big retirement home, grabbed a couple of bundles of papers and ran up the walkway to drop them in the outer foyer. He didn't notice the big black car stopped in the street until he returned and found James lounging against the old pickup, the Mercedes idling behind them.

"So, still trying to horn in on my turf, Paper Boy?"

"Shaunee's not anybody's turf, James. Just leave her alone."

"I s'pose you're going to make me, Paper Boy?"

Just then someone grabbed Drew from behind in a bear hug, pinning his arms to his sides. He was just aware that it was someone big when James drove his fist into Drew's face, forcing Drew and the man holding him back and off-balance. Before James could hit him again, Drew's aikido training kicked in. He stooped a bit, raising his right arm forcefully to push up the arms of the guy holding him and slip out of the bear hug. As he freed himself, he grabbed the guy's arm in a wristlock and twisted it down as hard as he could. He heard a snap and a groan, and the big guy was writhing in the street. But James was back again. This time Drew was ready, and he gave James a smashing blow to the head, which knocked him flat. Drew got in his car and sped off, blood running down his clothes and all over the truck.

He drove a few blocks, turned onto Broadway, and pulled into a parking space, lit brightly by the signs of adjacent stores and restaurants. His hand really hurt, but he got his cell phone out of his pocket and called home. His dad had been sound asleep, but he was instantly awake when he heard his younger son mumbling something about a fight and needing to see a doctor.

"Where are you, Son?" asked Alex, throwing off the covers and heading for his closet. Hearing that Drew was within five minutes of an emergency room, Alex told his son to drive there immediately and that Alex would arrive shortly.

Drew followed instructions, found a place to park and checked in. As he sat in the waiting room, he replayed the incident again and again, his mind bouncing all over the place. It happened so fast! All those years of aikido really paid off—at least in terms of self-defense. He couldn't really say that he'd handled his attackers without harm, which is what he should have done if his aikido was good enough. What would have happened if he hadn't been able to get loose from the big guy? It was pure joy to smash that punk James in the face! So much for facing an aggressor with calmness and without malice! Would James leave Shaunee alone now? What would this do to Drew's trumpet playing?

*****

Sylvianne woke up as Alex jumped out of bed and began dressing. He explained what was going on as he threw on his clothes and she said, "I'm coming too. It'll only take me a minute to get ready." In five minutes they were out the door, and ten minutes later they had parked and passed through the automatic doors into the ER. Drew was sitting in the waiting room, one hand elevated in a big ice pack, and the other holding another ice pack over his mouth. He attempted to smile, winced, and mumbled that he was glad they were there. "They said a doctor could see me in probably another fifteen minutes."

"Can you talk well enough to tell us what happened, Drew, or would you rather wait till you've seen the doctor?" asked his dad.

"It doesn't hurt too much to talk, but my mouth is so swollen that you might not be able to understand me. And it might start bleeding again."

"Let's wait until you've seen the doctor," said Sylvianne, her forehead creased with worry lines.

Alex went to check with the receptionist to see if any paperwork was required. All they needed was Drew's medical number, which he'd already produced. Drew's name was called, and all three of them were shown into an examining room. Another two minutes and a petite woman, thirtyish with blonde hair, appeared, introducing herself as Dr. Fredrickson. "Let's have a look at you."

She glanced at the chart. "Drew, is it? What happened?" she asked, looking closely at his mouth and then examining his hand.

He recounted the incident with James and his partner. "Where did you hit James, when you knocked him over?"

"I was aiming for the middle of his face, but I think I hit his forehead."

"Yes, I think that's likely. You probably didn't do as much damage to his face as his forehead did to your hand. We need to get some X-rays taken, but I'm pretty sure you've got a few broken bones. See how there's swelling and bruising around the fourth and fifth metacarpal bones? Can you make a fist for me, nice and slow?"

Drew tried, and grimaced. "Feels like it's popping in there, or something."

"Yes, see how those fingers bend toward your thumb? They shouldn't bend that much, which means they're broken. This is what we call a boxer's fracture. Now I need to stitch up your lip. You've got quite a cut there. Let's do that first. Lie down here, Drew." She indicated the examining table on which he was sitting. "I'm going to use a local anesthetic, so it won't hurt so much. After the stitches, we'll take you down to X-ray."

"I'll wait outside—I'm too wimpy for this," said Sylvianne, resting her hand on his shoulder. "I'll go to X-ray with you though." She slipped out to sit in the hall.

By the time they'd finished and got pain pills and were ready to go home, it was nearly three. Alex drove the pickup, and Sylvianne took Drew in the family car. She helped him get out of his bloody clothes, and he was asleep as soon as his head hit the pillow. She tucked the blankets under his chin, then stood in the doorway, contemplating the sleeping young man who had once been her baby. Her parents would have so much enjoyed seeing the boys grown up. Paul and Drew had the height of their strapping American grandfather, who'd met their petite grandmother in France as World War II was ending.

Alex and Sylvianne sat in the kitchen drinking cocoa, doubting they could get back to sleep. "I wonder if he's thought about how this will affect his trumpet playing? He certainly won't be able to play for quite a while, and depending on how badly his hand is broken, he might not be able to play at all. My God, what a shame that would be, after all these years of practicing! He'll be devastated if the band gets invited to the Essentially Ellington Competition and he can't go." Sylvianne's furrowed brow returned, and tears appeared in her eyes.

Alex put his arm around her. "Let's not assume the worst, Honey. I'm more worried about whether these guys are going to try again, or if they've had enough. I think we're going to have to go to the police—this is assault. I know he won't want to do anything that could be harmful to Shaunee, but this is beyond the two of them now." He studied his empty cocoa cup. "Come on, let's try to get some sleep."

*****

Not only did his mouth and hand hurt, but his face was black-and-blue, so Drew stayed home from school the next two days. Friday evening he got a call from Shaunee. "Hey, where've you been? I've been wanting to tell you about some more good stuff that's happening."

"Uh, well, I've got some stuff to tell you too, good and bad. I had a little run-in with James and one of his pals Wednesday night, and I'm kind of banged up. But so are they, I'm happy to say," he added with satisfaction.

"Drew, tell me what happened!"

He described the incident, trying to downplay it. There was silence on her end, when he finished.

"It has to be bad, or you would have come to school. Tell me how bad it is."

"I've got some stitches in my lip and some broken bones in my right hand. I saw a specialist today, and he said it could be fine in three to four months, but that's the soonest, and not a sure thing. If I do physical therapy, I've got a chance to regain the full use of my hand, and to play my trumpet again."

Another long silence, then, "I'll kill that bastard—I'll kill him! I'll go to the police. I know where to find him. He can't get away with this shit!" Then she was crying. "I'm so sorry, Drew. I'm so sorry! You were just trying to help me—and this is the reward you get for trying to be a nice guy! You should never have gotten involved with me!" she said, bitterly.

"Shaunee, it's not your fault, so don't go there. We just need to make sure this is the end of this stuff with James. Dad says we should go to the police and get their opinion. It could be that if we just threaten James with an assault charge, that'll be enough."

"OK, when can we go? I don't want to wait."

Drew suggested Monday, after school, when his dad could go with them. "We could go by ourselves, but I guess I'd rather have one of my parents with me. You OK with that?"

"Will he be mad at me? Even if he is, it's only fair. He'll think his son is hanging out with some kind of slut."

"Shaunee, I said don't go there—it's not your fault! He's not mad at you; he feels bad about the whole situation. He just wants to do whatever he can to help us both be safe. Look, there's something else we have to agree on. I've talked with my parents and Paul about what to say at school. I'm just going to say that I got jumped by a couple of hopped-up dopers looking for money, while I was running my route. I'll get a lot of sympathy, and maybe some street cred, and people will forget about it. You don't have to be involved in this at all."

There was another long silence. "Drew, you are something else. How am I *ever* going to make this up to you?"

"Just dedicate your first CD to me and give me 10 percent of the profits. That should take care of it!" he joked, trying to get her to lighten up.

"OK, Abercrombie, that's a deal." He could hear the smile in her voice.

*****

Drew was stretched out on the couch, his feet hanging over the end. It was late Saturday morning and he was trying to concentrate, not very successfully, on his history assignment. He'd be reading about the Civil War and then find himself wondering what would have happened if James had had a knife or a tire iron or a gun. He'd push the thought away, go back to the Civil War, and then find himself feeling really angry because he couldn't play the trumpet for three or four months.

"Hi, Big Guy," said his grandmother, Susannah, coming into the living room.

"Hey, Grams, what's happening?" he said, smiling and putting down his book as she perched on a chair across from him.

"Oh, nothing much. Will's been invited by the president to give meditation lessons at the Department of Defense. I won my fencing match and was offered a job as head chef at the Four Seasons, but I turned it down in favor of driving in the next NASCAR season."

"Super, Grams, can you get me tickets?"

"No problem—anything for my grandsons. Where is everyone?"

"Paul's at aikido, and Mom and Dad are on a grocery run."

"How are you?" She had that expression on her face that he'd seen so many times. The raised eyebrows that asked a question, the little smile that let you know she loved you, was concerned for you but wasn't going to intrude.

"I'm OK. Well, not sleeping very well . . . but it's probably the pain . . . which really isn't all that bad." He sat up and tried to gather the textbooks he'd scattered around the floor. He was awkward, trying to do it with one hand. "You've got that look on your face, Grams."

"What look?" she asked innocently.

"That 'I'd like to know how you feel and what you're thinking, but I don't want to ask' look," he replied, grinning at her.

"You know me pretty well!" She smiled and waited.

"I'm OK, really, Grams. It was just a fight. Guys get in fights all the time."

"This wasn't a shoving match on a soccer field or a playground, Drew," she said, pulling off her gloves and stuffing them in her coat pockets. "This incident may have a bigger impact on you than you think. Shall I make you some cocoa?" she asked, not wanting to lecture him.

They heard the kitchen door open and went in to help Alex and Sylvianne bring in the groceries. Drew's cell phone rang, so he left the room to take the call.

"Do you two remember when one of Will's students tried to immolate himself in class a few years ago?" Susannah said, as she helped empty the grocery bags onto the island. Her second husband was a professor of philosophy and comparative religion at the university, and the only grandfather Paul and Drew had known.

"God! How could we forget! But what made you think of that, Mom?" asked Alex.

"It was pretty traumatic, even though it ended well. It made Will think about a lot of things he'd taken for granted or was avoiding. He'd get angry because he felt so helpless—what could he do about the war, what could he do for this young man? Then he'd get depressed." She handed Sylvianne four packages of ramen. "This went on for a couple of weeks before he sorted it all out. I was just thinking that maybe Drew might have a reaction something like that."

"We were just talking about that on the way home from the store, Mom. He probably won't say much to us, but having a friend who's mixed up in prostitution and then being attacked while he's delivering newspapers is certainly exposing him to a different world than he's used to. I'd be concerned if he *weren't* a little upset by all this."

Drew's stitches, cast, and story got a lot of attention at school for a day or two, but it was old news fairly quickly. His father had an informal talk with a Seattle policeman who was a friend of a friend, and was told that a good next step would be to get word to James that Drew had the license number of the Mercedes, but he wouldn't press assault charges as long as James left Shaunee and Drew alone. They hoped that a threat would do the trick, since they didn't have a lot of evidence to get a conviction. Meanwhile, Drew and Shaunee were warned to be watchful.

5 SNOW CAMPING

Drew was careful to follow the doctor's instructions for regaining the use of his hand. He didn't start practicing until the swelling had gone down and the pain was minimal. He found himself frustrated at not being able to play as well as he was used to playing. He was first chair, but the second chair trumpet was almost as good. Drew began to worry about losing his first chair seat. He continued to attend practice, even though he couldn't play.

The second Saturday in December, they drove up to the foothills of the Cascades to cut their Christmas tree, a tradition of many years. Drew trailed his parents and brother as they wandered around the tree farm, debating the merits of this tree and that: too bushy, not bushy enough, too thin at the top. "You don't have much to say, Drew," his mother said. "Usually you're leading the charge for the perfect tree."

"Yeah, well, seen one tree, seen 'em all. Guess I'm just not in the mood this year." At lunch he ate his pizza mechanically and didn't participate much in the conversation.

The holidays came and went.

The Outdoor Program always had a snow camping trip in January. They'd go up to Gold Creek at Snoqualmie Pass and build igloos and stay all night. The snow was deeper than usual this year, great for igloos, and the forecast was for cold, clear weather. Everyone was looking forward to snowshoeing and skiing in good snow, instead of the wet or icy stuff they usually had. In the school parking lot at eight on a Saturday morning, about fifteen campers, including chaperones, piled a mountain of down, fleece, food, snowshoes, skis, packs, and other high-tech gear into the drivers' cars. Two hours later they were chattering and laughing, throwing snowballs, loading their packs, strapping on their skis and snowshoes, and heading into the woods on a frigid sunny morning.

Paul and Drew were expert igloo builders, since they'd been snow camping for years with their dad. They even had special tools they'd designed and made for cutting snow blocks. Each of them had a little group of campers to instruct, and they showed them how to start by digging out a hole, then building up the walls of snow blocks in a spiral to form the dome, finishing with an entrance tunnel. It took a lot of technique to do it right, and by the time it got dark, there were some weird-looking structures dotting the landscape. Some couldn't get the spiraling angles right and ended up putting a tarp or a tent fly over the open top of their igloos. Some elected to sleep in their tents.

There were some very cold campers the next morning, but no one had frostbite and they had learned what to do and what not to do the next time they went snow camping. They had about an hour of free time after breakfast before they had to break camp, so some of them were going off for short snowshoe hikes or ski runs.

Paul, Drew, and Cathy Walther were snowshoeing through the trees when they heard a frantic female voice yelling for help. "Sounds like she's down there, just past that little rise," said Paul, pointing. He yelled back, "Where are you, keep yelling so we can find you!"

"Down here, we need help! Gene's fallen into the creek, and he can't get out!"

They came to the top of a little hill and could see immediately what had happened. Gene and Delia had tried to cross on two parallel logs that lay across the creek, covered with snow, and Gene had fallen.

"I've done something to my ankle," shouted Gene. "I can't stand on it! Help me get out of here—I don't know what to do!" They could hear the desperation in his voice.

"OK, Gene, hang on. We'll figure something out," Drew yelled down to him.

Paul said, "I think we should tell Delia to go back the way she came and tell people at camp what's happening. They could come back with some sleeping bags and anything else that might be helpful. Meanwhile, we can try to get him out of there. Got any rope in your pack, Drew?"

"You know I never go anywhere without my climbing gear. Yeah, let's see what we can figure out."

Cathy called down instructions to Delia, who immediately turned around and started back the way she'd come.

"Guys, I'm freezing—I can't stay here much longer," Gene called up to them. "What do you want me to do?" He was standing in about six inches of water, but half his clothing was soaked. He had managed to get his snowshoes off and had stuck them into the snow covering the side of the ravine.

Paul called back, "We're going to throw down a line. Fasten your snowshoes to the line first, and we'll get them up, then we'll throw the line back for you. Fasten it under your arms with the carabiner, and we'll pull you up."

By this time, Drew had unloaded his climbing rope from his day pack, hooked a carabiner on it, and they threw it down to Gene. They had the snowshoes in five minutes and threw the line back down to Gene. He slipped it over his shoulders and yelled that he was ready.

Paul and Cathy had been looking at the side of the ravine. It was about a forty-five degree angle, with bumps of snow protruding, covering rocks and brush. "I think you can use your hands, one knee, and your good foot to climb with, and we'll pull on this end," Drew told Gene. They wrapped the rope around a tree and began pulling. It was very slow going. Gene was wet and heavy, awkward with cold, and the rope kept getting hooked on roots under the snow.

"I'm going down to see if I can push him up," Drew said. "He's so cold and tired, he can't help." Drew carefully worked his way down the side of the ravine, positioning himself under Gene. "OK," he hollered to the others, "when I yell 'pull,' you pull and I'll push. Ready, pull!" That got them another foot. Drew moved up, put his shoulder under Gene and yelled, "Pull!"

Just as he yelled, Gene's good foot slipped right onto Drew's hand, which took all Gene's weight and was crushed against the rock Drew was holding on to—the hand that was barely recovered from his run-in with James. He grunted in pain, shoved up on Gene with his left shoulder and got his right hand free. They gained another foot. After fifteen minutes, Gene was about three feet from the top of the ravine and reinforcements had arrived, a half-dozen people on snowshoes, ready to help. Five more minutes and he was sitting on the snow at the top.

Someone had brought one of those roll-up plastic sheets used for sledding. They got a splint on Gene's ankle to keep it immobilized and then had him squirm into a down bag and onto the sled. They took turns pulling, two at a time. It was ungainly because the snow was soft and the sled kept sinking. They finally decided that he should put on one snowshoe, and two people would help him walk, with his arms around their necks. At least the exertion would help keep him warm. It took them another twenty minutes to get back to the campsite. Everything had been packed up except some dry clothes and another sleeping bag.

"It's another quarter mile to the parking lot. Can you make it, Gene?" Paul asked.

Just then they saw the Snoqualmie ski patrol coming up the trail with a rescue toboggan. They got Gene, wrapped warmly, onto the sled and out to the parking lot in no time. Then they loaded him into a van and took him to the hut for injured skiers. His carpool followed, and the rest of the group started for Seattle.

Cathy had packed a plastic bag full of snow and wrapped a scarf around it for Drew's reinjured hand. After they dropped their passengers and gear off at school, where families were waiting to pick them up, they drove home. "How's the hand?" Paul asked his brother.

"It fuckin' hurts! What an asshole that Gene is, to pull a stunt like that—he should have known better! Wasting everybody's time, and now I've got to go to the doctor again and make sure everything's OK with my hand. More weeks before I can play again, and I might not be able to go to New York for the Ellington Competition. I'll kill him if I don't get to go!"

"Hey, I know you're upset. I would be too," said Paul. His brother glanced at Drew's stony face as they pulled into the alley behind their house. "But maybe you're too upset. The whole purpose of going on these camping trips is so people can have accidents without serious consequences and learn what *not* to do. I know your hand hurts, but Gene's probably fine, and nobody who was on this trip will ever try something stupid like that in the future." He stopped the car in front of the garage. "Besides, you don't know that you won't get to go to New York, and even if you don't go this year, there's always next year. I think you need to chill, Bro."

"Well, I'm not feeling very chill right now, and I don't want one of your big-brother lectures," Drew said, slamming the truck door. "Just leave my gear. I'll come get it later." He stomped into the house.

Paul was annoyed. Big-brother lectures? What was that all about? But he put all their gear away; it would be hard for Drew to manage with a swollen hand.

After dinner Drew sat propped up on his bed, trying to concentrate on chemistry. His mind would wander off to finding his tires slashed, to his stupid remark about the Christmas tree, to his outburst about Gene. Paul was right; he needed to chill. What was going on? He dragged his mind back to chemistry.

Then something his grandmother had said bubbled into his thoughts. "This incident may have a bigger impact on you than you think." Was that it? Was this some kind of post-traumatic stress stuff going on? But it wasn't *that* traumatic. He had a few stitches, minor broken bones—no big deal. He did, however, admit to himself, that he felt a little twinge of . . . something, every time he saw a black Mercedes.

He got up and went into the kitchen, where his mom was finishing a grocery list. "Hey, Mom," he said, sitting down at the island, "have I been a little weird the last few weeks?"

She put down her pencil and gazed at him thoughtfully before she said, "Well, I don't know if *weird* is the right word, but I don't think you've been your usual happy-go-lucky self since the James incident. What makes you ask?"

"Yeah, I definitely don't feel happy-go-lucky," he said, dryly. "But why would that be. It's not like I got paralyzed for life or something."

"Those guys were really trying to hurt you, Drew. It was a premeditated assault. That's never happened to you before, and it could have turned out a lot worse." Sylvianne sat down beside him. "It's probably sinking in unconsciously, and that's kind of upsetting. Remember when that guy attacked your dad at the soccer game when you were little? All the kids were so shocked to see grown-ups—parents—behaving like that, when kids are always told fighting is bad."

She got up to get him a dish of ice cream. "This James thing is a more serious example of some really bad stuff in the world, and it can affect you personally. Same with Shaunee's situation. I know you know about prostitution, but to have a friend almost get into that, it's . . . sobering . . . to say the least. So, in answer to your question, I think you've been 'processing' all this for the past couple of months."

They sat there for a few minutes while he stirred his ice cream and chocolate sauce around in his bowl. Then he said, "Hmm . . . Thanks, Mom. Back to chemistry."

6 A MYSTERY

In early February Paul came home from school one afternoon to find a letter from the University of Washington Admissions Office telling him that his acceptance for the coming fall was in jeopardy due to the low GPA of the semester he'd just finished. Paul was stunned. He'd received five As and a B in calculus for that semester. He immediately called the woman whose name and number were listed in the letter. He got her voice mail and left a message.

"Ms. Chastain, this is Paul Emory. I just got a letter from you saying that my acceptance for this fall was in doubt because I got bad grades. There must be some mistake because I got a 3.8 this semester. Please call me . . ." Beep. He got cut off and redialed. This time Paul left her the phone number.

His dad came into the kitchen, carrying a bag of groceries. "Hi, Son. How was your day? Hope it was better than mine. I was so busy, I almost forgot to get the stuff for the stir-fry. My turn to cook tonight." He put the bag on the island and began unloading it.

"Dad, the weirdest thing just happened. I got this letter from the U saying I got bad grades last semester, and that my acceptance was in jeopardy. I just called the lady who sent the letter, but I had to leave a message."

"Well, that's pretty strange—and worrisome. But I'm sure we can get it straightened out. You have a copy of your grades, don't you?"

"Yeah, I just happened to keep it; normally I throw out all the paperwork once the semester is over, but I just haven't got to it yet this time. Usually if you want a copy of your transcript, you just go to the office and they print one out for you, so you don't need to keep what they send you each semester."

"So how did the U get this mistaken information?" he asked, putting groceries in the cupboards and refrigerator.

"Hell if I know," said Paul. "What a pain! Maybe they got someone else's grades instead of mine. I know the colleges and universities that accept you ask for your senior year grades. They don't want the students who slack off in their senior year, so they ask for updated transcripts from those they've accepted. When this lady calls back, I'll ask her how mistakes like that could happen."

Ms. Chastain called back the next day while Paul was at school. He returned her call as soon as he got home, but got her voice mail again. He opened his laptop and Googled the UW Admissions Office where he finally found a phone number for a secretary, who gave him Ms. Chastain's e-mail address. He sent off a message offering to bring in his transcript or whatever she needed to clear up the mistake. In that afternoon's mail he found a letter from another college, which had accepted him—with the same message. He had trouble concentrating on his studies that evening.

The next morning Paul went to the guidance counselor's office at lunchtime. He explained what had happened to Mr. Johnson. "Where is this coming from? How could this be?"

"Hmm," said Mr. Johnson. "I don't think this has ever happened, at least in the six years that I've been here. Let me walk you through the system, and let's see what we can figure out. First, all the teachers enter their grades online. They can keep track of them any way they want up until the final grade, but they have to be able to produce their records, in case someone questions a grade." He stopped to think, swiveling his chair toward his window. "Then they enter them into the system at the end of the term. What's in the system is what we print out when someone wants a copy, or what we e-mail to the universities that students are applying to."

"Could someone hack into the system?" asked Paul.

"Well, I suppose so, but I'm not an expert on that. Why don't we talk to Mr. Pietre? He's our IT expert, the one who keeps everything working for us." He dialed a number. "Hey, Pete, got a technical question for you. Are you free? OK, thanks. He'll be here in a minute, Paul."

A stooped man with thick glasses and wrinkled clothes came into the office. Mr. Johnson introduced Paul and explained the question.

"Could someone hack in? Sure, it's an old system, poorly built, lousy security features. You know how the district is always trying to save money and get the cheapest thing." He sat on the corner of Mr. Johnson's desk. "This system is a case in point. This one doesn't even need to be hacked. It allows the 'administrator' to go in and change records, and we've got students who work in the office doing data entry who have access as 'administrators.' I've told the principal and assistant principal this presents all kinds of potential problems, but they're just hoping nothing bad will happen because nothing has."

"How do the transcripts get sent to the universities?" asked Paul.

"They're generated automatically and sent to the names and addresses that the students supply. There's a place on the screen to mark when an additional transcript is to be sent after the original one. If that's marked, the system will forward another transcript. In most cases it's marked, because most universities want the seniors' grades."

"So, it sounds like they probably didn't send the wrong transcript. Somehow the grades on mine got messed up. Could that happen by mistake, or would it have to be on purpose?" asked Paul.

"I think it could be either way," said Mr. Pietre. "I'll go print out a copy right now; I don't want to ask someone to do it. If this is some kind of sabotage or game or something, I don't want to tip off the perpetrator. I'll be right back."

"I gotta go to class, Mr. Johnson. OK if I come back later?"

"Sure, give us a few days and we'll get to the bottom of this."

7 ELEKTRA

Drew was in the school theater, having just confirmed arrangements with his brother for a meeting they were going to that night. As he was about to leave, she came in the stage door, carrying a precarious stack of props. Leo, one of the actors, walking backward and talking to someone, plowed right into her, scattering the props all over the backstage. "Damn! Why don't you watch where you're going!" she exclaimed.

"Sorry! I'm really sorry—I just wasn't paying attention," said Leo. "Here, I'll pick it up for you." They were both on their hands and knees, picking up silverware, sweaters, and a lot of other items she was taking to the set for the rehearsal. Drew came over to help. Then they were standing, their arms full of props, and Drew was looking into the greenest eyes with the longest eyelashes he had ever seen. He dropped the football he'd just picked up.

"You've bent my lamp, Leo!" she said. "And the vase is broken! What a pain!"

"Hey, I can bend the lamp back in shape," said Drew, taking the lamp from her.

Leo said, "I'll get you another vase—they have thousands at Value Village."

"I know that, you idiot, where do you think I got all this stuff?" she huffed.

She was pissed off. "We're already behind schedule, and now I have to mess with *this*! Just put that stuff over there on the table," she told Leo and Drew, who had finished bending the lampshade holder back into shape. She pointed with her chin. "OK, everyone, let's run the third scene blocking," she told the actors who were gathering on the stage. She dropped her jumble of props on the table and began conferring with the lighting tech. Drew left the lamp on the table and tiptoed off the stage.

He was back at six forty-five, early to meet Paul, and hoping to score points with Whoever She Was, balanced at the top of a twelve-foot ladder, adjusting a spotlight. She had a dancer's body—long and slender, the kind of body that looked really good in skinny black jeans and a black turtleneck. A nose ring and curly black hair in a ponytail that spouted out the top of her head like a fountain contributed to her aura of "don't mess with me."

Ms. Dawson, the drama coach, called out, "OK, folks, nice job. See you tomorrow." The actors were chatting, gathering their coats and books, and leaving in twos and threes. Paul was talking with his leading lady, so Drew went over to the ladder. "Hey, I brought you a new vase. Will this do?" He'd taken one from his mom's back porch collection, hoping it wasn't anything special that she'd miss.

"Yeah, that'll do. Thanks," she said, gruffly. He steadied the ladder as she climbed down.

"Who are you, anyway?" she asked.

"Drew Emory, Paul's brother. Who are you?"

"I'm the stage manager, Elektra Stephanopolis. And I don't like smart-ass comments about my name."

"I like your name; it has lots of . . . energy. It suits you," he said, grinning at her.

"Well, that's a new one! Guess I should be glad they didn't name me Windy."

"Or worse, Coal or Nuclear." She couldn't help laughing.

"I was wondering if you'd like to go out for coffee," said Drew. He noticed that the top of her head was about even with his chin.

A look of surprise passed quickly over her face, but she said, "Sure. Would you mind taking me to Bing's, down in Madison Park? I always take the bus down there after rehearsals and have dinner."

"No problem. We can just drop Paul off at a meeting, and I'll pick him up later."

While she got her coat and books, Drew told Paul about the change of plans. "Cover for me, Bro. This chick is outta sight. I'm not passing up a chance to get to know her. You can sign me up for whatever they need help with."

"Watch it—she really comes on strong," said Paul. "But underneath she's kind of sweet. She brings cookies for the cast, after she bullies us through the rehearsals. But she really knows her stuff." They walked backstage to meet Elektra. "She's been doing theater since she was little—took a lot of classes at the Seattle Children's Theatre. We're lucky to have her. You'll have your hands full with this one! Hey! What a great pun—I can hardly ever do that." He pretended to leer at his brother, who grinned back.

"Thanks for the intelligence. I'm sure I can impress her with my ignorance of the theater."

*****

Elektra talked; he listened, nodding or shaking his head or laughing. She was intelligent, funny, very intense. He was glad she'd chosen a table, so he could sit adjacent to her; their knees bumped. She had beautiful hands, which she waved around while talking. He couldn't believe how so slender a girl could eat so much! While he ate a piece of apple pie with ice cream, she had a double hamburger, a huge pile of french fries, a salad, and a chocolate sundae for dessert. "Hey, it's eight forty-five. Don't you have to pick up your brother or something?"

"Oh yeah, guess I have to hit the road. Let me get the check, and then I can take you home."

"Not necessary. They'll just put it on my tab. I eat here a lot," she said, getting up and waving at the hostess. "And I just live a couple of blocks from here, so I'll walk home. It'll be fine. Go ahead and pick up Paul."

"No, no, I'll walk you home first." They went out into the damp February cold. She lived in a big house on Lake Washington, not far from the little Madison Park shopping area. All the lights in the house seemed to be on. "Looks like my mom's back from Athens. She and Papa travel a lot." They stopped on her doorstep. "Well, thanks for the ride and the company, and for walking me home. See you around."

"I hear you bake cookies. Would you like to come over to my house and I'll help you make some, maybe Sunday night?"

She considered. "Sure—sounds like fun."

"OK, I'll pick you up about seven thirty. See you soon."

On the way home, Drew realized he was, as his grandmother would say, "smitten." Elektra was fascinating—and those green eyes! He could hardly wait for Sunday evening. He almost forgot to pick up Paul. When they got home, they walked into the living room where his folks were reading. "I've invited someone over to bake cookies Sunday night. Have we got everything we'll need, Mom?"

"Yes, unless you want something exotic, we've got the basics, including chocolate chips and raisins. Who's coming?"

"Her name is Elektra. Paul knows her better than I do. She's the stage manager for the theater program. I just took her out for dinner. She's really neat—you'll like her."

"He neglected to mention that she's really hot," added Paul, poking his brother. "She looks a little Goth at first, but she's not really. Elektra's very serious about drama. She's on your case if she thinks you're just messing around and not working hard." He plopped down on the sofa. "There's something kind of funny about her though. Sometimes it's like she's just run out of energy or something. Gets quiet, acts like her mind's a million miles away. Then, after a while, she's her usual high-energy self."

Drew was impatient for Sunday evening. It seemed like months before he could go pick her up. She took him into the living room to meet her mother, a statuesque woman with dark hair and eyes, not pretty but very attractive. She too was dressed in black, casual but elegant slacks and a very soft-looking sweater. She was polite, but seemed to Drew a little bland, or like she wasn't quite there. He couldn't put his finger on what it was. "I'll be back by eleven, Mom," Elektra told her.

Sylvianne was rummaging through the cupboards, getting out the flour and sugar and cookie sheets when they came into the kitchen. "You must be Elektra," she said, smiling and extending her hand, "I'm Sylvianne."

"This is my dad, Alex," Drew said, as Alex walked into the kitchen.

"Hi, Elektra," Alex said, shaking her hand. "We've heard you don't allow any slacking off from the cast. We're looking forward to seeing the production."

"Yeah, I make them toe the line, and when they work hard, I make them cookies."

"OK," said Drew, "let's get to it."

"Have fun, you guys. I've left my cookbook on the island, in case you need some inspiration." Drew's parents diplomatically adjourned to the living room.

"Shall we make chocolate chip?" asked Drew. That was his favorite.

"Noooo. Too boring!" She was looking through the cookbook. "How about this one—Irish Christmas cookies. Looks like shortbread with caraway seeds. That looks different."

"I *hate* caraway seeds."

"OK, how about pumpkin? Do you have any canned pumpkin, by chance?" Drew went to ask his mom.

"Yes, there's a can left over from Thanksgiving; it's in the pantry."

Drew got the pumpkin, and Elektra looked through the cupboards. "Your mom's got some pretty neat shit here," she said admiringly. "Look at this, *quatre épices*—I love this stuff! I'll bet it would go good in the cookies. And these are fantastic cookie sheets. Cool!"

"You seem to know a lot about cooking. Does your mom like to cook?"

Elektra laughed. "She never cooks. I learned from Elena. She's our—what? Everything. Cook, housekeeper, nanny, you name it. She's been with us since my brother was born. Let's see, he's eight years older than me, so that would make it about twenty-five years. She's part of the family."

They mixed up the dough and talked and joked. When Sylvianne came in to refill her coffee cup, they were laughing and feeding each other cookie dough.

After the baking was done, they sat opposite each other in the breakfast nook, drinking milk and eating warm cookies. "Mmmm— these are really good. What's different about them?" Drew asked. "They sort of taste like pumpkin pie, only peppery."

"Yeah, it's the *quatre épices*; it's basically pumpkin pie spice with pepper. I think they turned out really well. Would you e-mail me the recipe?"

"Sure, if you'll go to the junior prom with me."

He'd startled her, as he hoped to. But she recovered fast. "It's in two weeks, isn't it? I thought you were supposed to, like, have your prom date lined up months in advance. Am I the alternate?"

"I didn't know you months ago or I would have asked you then. No, you're not the alternate." He looked at her expectantly.

"Sure, OK." She smiled at him. "Thanks." She took another cookie (her sixth, Drew was counting) and said, with what he'd come to think of as her intense look, "So. Time for true confessions. Might as well get it over with all at once. I'm bipolar. My family is really rich. My little sister drowned six years ago in a boating accident. She was five and I was ten, and we've all been basket cases ever since." She tried to look nonchalant as she stopped for a drink of milk.

"My brother's in grad school, my mom's on Valium, and my dad tries to take care of her by hauling her around on all his business trips. They've basically forgotten they have another daughter. So Elena takes care of me—or tries to. I pretty much take care of myself. Questions?"

Drew had been watching her face. With one finger he lightly touched the back of her hand. "Um . . . that's a lot to take in. I'm really sorry about your sister, Elektra. I know that doesn't help, but I still feel bad for you."

"Thanks," she said briskly, and got up to wash the cookie dough bowl and beaters. "You got any confessions? Anything I ought to know about you I don't already know, like you're a good student, you do aikido, you're a fabulous trumpet player, and most of the girls in school would give anything to go out with you."

"Did your sources tell you that I stole some candy when I was eight and my dad made me take it back and apologize? Or that I deliver twenty-five-hundred copies of the *Capitol Hill Times* every Wednesday night?" He was trying to lighten things up a bit and hoping she didn't think he was trivializing what she'd told him.

"No, I didn't get those juicy bits! But I guess I can still go to the prom with you. Only, no flowers. I'm not a flower kind of girl."

On his way back from taking her home, Drew thought about what she had told him. Maybe the bipolar thing accounted for what Paul had said about her. And maybe the Valium accounted for her mom's sort of vacant look.

*****

Elektra wanted Drew to see one of her favorite movies, so he'd come over for a movie night. They made popcorn in the microwave and took it into the media room, settling close together in front of an enormous HD screen. "What are we seeing?" he asked.

"It's a surprise. I don't want you to make up your mind ahead of time about whether you'll like it or not."

"I'm hurt that you think I'm not open-minded," he said, stuffing more popcorn in his mouth.

"You aren't hurt, I can tell. But everybody has preconceptions. What if I said we were going to watch a new James Bond movie? You'd say, 'Super, I love James Bond!' Or if I said we're going to watch a Hugh Grant film, you'd say, 'Oh, he's such a pansy.' Anyway, this is one of my favorite films, so you'd better like it—or else!"

He casually put his arm around her, placed the popcorn between them, and they watched *Tango*.

As the credits were rolling, he said, "I loved it! One of the best films I've ever seen! Let's watch it again! Buy me my own copy!"

She jumped on him and began tickling him. "I'll teach you to make fun of my favorite films!" They laughed and rough-housed until she finally shrieked at him, "Stop, stop, it's no fair, you're so much stronger. I'll never win!" She stood up and took his hand. "Come on, I'm going to show you the ballroom."

He got up and followed her into the hall and up to the third floor. "You've got a ballroom?"

"Yeah, it's really neat. It was our playroom when we were little, but when my sister died, my mom cleaned it out, got rid of everything. I was lucky Elena saved my teddy bears for me. So, anyway, it's back to being a ballroom. I come up here and dance by myself sometimes."

It was about twenty-five by fifty feet, with hardwood floors and a pitched roof with dark beams, totally empty except for an audio system in one corner.

"This is an awesome room—what a great place for a party! Did you ever think about that?"

"No, but I will. OK, Handsome, you're going to learn the tango!"

"What! You just showed me the best tango-ers on the planet and now you want me to dance like that? I can't dance!"

"Oh, shut up. You do sports and play music. Don't tell me you can't dance. You have to try or you're going to be in serious trouble!" She had her no-funny-business look, so he figured he'd better try.

"So here's the basic step. This is American tango, and it's a lot simpler than Argentine. I'll go backward, you come toward me on the opposite foot—like if I'm going back on my right foot, you're coming forward on your left, OK?"

He nodded.

"Watch first. I go back right slow, back left slow, back right quick, then I take a little quick step to the left, drag my right foot over and pause on my left foot, ready to repeat the whole thing, starting back on my right foot. Got it? It might help if you say it to yourself; for you, it would be left, right, left, side together, pause, then repeat. OK, go when you're ready, and I'll follow your lead. Don't look at your feet either."

Drew focused on the wall behind her and repeated the directions, moving forward. She watched his face and moved back exactly when he moved forward. They went through the pattern three times.

"You've got it. It's a lot easier to music." She went to the sound system, punched a button and "Blue Tango" began. "All right. You did so well by yourself, now you get to dance with me." She placed his right hand in the middle of her back, then showed him how her right arm and his left were together from the elbow to the hand. "You have to dance close for tango."

"Fine with me." He grinned at her and off they went. In a minute, he had it. "Hey, this is fun!"

"It gets funner. Now I'm going to show you a turn. So, at the pause, we make a right-angle turn, arms extended, side by side, and we do the same foot sequence. You have to turn me with your hand; otherwise, I won't know what you're going to do." She demonstrated, and they practiced a few times. Then she showed him how to get back to the original position.

"So, when you do this dance, you have to have *attitude*. Snap your head around for the turns and look like one of those guys in a *GQ* ad. All smoldery or something. What do you suppose they're thinking about to get those looks on their faces?"

"They're probably pissed off because they've flunked their tango lessons."

She burst into laughter. Then they resumed their practice. Another five minutes and he had the turns down.

"I knew you wouldn't have any trouble with this, but I didn't think you'd get it, like, *this* quick. Congratulations, Handsome. Two more steps and you get to quit. These are very romantic." She showed him how to do *ochos* and a *corte*.

"Now comes the fun part! You have to hold me really close; we're, like, glued together from the waist down—think you can manage that?"

"I know I can manage that, but I might forget to dance!"

"Think about cold showers or something. OK, you're the lead. You have to decide which steps to do when. I'm going to get us a new song." She punched another button. He pulled her very close, waited for the right beat, and they were doing the tango.

It was a long piece. They danced for six or seven minutes. He didn't want to let her go when the music stopped. "Hey, that was wicked cool! I had no idea it would be so much fun. Thanks, Elektra." He really wanted to kiss her.

8 SOLVED

A few days after his meeting with Mr. Johnson and Mr. Pietre, Paul had an appointment to stop back at Mr. Johnson's office. He found the two men studying a piece of paper. "Here's a copy for you, Paul. It's your transcript. Do you see any errors?"

Paul sat down and studied his transcript. "Yeah, here's one. In my freshman year, this says I got a C in English. I never got a C in my life. And here, it shows that I got a B instead of an A in biology. And in my sophomore year, two As have been turned into Bs. And here's a C from last year. And then first semester, this shows I didn't even get a 3.0, when I got a 3.8. This is really screwed up!"

"You can say that again!" said Mr. Pietre. "Paul, do you have a paper transcript of your first three years?"

"Yeah, I asked for one, I can't remember why. But I know I've got one somewhere."

"And you have a paper copy of your first semester's grades from this year?" Mr. Pietre asked, perching again on the corner of the desk.

"Yeah, I do."

"Well, that means someone's done this in the past couple of weeks, whether by mistake or on purpose," Mr. Pietre said.

"Who's working in the office, Pete, or who has access to the system?" asked Mr. Johnson.

"Hmm, let me see. The principal and vice principal, but they haven't got a clue how to change anything. All they can do is print stuff out. They'd ask Marsha, the school secretary, if they needed something." His fingers tapped on the desk as he thought. "Besides me, there are about five girls who work in the office at various times, mainly doing data entry. Marsha trains and supervises them. Right now we have Lavonne Davis, Susan Patterson, Vickie Woo, um . . . Tricia Jarvis . . . and Delia Wallace. No, Delia quit about two weeks ago, said she needed more study time. So that's it. You know any of those girls, Paul?"

"Yup. Only one. And her boyfriend really doesn't like me. Maybe I shouldn't jump to conclusions, but I'd say she or they are the likely . . . What did you say? Perpetrators." The two men watched him study the copy of his bogus transcript as he told them who he thought might be responsible. "I can't believe this! Just because he doesn't like me?" Paul looked from one to the other. "Now what? Is there any way to prove this? That they did it or didn't do it? And what do I do about those false transcripts that've been sent out?"

"I'll take care of that, Paul," said Mr. Johnson. "I'll get in touch with the admissions offices where you applied and let them know that corrected copies will be coming, that there was a glitch. I don't think you need to worry about that."

"Thanks, Mr. Johnson. If you'd call the UW first, I'd appreciate it. That's where I really want to go, and I don't want that to get screwed up. I'd like it to be corrected with the other schools too, but that's not as important right now."

"Pete, how do we go about seeing who might have done this?" said Mr. Johnson.

"Let me think about it tonight; I'll have some ideas for you tomorrow. Meanwhile, Paul, don't do anything rash. We don't know that it was Delia, or that it was intentional, so just keep this under your hat for a while, OK?"

"OK, Mr. Pietre. I'm pretty steamed, but I know we're not sure yet, so I'll try to just let it ride. I really appreciate your helping me out with this."

After the fiasco of falling in the creek during the snow camping trip, Gene had resigned as president of the students' Outdoor Program, citing a heavy class load, which prohibited extracurricular activities. The vice president declined to serve as president, saying he'd only taken the VP job so that he could list it on his college applications (which wasn't entirely true). He nominated Drew, who had been immediately elected.

When Paul got home from school, he plopped down on the sofa with a bag of cookies and a glass of milk, thinking about the transcript mystery. Could it really be Gene behind this? He thought back through their interactions this year: outmaneuvering Drew to get himself elected as president of the Outdoor Program, getting bailed out for his poor choice of Delia as the Survival School coordinator, having to be rescued on the snow camping trip, the hint of competition for the lead in the school musical. Also, someone had told Paul what Gene said about him after Paul and Greg left to get something to clean up Greg's mess in the book-throwing episode. Something about being a show-off, and how Georgina had defended him, making Gene look bad. He and Drew had never done anything to harm Gene; if he came out looking bad, it was his own fault!

At dinner Paul brought his family up to date on what he'd learned that day and his thoughts about Gene. "If you're right, that guy's a scumbag!" said Drew. "I hope he gets everything he deserves."

"Well," said their father, "as Mr. Pietre said, you need to keep this under wraps until we know more. Maybe it wasn't Gene at all."

"You haven't said anything, Mom. What do you think?" Paul asked.

"I'm wondering why, if it was Gene, he'd do such a thing. It's not like you guys had an open feud going, like you'd actively done something to harm him. So it must be something in him. Maybe he's projecting some anger or frustration on you, something he doesn't want to recognize in himself. Maybe he's jealous or envious. That doesn't excuse the behavior—if he is behind all this. But at least it's a possible explanation."

"He must be pretty messed up to try this shit," said Drew. "If he's hacking into school software and he gets caught, he's going to be totally screwed. He's probably breaking some law or something." Drew scooped another big helping of mac and cheese onto his plate and passed the bowl to his brother.

The next day before class, Paul stuck his head in Mr. Pietre's office. "Any news?"

"I've learned some interesting things. Why don't you come to Mr. Johnson's office at lunchtime and I can fill you both in."

At noon Paul wolfed down his two sandwiches and a carton of milk, then knocked on Mr. Johnson's open door. "Come on in, Paul."

"Well, we know more now, and it's not good," said Mr. Pietre. "There is a feature in the system that allows you to look up when changes were made, the date and time, and who made them. Like in Word, you can see when your last edit occurred." Paul and Mr. Johnson nodded. "I don't think this feature is known to anyone but me. If it were, Delia would have known they could get caught and this probably wouldn't have happened. So I looked up the history for the changes to Paul's transcript and found that they were made two weeks ago today, at 11:30 a.m., by Delia Wallace. On a hunch, I looked at Gene's transcript and found that there had been changes to his on the same date at about the same time. It doesn't tell me what the changes were, so we'd have to get a paper copy—or just ask him or Delia. No changes have been made to her transcript since the teachers put in last term's grades."

The room was silent, as each of them weighed the implications of what they'd discovered.

"Now what?" asked Paul.

"Now what, indeed!" said Mr. Johnson. "Obviously, Delia has to be asked about this and the records have to be restored."

"And we need new procedures so that it can't happen again," said Mr. Pietre. "I'll take care of that. I think Mr. Johnson and I need to talk to the principal, Paul. We'll see what he has to say and go from there. So you'll have to remain mum about this a while longer."

Mr. Johnson told Paul he'd talked to Ms. Chastain at the UW. "She understands she received misinformation and that corrected info will be coming soon. She says there's no problem with your admission if you got a 3.8 last semester. And we'll make sure corrected transcripts go to the other colleges as well."

"Any idea why Delia would do something like this, Paul?" asked Mr. Pietre, eyebrows raised.

"We were talking about this at dinner last night. My family knows what's going on, but you don't need to worry about them saying anything to anyone. My mom was guessing that Gene was jealous of me or Drew for some reason. There've been a few little incidents with Gene, nothing major, nothing I could imagine someone risking this kind of trouble for." Paul looked from one man to the other. "Delia's a sophomore going with a senior, so maybe he talked her into it. I hardly know her, and I can't remember anything that I might have done to make her angry at me. So it's a mystery to me."

The following Tuesday, Paul's first-period teacher told him that Mr. Johnson would like to see him at lunch. Paul had seen Gene in the halls the past few days, but they had no occasion to talk and Gene seemed normal. Mr. Johnson offered Paul a seat and closed the door to his office. He stood in front of his window. "OK, here's the update, Paul. Mr. Pietre and I briefed the principal right after we last talked to you. He conferred with the district person in charge of incidents when students have broken the rules or engaged in inappropriate conduct."

Mr. Johnson sat down heavily in his chair. "We were advised to meet with Delia and get her story, which we did, this morning. She admitted immediately that she'd made the changes, didn't try to cover it up at all. She was very upset, crying, worried about getting kicked out of school, what her parents would say, and so on. You can imagine. She said that Gene had asked her to make the changes to both his and your transcripts, and she did it knowing it was wrong, but thinking they wouldn't get caught. So we called Gene in and confronted him, and at first he denied it. But when we told him Delia had confessed, he admitted he'd put her up to it."

"Did he say why he did it?"

"I asked him, but he didn't really answer. He said he was sorry, but I had the feeling he was sorrier that he got caught than that he'd done something wrong."

"So what will happen to them?"

"Both of them will be suspended for a week, and that suspension will be in their permanent records," said Mr. Johnson. "They have the right to appeal, but I don't think they'd have a chance of winning."

A week after his suspension was over, Gene was back in school, spreading a story of a family funeral he'd had to attend on the East Coast to account for his five-day absence. He and Delia were no longer seen together. On his way to the parking lot one night, Paul passed Gene, who was just unlocking his car. Paul stopped. "Why'd you do it, Gene? What did I do to you that was so bad? I just really want to know."

"It wasn't anything you did; it's who you are!" Gene spat out. "You and your brother think you own the world, like you're the coolest guys ever. I just wanted to take you down a peg or two. You don't deserve *all* the looks and brains and talent. I'm just sorry I didn't get away with it! I suppose you're going to spread it all over school and gloat and try to make me look bad. Anything to make you look better than other people."

Paul just looked at him. Then he said, "Listen, dude, if anyone finds out about all this, it won't be from Drew or me. All I've got to say is you are hella fucked up." Paul walked to his car, got in, and drove home.

9 IMAGININGS

"You look really handsome, Drew," said his mother. "Have a wonderful time, and don't forget to take pictures. I can hardly wait to hear about what she wears!" Sylvianne and Alex were sending Drew off to the prom. "Have fun, Son. We'll look forward to hearing all about it tomorrow."

Drew arrived at Elektra's house at eight. He rang the doorbell and heard her calling him to come in. She was walking down the elegant curved staircase, wearing a black dress that looked like a leotard on the top—clingy, long-sleeved, and formfitting down to midhip, with rows of black tulle ruffles to just above her knees. Her hair was slicked back, and she had a chignon hairpiece at the nape of her neck. Black platform sandal stilettos with a strap around the angle, and bright-red lipstick completed her ensemble. She looked like she was ready for a tango competition.

"Wow, you look terrific! How did you get your hair to look like that?"

"Three hours at the hairdresser's is all it takes. You don't want to know more than that."

"I have to take your picture; I promised Mom." He got out his cell phone as she posed prettily.

Picking up a three-quarter-length silver fox jacket from a bench in the foyer, she handed it to him. "Here, be a gentleman."

She turned around for him to help her into the jacket, and he was stupefied. Her dress was backless, tapering to a V at her waist, and right at the V was a little red rose tattoo. "Do you like it?" she asked, coyly.

"Yeah, I like it—totally! I like all of it—the dress, the back, the tattoo, the girl. You sure know how to make an impression, Elektra!" She slipped into the jacket and turned around to give him a head-to-toe inspection.

"You look . . ." She paused, noticing his cuff links and the studs in his tux shirt. "Speaking of studs"—she gave him a suggestive smile—"these are awesome! Where did you get them?" Drew's jewelry was made of little gold nuggets.

"My great-great uncle, or some distant relative, dug them out of a stream in the Klondike, and somehow my dad ended up with them."

"Very tasteful. You wouldn't even know they were nuggets unless you saw them up close. Nice." She dropped her bantering tone for a moment. "You look really handsome, Drew. All the girls are going to be so envious of me. Shall we go?"

On the way to the Sheraton, Drew noticed his hands tense on the steering wheel as they passed a black Mercedes. He reminded himself to relax—that was all in the past.

At the hotel, they checked her coat, which she had informed him on the way was made from farm-grown—not wild—fox and purchased secondhand. So no wild animals were killed for her.

"Here, I had to bring you a flower." He handed her a long-stemmed red rose.

"Oh, OK. I can deal with this. It's perfect." She stood in front of a mirror in the hallway and broke the thorns and some of the leaves off the stem, dropping them into a dried flower arrangement on a table in front of a mirror. Then she plunged the stem through her chignon so that it stuck out on both sides, like an arrow. It was just the zany touch that was so Elektra. He collapsed, laughing, into a chair next to the mirror. When he could breathe again, she said, "Thank you, Drew—you are so sweet!"

If they'd been frowning, they'd have looked like an ad in *Vogue* as they walked into the Sheraton ballroom. Heads turned and conversations stopped while glances and stares of amazement, envy, and admiration came their way, which they both thoroughly enjoyed—though Elektra pretended she didn't even notice. She graciously accepted compliments and didn't hesitate a second when asked, as she was several times, where she got her dress:

"Goodwill—they have really nice things there." Elektra had a dance style all her own and seemed to go off into a trance when they played a song she especially liked. They danced and danced, talked with friends, took pictures on their cell phones, and had a wonderful time.

When the band took a break, recorded music was piped in, old-fashioned slow music. She looked at Drew expectantly. "Where am I supposed to put my hand?" he asked, feigning embarrassment.

"Where do you think, idiot?" She put her arms around his neck, so he put his arms around her, his hands on her bare back. A piece of paper could not be slipped between them.

After two hours of dancing, they were ravenous. "Where shall we go? I haven't made a reservation anywhere. How about El Gaucho—it suits your dress."

"I love that place. Especially the desserts. Why don't you call and see if it's too late?"

If they could get there in fifteen minutes, they could still be served. They arrived just in time and were shown to their table, amid smiles and admiring glances from the other diners.

When the waiter offered her a menu, Elektra said, "Thank you, I don't need a menu. Caesar salad and filet mignon, medium-rare, please. And could we have a chocolate ganache to go, please? Thanks."

"Same for me, thanks," said Drew, handing back the menu.

"Too bad we can't have wine. What a drag! But I have a nice bottle at home, and we can drink it with our dessert."

"Sounds good to me!" Drew said.

As they waited for their salads, Drew asked Elektra about being bipolar. "Why did you think you had to tell me?"

"Well, I get a little weird sometimes, and if we're going to, like, hang out, I wanted you to know."

"What do you mean by weird?"

"Ummm, when I don't take my medication, which I don't usually because it makes me feel like a zombie, sometimes I get really high, busy, happy, you know, and then I get depressed—no energy, can't seem to get anything done. It's a bummer."

"Can't they, like, adjust the medication so you don't feel like a zombie, but it still works?"

"I don't know; I just can't be bothered."

Their salads arrived and conversation slowed for a while. Then Drew said, "What causes it, do they know?"

"It's some kind of chemical imbalance."

"But where does that come from? Are you born with it, or can it come from something that happened to you?"

"I don't know. I've never really thought about it. I should, like, check it out. If it's something that happened to me, maybe I could work it out in therapy. That stuff can be really useful, you know? My whole family had therapy when my sister died. I could see that it helped my dad, and maybe it helped me a little. But my mom—no way."

Their steaks arrived and there was another lull in the conversation as they launched hungrily into their main course.

"So tell me about Shaunee. There're all kinds of rumors floating around about you two."

"She's just a friend. She was . . . in a difficult situation and I helped her out. That's all."

"Rumor has it that you beat up a bunch of guys for her and ruined your hand and will never play the trumpet again. Is that true?"

He laughed. "Rumor is really amazing, isn't it? No, I managed to fight off two guys and get away without getting beaten to a pulp, and my hand seems to be healing OK. I'm just worried it won't be well fast enough for me to go to the Essentially Ellington Competition. I'll be really bummed if I can't go."

When they arrived at her house, there were a few lights on. "Are your folks home?"

"No, they went to Vancouver for the weekend. I told them I had a test Monday, so they wouldn't bug me to go along. Elena's here. She has her own apartment; she won't bother us."

They took their dessert into the kitchen. Elektra threw her coat over a stool and opened the red wine that was sitting on the huge granite-topped island. She got out two red-wine glasses and a couple of forks and napkins, and they sat down at the island, close together, and drank their wine and ate half of the dessert out of the box. She was talking a mile a minute, making him laugh with her stories.

"C'mon, bring your wine and I'll show you the rest of the house." She took him on a tour of the elegant old mansion, showing him the library, the guest suite, her parents' master suite with a marble bathroom and sunken tub. "And this is my room. You can come in; it's OK."

It was a very large corner room, facing the lake, with big windows on two sides. There were floor-to-ceiling sheers over the windows, with shimmery drapes that puddled on the floor. It was all off-white: Berber carpet, sheers, drapes, bedspread, furniture. Except for the books and papers on the desk in front of one of the windows, it was very tidy.

"Wow, this is really beautiful! It's not what I would have expected. I never thought about it, but I guess I would have expected posters of great actors and, I don't know, lots of stuff. My mom went through what she called her *Architectural Digest* phase. I used to look at those magazines sometimes. This looks like something you'd see in there. Did you do it yourself?"

"Yeah, pretty much. My mom made me talk it over with an interior designer, who drew it all up so Mom could approve. I think she was proud of me, but she never said anything."

"Why wouldn't she tell you she was proud of you?"

"I don't know; she just doesn't say stuff like that." She turned off the light and led him back down to the kitchen.

"Let's go look at the stars." She grabbed her coat and was out the French doors that led to the backyard before he knew it. She ran down the walkway that crossed the lawn and out onto the dock. He followed, more slowly, not sure of his footing, even though there was moonlight.

"Drew," she exclaimed, as he walked out onto the dock, "are you going to kiss me or not?" She stamped her feet and waved her arms. "I've been wanting to kiss you since you dropped the football. I'm dying here!"

That kiss, and the next one, had been dreamed about for some time, and were all the more passionate for the wait. At the end of the third kiss, Elektra went limp in his arms and would have fallen to the deck if he hadn't been holding her so tightly. "God! That was better than I imagined!" She stood up and said, "More, please!"

They kissed again, then Drew said, "Elektra, it's freakin' cold out here! We can do this inside. Come on." He took her hand and pulled her down the dock to the lawn.

"But, Drew, it's so romantic! It's just how I imagined it would be." She was resisting going in.

So he picked her up and carried her to the house, saying, "Look, lady, I'm not wearing a fur coat. And besides, I had imagined some things too—like some heavy-duty making out on your nice big sofa."

"Oh, well, in that case, I'm OK with going in. We can have some more wine too." In the kitchen, she poured more wine and they went into the dimly lit living room. Taking off her coat, she said, "Here, we can use this for a blanket."

He threw his suit coat on a chair. "Would you unhook this tie for me?"

"I'd love to," she said, reaching around his neck to unhook the fastener on his tie. He unbuttoned his collar.

"Anything else I can do for you?" she asked suggestively.

"There's only one more thing. That rose has got to go! I don't want to get stabbed."

She giggled. "No problem." She began taking hairpins and hidden clips out of her hairdo and the whole thing came off. "There, is that better?"

"Much! Now, how about the shoes? They're just as dangerous." He dropped to the sofa and pulled her down beside him. "Give me your foot. OK, now the other one. Your feet are freezing! Turn around and put your feet on the sofa and then cover up with your coat." She did as instructed.

"OK, have you got it just the way you imagined?" she asked. "You're as bad as me!"

"Yeah, except now you kiss *me*."

She complied.

"Sweet Jesus, I love this dress! There's hardly any of it! He was running his hands up and down her bare back. "S'pose you could wear this every time we go out?" he asked.

"Oh, are we going out again?"

"You bet!" he said, kissing her neck. "You're funny and smart, you bake cookies . . . and you *feel* so good!"

They were soon lost in the pleasures of their bodies. The fur coat lay in a heap on the floor. His shirt was untucked and her hem was quite a bit north of her knees when she pushed away from him a bit and said in a slightly wobbly voice, "Drew, I need to tell you something."

"Can't you tell me later?" he asked, pulling her back to him. "I'm really not interested in talking right now. I've got much better things to do."

"No, I need to tell you now. But I want you to keep holding me close, OK?"

"OK, no problem," he said, trying not to sound disappointed as she nestled her head on his shoulder.

"I know you're not supposed to talk about other guys with the guy you're with," she began, hesitantly. "But . . . This is awkward, so I'll just spit it out. I've had sex three times and . . . it wasn't really all it was cocked up to be. It was disappointing, and I don't want to be disappointed with you. I like you a whole lot, more than I've ever liked any guy, and I don't want to spoil it." She lay against his chest, fiddling with his shirt studs.

After a moment he said, "So you're assuming that I want to have sex with you—and you're right, I do—but that it won't be good and it will somehow ruin what we've got going, or something. Is that right?"

She nodded.

He was quiet again. Then, "Would you be willing to tell me about those three times? I don't want the details or anything, just when and who were they?"

"The first time I was fourteen, and it was a kid I'd been friends with all through grade school. It was the first time for him too. We both just did it because we were curious. It was awkward, and it didn't feel good to me, but I think he liked it. I'd heard that the first time was usually not good, so I figured it would be better the next time." She nestled closer to him. "The next time I was almost sixteen, and it was with the gardener's son at our friend's house in Aix. My family was staying with them for a few weeks. He was really hot, kind of Greek-looking, a couple of years older than me. He seemed to know what he was doing, but it was all over in about five minutes and we left the next day." She looked up at Drew, but couldn't guess what he was thinking, so she went on.

"The last guy was a friend of my brother's. He's a lot older, and I kind of had a crush on him for years, and he knew it. About six months ago, we were at a wedding, and I got a little high, not drunk, but . . . Anyway, he said it was great, but I didn't think it was great. I can't figure out why women want to do it, other than to make their boyfriends happy or something." She turned to face him.

"But Drew, I love being with you. I really like kissing you and I like being close and having you touch me. It's what I thought it would be like, having sex. God—sometimes I get turned on when you just look at me! But it wasn't like that with the others. I just sort of felt . . . used." She looked down and began fidgeting with his studs again. "What do you think? Is this our last date?" she asked, trying to sound nonchalant. The minute or so before he replied seemed to her like eternity, even though he was running his hand up and down her arm while he thought.

"Nope, not our last date," he finally said. "But there's a lot to think about."

"Like what?"

"Like what it would take to change your mind. Whether you'd feel I was pressuring you and was just like those other pricks. Like how it would feel to be in the middle of hot making out, always knowing that you only wanted to go so far. Maybe that wouldn't be frustrating for you, but it sure as hell would be for me! I'm sorry you had bad experiences, and I can see why you feel the way you do. But I didn't have bad experiences, and I'm pretty sure the girls I was with liked it—not that there've been all that many. But enough . . ."

"Oh shit. I've ruined it," she said in a little voice.

"Hey, you haven't ruined it," he said softly, caressing her cheek, damp with tears. "I still want to hang out with you—a lot. Can we just, sort of, let this lie for a while and see what happens?"

"Yeah, I'm up for that. I'm really glad you're not leaving me, at least not for a while."

"Elektra, it's time for me to go. It's two thirty."

"But I don't want you to go."

"I don't *want* to go, but I have to go. I'll call you tomorrow afternoon." She walked to the door with him and kissed him passionately. He dragged himself out the door, wishing the evening had ended differently.

10 THE ACCIDENT

Susannah and Will rushed through the double doors into the ER waiting room. "I'm looking for Paul Emory," said Susannah, nearly breathless, to the receptionist. "He's our grandson, and he was brought in about thirty minutes ago. He was in a car accident. His parents are on their way home from Canada. Can you tell me anything? Where he is, who his doctor is, anything?" she asked.

The receptionist told Susannah that Paul was with an ER doctor, who would come give them a report as soon as the staff knew what the situation was.

They were just about to sit down when Drew arrived, having been dropped off at the ER by his friend, Tom. The boys had been hanging out at the Emory's house when Drew got the call from the police. Drew had called his parents and then Susannah and Will.

"Drew, did you get any information from the police at all? Do they know what happened?" Susannah said.

"They didn't tell me much, Grams. Paul was in the passenger seat; his friend Ron was driving, and I guess he got distracted and drove over the center line." Drew was twisting and untwisting his baseball cap as he talked. "They were hit by a semi. The driver of the truck was OK, but Ron was killed. I didn't know him very well; he and Paul had just started hanging out together last summer."

"Are Alex and Sylvianne driving back, or flying, or what?"

"They weren't sure. They were going to check the flights," he answered.

"I think it would probably be faster to drive," said Will. "The weather isn't bad, and it's late, so there shouldn't be a line at the border. They could make it in three hours. It would take that long to go by air, by the time you add in the trips to and from the airport, and then what would they do with the car? So I imagine we'll hear from them soon, and that they'll be driving."

Will was right. Drew's cell phone rang fifteen minutes later, and he went outside to talk to his parents, who had just crossed the border on their way back from Vancouver. He didn't have any more information to pass along to them.

The three of them sat in the waiting room in dazed silence, watching the other people coming and going. A mother came in with a screaming baby; a middle-aged man staggered in with a bad cut on his forehead; a family of three seemed to be waiting for a mother or grandmother, who, it was gathered from overheard conversation, had passed out on the street and hit her head.

Susannah was sitting between Will and Drew, holding both their hands. She was meditating, thinking that being calm was the best way she could help right now, and meditating was the best way she knew to be calm. Thoughts of her two grandsons kept slipping into her meditation.

When she and Will were married, fourteen years ago, the boys were children. Drew and Paul were just a year apart, and they had always been close, with a minimal amount of sibling rivalry.

Susannah contemplated the unthinkable. She couldn't stop her thoughts from going there. What if Paul died or was crippled for life? She had always dealt with fear by imagining how she would behave if the worst happened, going into her head to avoid the scary feelings. That wasn't helping now that they were facing a potentially terrible reality. She was shaken to her core.

*****

The brothers had become grandsons to Will when he married Susannah. He had been their soccer coach, helped them with homework, taken them on outings, and grown to love them. He felt as if he were sinking in a sea of fear. Fear of loss. What would it be like not to have this fine young man around, not to watch him mature, get married, have his own children? How would Susannah cope with the loss of her grandson and the effect of that loss on her own son? It would put a hole in their lives, one that would always be there.

*****

Drew held his grandmother's hand, and his thoughts ricocheted from one thing to another: his parents driving back from Vancouver, would they be careful or would they have an accident too? What would it be like if Paul died, if Drew didn't have a brother anymore? Where would Paul go if he died?

Arms slipped around Drew's neck and he breathed a familiar scent. Elektra. He kissed her cheek, then stood up. "How did you know?"

"Tom called and told me. I took a taxi." She was very pale. They sat down next to each other and held hands, across from Will and Susannah.

They had been at the hospital thirty interminable minutes when the ER doctor came to give them a report. "Hi, I'm Doctor Rawlins; we've sent Paul to the operating room and called in an orthopedist and a plastic surgeon. We think he's going to come through this just fine, though it may be a long recovery. He has a broken leg and a broken arm, and those should heal with no problem. His face is another matter. It got pretty banged up and may need reconstructive surgery. He's a very lucky young man; this accident could very easily have blinded him or been fatal. You can wait here, and someone will come and tell you after he's out of the OR. He'll be in the recovery room for about an hour, then he'll be moved to a room where you can be with him."

They thanked Dr. Rawlins and waited while Drew went outside and called his parents to tell them that his brother was not in a life-threatening situation, and that one of them would be with Paul until they arrived.

"I wish there was something I could do, Ms. Emory," said Elektra. "I feel so helpless."

"Your being here for Drew is enough, Elektra. We really appreciate your coming. Are you OK, though? You look very pale."

"Oh, I'm fine, thanks. Just anxious, like you."

They sat, relieved but still tense, for about ninety minutes more in the waiting room while the surgery was under way. Then Paul was wheeled into a post-op recovery room and the plastic surgeon, Dr. Thomas, came to give them a report. "The fractures are straightforward and should heal just fine," he said. "But when the air bag went off, it splintered Paul's glasses, and some fragments of the frame were driven into his face. There was a bad cut to his eyelid, which I've sewed up. He'll have a scar, but we won't know for a few weeks whether he'll need more corrective surgery. If that's the case, it will be a matter of six months to a year before we'd want to do that."

An hour later Paul was transferred to a room where they could visit him, one at a time. Drew went in to see Paul first. He was gone for about ten minutes. His hands were shaking, and he had tears in his eyes when he came back. "There's all these tubes and machines, and his face is all, like, swollen and bruised. That cut on his eye looks really scary. But I held his hand and told him it was going to be OK, even though I know he couldn't hear me." Susannah put her arms around him and gave him a big hug. Will left to visit Paul.

"At least we know he's not in danger of dying. My God, such a relief!" said Susannah.

Drew looked exhausted. She said, "Here's some money. Take Elektra home in a taxi. Will and I will stay until your folks get here."

"No, I can call Tom. He said he'd be glad to give me a ride back home, and he's still up. He never goes to bed before midnight. He and his sister will want to know how Paul is, anyway. She's had a crush on Paul ever since they were freshmen."

"Take the money anyway. You can buy him a thank-you burger at Dick's. And tell him to drive carefully." Drew smiled at her, gave her a big hug, and put the money in his jeans pocket. "I'll talk to you soon, Grams." He and Elektra went outside and called his friend, who promised to pick them up in fifteen minutes.

Arms around each other, they waited for Tom. "Want to come with us for food?" She nodded.

"Good. I'd like to have you around. My hands are still shaking." She hugged him tighter.

They ate their fries and burgers without the usual banter, and then took Elektra home. Several lights were on at her house. "I told Elena what happened, so she's waiting up for me. Are you sure you're OK, Drew?"

He got out of the car too and hugged her again. "I'm fine. Thanks for coming. I appreciate the moral support." He kissed the top of her head. "I'll call you tomorrow and give you the latest."
*****

Susannah tiptoed into Paul's room. It was indeed, as Drew had said, a frightening sight. There were drips and cords and monitors and bandages—all very overwhelming. As she sat down beside Paul, she worried about Sylvianne's reaction. The arm not in a splint was nearest her, and it was covered with minor cuts and scratches. She put her hand lightly over his, sat back in the chair, and meditated. Some time later, a groggy voice said, very slowly, "Is that you, Grams? I can smell your perfume."

"Yes, darling, it's Grams. You're going to live, so don't worry. Your mom and dad are on their way. You're going to need to rest to get well."

He drifted off, as did she, her hand over his. About an hour later, she felt Sylvianne's hand on her shoulder. Susannah got up from her chair and gave her a big hug. "He was conscious long enough to recognize me. I told him you'd be here soon and that he should go back to sleep. Sit here, Sylvie. I'll just stay a moment with you. It's a big shock at first, to see him like this."

"I'm so glad you were able to get here right away. It was a nightmare for us driving back from Vancouver, not knowing whether he would be alive or not when we arrived. What a relief to get that call from Drew! Alex is talking to the doctor and will be here soon." Susannah could see the strain in her face, even in the dim light. They talked quietly for a few minutes, until Alex came in. Susannah hugged him and went back to Will in the waiting room.

Alex told Will there was no need for the grandparents to stay, and that Alex and Sylvianne would call them early in the morning with a report on Paul's condition.

*****

They had finished breakfast by seven thirty, and were both at work on their computers, waiting for a call from Alex, which came about eight. Paul had slept most of the night, but was awake a couple of times. He wanted to know how his friend Ron was, and they couldn't avoid telling him. And he wanted to know the extent of his own injuries. They told him that he would get the best report from the doctor the next day. Alex asked if Susannah and Will could take turns sitting with Paul while they went home to eat and sleep. They'd plan to come back after lunch. It was agreed that Will would drop Susannah off in about thirty minutes.

Paul's parents left as soon as Susannah arrived. Paul was the only patient in the two-person room, and he was awake. Susannah sat down in a comfortable chair next to his bed. She had brought a couple of magazines and books, things she thought might interest Paul, if he wanted her to read to him.

"Good morning, Paul," she said. "Is there anything I can do for you? I've brought things I could read to you. Or I could turn on the TV if you like. Have you had breakfast yet?"

"I'm not very hungry. Maybe it's the anesthetic, or stress, or something." He was quiet for a few minutes, and then said, "Grams, could you ask Drew to bring my iPod. I'd like to listen to my music. Tell him it's in my backpack, in my room. Thanks."

A few minutes later, he said, his voice barely more than a whisper, "Grams, this is so unreal. I can't believe Ron's dead and I'm lying here with casts and bandages and drips and all this stuff."

"Yes, I'm sure it seems like a bad dream, Paul. How are you feeling, emotionally?"

"I'm all over the place. Sometimes I'm just so happy that I'm alive. Then I worry about school. Am I going to be able to finish everything and go to college this fall? And what will I look like? Are people going to be scared of me when they see my face?" He shifted his position and grimaced.

"Then I think that's so petty, compared to what Ron's family is going through. I feel guilty. Why am I alive and Ron isn't? I'm really sad for Ron's family. If they have a service for him, I wonder if they would even want me to be there—I'd be a reminder of their bad luck." He fell silent.

"I'm sure you're right that this is a very difficult time for Ron's family, Paul," said his grandmother. "Since we don't know them, it's hard to guess how they'll react. I suggest you talk with your mom and dad about this. I know Alex would be willing to call them and offer to help in any way, and he could find out how they feel about seeing you. Then you'll know, and that will probably reduce your worries."

After a few minutes, she said, hesitantly, "You'll be puzzling over this event for a long time, Paul. There aren't any easy answers to such big questions. It may take years for you to work out answers that make sense to you. And you may look back years later and see how your life was shaped differently because of this accident than it would have been otherwise." She paused, and then went on. "Some consequences will be clear right away; you probably won't be able to play the lead in the play you've been rehearsing for weeks, as you were expecting. I'm sure that will be a big disappointment. And it will be a big opportunity for someone else who never thought he'd have a chance. Isn't it interesting how intertwined our lives are with others—in ways we don't often think about?

"But one thing I'd advise, Paul," Susannah continued. "Try to let go of the guilt. It wasn't your fault that Ron died and you survived. There wasn't a thing you could do about that. Feeling guilty would be useless. Find some positive way to express your gratitude for being alive and to make up for Ron's death, to the extent that's possible." Susannah knew it was impossible to rationally talk one's way out of emotions, but she hoped that her advice might help Paul a little with the guilt.

Paul drifted off to sleep again, and Susannah sat reading her book. After a while, there was a very quiet knock on the door. Susannah looked up to see a young woman standing hesitantly in the doorway. "Hi, I'm Georgina. I'm a classmate of Paul's, and I just came by to tell him hi and volunteer to bring him anything he needs from school . . . when he's well enough to think about that."

Susannah got up and went out into the hall to talk with the young woman without waking Paul. "That's very kind of you, Georgina. What a lovely name!"

The young woman blushed and looked at the floor. She was a bit taller than average, but she slumped. She wore jeans, a sweatshirt, scruffy shoes, and a battered knapsack, and her thick dark-blonde hair was pulled back into a long, untidy ponytail.

"Thank you. But nobody calls me Georgina; everyone calls me George. Will you tell Paul I came by? Here's my phone number and e-mail." She handed Susannah a scrap of paper. "Just let me know if I can help out somehow. I'm guessing you're Paul's grandmother, is that right?"

"Yes, I am. My name is Susannah Emory," she said, extending her hand.

"I'm pleased to meet you," said Georgina, politely shaking hands. "I've got to be going now. He's going to be OK, isn't he?" she asked anxiously, thrusting her hands into her coat pockets.

"We don't know yet how long it will take for the injuries to his face to heal. But the doctors don't think the broken bones will be a problem. I'll be sure to tell Paul about your offer of help, Georgina. Thanks very much."

The young woman left quietly, and Susannah watched her walk down the corridor, eyes down, with occasional quick glances at her surroundings.

The next morning, Paul and his parents, brother, and grandparents met for a conference with Paul's doctors. He wouldn't have to stay much longer in the hospital, but would have to be in a wheelchair to move around, until he could manage crutches and a walking cast. His face would be swollen for three to five days, but he wouldn't have a lot of bandages, just stitches. The sutures could be removed about a week after the accident, if all went well.

After the doctors left, the family talked about whether they needed a temporary ramp to get the wheelchair into and out of the house, and about turning the dining room into a bedroom until Paul could negotiate the stairs to his room.

"Sorry to be such a pain, Mom and Dad," Paul said to his parents. To his brother he said with a feeble smile, "You won't have any competition for the truck for a while, Drew."

"Hey, man, I'd rather have competition for the truck than a brother in two casts. We can fight over the pickup later."

"Don't worry about the household adjustments, Paul," his mother said. "We'll do fine. We're just glad you're alive—a little inconvenience is nothing!"

Drew went to his grandparents' for dinner, since his folks were going to stay with Paul for the evening and would eat at the hospital cafeteria. Since hungry grandsons were frequent visitors, Susannah always had something she could cook without much preparation. This evening she made a green salad and boiled some frozen ravioli, covering them with a red sauce and Parmesan cheese.

About halfway through his dinner, Drew said, "I can't believe we used to fight over who gets to drive, or who gets the truck for something, or who ate the last piece of pie! He coulda been dead!"

Will and Susannah exchanged a glance. Will said to Drew, "Makes you think about what really matters, doesn't it?"

11 MELTDOWN

For a couple of days Drew didn't see Elektra in the halls between classes as he usually did. He was preoccupied with helping his family rearrange the house to bring Paul home, and he had his classes and jazz band rehearsals. He asked one of her classmates if she'd seen Elektra. "She was here yesterday, kind of spacey, though. But she wasn't here today." He called her and texted, but didn't hear back.

Ms. Dawson, the drama teacher, passed Drew in the hall and stopped to express her concern about Paul. She asked Drew to send the regards of the cast to Paul, and to tell him not to worry; their stand-in could take over since Paul wouldn't be recovered enough in time to continue with the play. "Oh, Drew, have you seen Elektra? I'm a little worried because she missed a rehearsal yesterday. She's never missed one before, and she didn't call."

"I'll try to find out what's going on, Ms. Dawson. I've been calling, but I haven't got through to her yet." He had to go to a planning meeting for Desert School that evening, so he was really tired by the time he got home at ten o'clock. Still no call or text from Elektra.

About midnight his cell phone rang. "Drew, I'm scared. Can you come over?"

"Elektra! What's wrong? Is somebody trying to get in?"

"No, I'm just scared. No one's here. Can you come over?"

"Sure, sure, I'll be there in twenty minutes. Will you be OK until then?"

"Yes, I'll be waiting."

He pulled on his sweatpants and sweatshirt, stepped into his shoes without socks, grabbed his keys and down vest, and left quietly. When he arrived, every light in her house was on.

He rang the bell. "Drew, is that you?" She must have been standing there waiting for him.

"Yeah, it's me."

He was shocked when she opened the door. She was very pale and had black circles under her eyes. She looked like she'd been crying and like she'd lost weight. How could she lose weight in three days? She was barefoot, wearing pink pajamas, and what looked like a very old pink bathrobe.

"Hey, girl, tell me what's wrong," he said gently, trying to put his arms around her, but she slipped away and wandered into the kitchen. The kitchen island was littered with apple cores, leftover pizza, and takeout boxes.

"Thanks for coming, Drew. I was just really scared." She looked at him blankly. He finally got his arms around her. She was very cold and shaking.

"Elektra, it's really cold in here and you're freezing! Do you have some slippers?"

"Up in my closet. But I'm fine."

"You wait right here. I'm going to get something to warm you up." He ran up the stairs to her room and opened the doors to her closet. Her shoes were all lined up in a row. He grabbed a pair of red suede booties with bows on the toes and ran back down the stairs, stopping in the hall to look in the coat closet. Sure enough, there was the fox coat, which he brought with him to the kitchen. She was still sitting where he'd left her, staring into space. He made her put on the coat and slid the slippers on her feet.

"When was the last time you ate?"

"Oh, I don't know. I think I had some pizza yesterday."

"Would you eat something hot if I fixed it for you?"

"I guess so. I'm sorry I'm so much trouble."

He looked in the refrigerator. A few eggs, some milk, a loaf of bread. "Looks like Elena hasn't been shopping lately. Where is she, by the way?" He got out the eggs and bread.

"Uh, she had to go visit her daughter."

"Elektra, why is every light in the house on?"

Tears escaped from her red-rimmed eyes. "I just feel like someone's here when the lights are on. I like to have lots of lights on."

By now he'd figured out that she was probably at the down end of a bipolar episode. He made some scrambled eggs and put bread in the toaster. "Have you got any cocoa?" She pointed to a cupboard in which he found some instant cocoa.

"I want you to go upstairs and get in bed, so you can get warm. I'll bring this up when I'm finished. OK?"

"No, I want to stay with you. I don't want to be alone."

"OK, sure, no problem. It'll just be a few more minutes. He found some jam in the fridge and spread it on the toast. Then he heated some milk in the microwave and dumped in some cocoa.

"Can you carry the cocoa?" She nodded. "OK, let's go upstairs." He followed her up the stairs, carrying the plate of eggs and toast.

There was what looked like a nest of shawls and afghans on the bed, and crumpled tissues littered the duvet and floor. She set her cocoa on the bedside table and climbed under the covers, propping herself up with the pillows. "I need you to eat all of this, Elektra. It will make you feel less lonely," he told her, smiling.

She smiled back wanly and began to eat. She finished all of it— three eggs and two pieces of toast.

"Now, while you drink your cocoa, I'm going to go turn off some of the lights, the ones you can't see anyway, OK?" She nodded.

He moved quickly from room to room, turning off floor lamps, table lamps, sconces, overhead lights. He must have turned off a couple dozen lights. He left the light on in the hall outside her bedroom, but turned off the ceiling lights in her room, leaving only her bedside light and the bathroom light on. She sat propped against her pillows, cocoa on her lap between her hands, with her eyes closed.

He picked up all the used tissues and went into her bathroom to throw them in the wastebasket. The medicine cabinet was open, and there were nineteen apparently identical bottles of pills neatly lined up on the shelves. So she wasn't taking her medication. In the wastebasket he found a bag from a drugstore, and he dumped all the pill bottles into it. He was taking no chances. He went out to the hall and set the bag down at the top of the stairs.

Taking another look around the room, he noticed her laptop was open on her desk, glaring into the now dimly lit room. He went over to close it and saw her calendar on the screen. There was nothing on it except the dates of her parents' arrivals and departures. He scrolled back through the weeks; it looked like they had only been home for about two weeks in the last two months.

She finished her cocoa. He took the cup out of her hands and set it on the bedside table; then he sat down on the bed and pulled her close. She was crying again. "Now. Tell me why you're scared, Elektra."

"I was scared that Paul would die," she said between sobs, "and . . . and you'd be sad . . . like me, and you'd . . . get all weird, like me." She broke down completely and buried her face in his sweatshirt. He let her cry.

When she seemed to be calming down, he said, "Paul's not going to die. He might have a scar, but he's going to be fine. And I'm not going to be sad or weird. Elektra, are you having a bipolar event, or whatever it's called?"

She nodded.

"That's what I thought. Is this what happens when you don't take your meds?"

"Sometimes. Usually I just get a little down, but I can get myself out of it."

"Elektra, where's Elena? Why didn't she notice what was going on? She's supposed to be sort of taking care of you, isn't she?"

Elektra began sobbing again and clung to him desperately. "She's not here . . . she's gone . . . I mean . . . there's . . . no Elena . . . I just made her up. There's no one here but me." She took a shuddering breath and went on, her voice muffled in his sweatshirt. "At first it was a game. I'd talk to her in the kitchen or while I was doing the laundry . . . We'd discuss what groceries to order from Amazon. It was fun telling you about her, to see how long I could fool you. But I can't keep it up anymore. Now there's no one."

He was dumbfounded. He tried to keep his voice even. "You mean you've been alone, basically for months, in this big house, turning the lights off and on, eating by yourself, putting flowers in the hall? Do you do the cleaning too?"

"No, the housekeeper and the gardener come every week, and the security people drive by every day. Papa arranged for the bills to get paid, and I call or e-mail him if something unusual comes in the mail."

"I looked at your calendar when I went to close your laptop. Looks like your folks are due back day after tomorrow."

She had stopped crying. She sat up and blew her nose. "Yeah, they'll be back for a while. And then they'll leave again."

"Elektra, you can't go on like this. You have to tell them this situation isn't OK. It's not right for you to be so alone. You never mention friends. All you've got is me. You need your family."

"I don't want them to worry about me. Most of the time I do fine. I just fall apart once in a while. But it's usually not this bad." She blew her nose again.

"What would you have done if I wasn't around?"

The tears came again. "I don't know. I'm just so glad you were around." They just looked at each other.

"Hey, are you warm yet?"

"Almost."

"Why don't you go take a hot bath or a shower or something. It'll make you feel better. I'll stay here with you tonight."

"OK." She climbed out of bed and went into the bathroom. While she was showering, Drew lay on her bed, wondering what to do next. He didn't want to leave her alone the next day; he didn't think she'd be ready to go back to school, but he couldn't be with her all day. He knew his mother had a meeting in the morning and was tutoring all afternoon. Grams! She'd do it, if she could get out of whatever she might have planned. Now, if only Elektra would agree.

She padded back into the bedroom in her pink pj's, her hair damp and her face not quite so pale. She slipped under the covers. He got up, turned out the light, took off his shoes and sweatshirt, and got in beside her. She snuggled up to him, gave a sigh, and was asleep in two minutes. He lay there a long time, thinking about what had happened in the past two hours. He also couldn't avoid thinking about being in bed with her, how often he'd thought about what that would be like, and about how different it had turned out from his fantasies. Then his thoughts returned to what he should do tomorrow. He finally dropped off to sleep.

*****

His cell phone alarm went off at the usual time, six thirty. He fumbled for it, turned it off, and sat up. Elektra was still sound asleep. She looked so much better than she had a few short hours ago. He took his phone down to the kitchen and called Susannah; he knew she'd be up. "Hi, Grams. Sorry to call you so early, but I've got a problem and I'm hoping you can help."

"I'll sure try, Drew. What's happening?" He could hear the concern in her voice.

"Elektra had a, uh, meltdown last night. I think Paul's accident reminded her of her sister's death and she kind of freaked. It's got something to do with being bipolar too, I guess. Anyway, I stayed with her last night, but I can't stay all day, and I was wondering if you'd be willing to come over to her house for the day, if she's willing. She's so independent, she might not agree, but I know she likes you, and I don't think she should be alone. What do you think?"

"Of course, I'll come, Drew. I don't have anything today that won't wait. I'll bring my laptop and some books, so if she doesn't want to be social, she won't have to. She might feel kind of awkward. But I'm so sorry to hear about this—whatever it is—and I'd do anything I could to help her. What time shall I come?"

"I'll call you back after I've talked to her. I'm going to suggest eight. Will that work?"

"Yes, I can make it work. Give me the address."

After he finished talking with Susannah, Drew ate a couple of pieces of leftover pizza, drank a glass of milk, and went back upstairs. He sat down on the bed and kissed Elektra on the cheek. She opened her eyes sleepily, and said, "I smell pizza."

He laughed and said, "That's my girl: the food gets her every time. Are you awake enough to talk to me?"

"Mmm-hmm." She sat up and tousled her hair with both hands. "You're not going are you?"

"I have a proposal for you. I don't want you to be alone today. I think you need a little more time to feel better, but I can't stay with you all day. Grams would like to keep you company, if that's OK with you. She'd really like to do it. She can just read or work on her stories, or you two can hang out, whatever makes you comfortable. How does that sound?"

Elektra considered, then said, "I'm embarrassed to inconvenience her, but if she doesn't mind, I'd really like for her to come. I like her a lot."

Drew gave her a relieved smile. "Good! I'm really glad you're up for this. You can sleep a lot and eat a lot, and just rest. I'll call her and tell her eight is OK. I've got to go, Elektra. I can barely make it home to get some clothes and get to my first class on time. You'll be fine. Grams will be here in a little more than an hour. I'll call you later today and tell you when I can come over. Answer your phone!"

*****

Susannah rang the doorbell just after eight. Elektra was dressed in her usual black jeans and turtleneck, but she was also wearing a bright-red sweater and red slippers. Her customary energy was missing, and she had circles under her eyes. "Come in the kitchen, Ms. Emory. I'll make you some coffee."

"Please call me Susannah, Elektra. We don't need to be formal. I'd love some coffee, decaf if you have it."

Elektra got out the coffee and fiddled around with a very elaborate espresso machine, making an Americano for each of them. While she was making the coffee, Susannah admired the kitchen and the view. "We've got a lovely day, haven't we? This is such a pleasant room with the sun streaming in. I'll bet your family loves to be in here."

"Yeah, when they're around, we do sort of hang out in here a lot." She sat down on one of the stools at the island.

"Elektra, I don't want to intrude. I'd just like to do whatever would make you comfortable. If you feel like chatting about anything, that's fine; if not, that's fine too. I brought things to do, nothing pressing, but I want you to know that you don't need to entertain me. So I'll just follow your lead."

"Thanks, that's really nice of you. I'm a little embarrassed to ask you to come, but I really appreciate your being here. I should tell you that it's really, like, hell when I'm coming out of one of these . . . downers. I get exhausted and I feel physically sick. So I probably won't be very good company. I'm sorry." She looked at Susannah apologetically.

"Well, how would it be if I cooked some breakfast for you? I don't get to cook breakfast very often because Will and I always have the same thing. It's nice to cook for young people with good appetites. What do you like?"

"I like pretty much anything. I don't know how much breakfast stuff we have, though."

"How about if we just browse through the cupboards and see what we can find?"

"Sure, let's do that."

They started opening doors and telling each other what they found. "Here's some flour: rice, potato, whole wheat, non-gluten. And all the other basics: salt, baking powder, sugar, and so on," said Susannah.

"Every spice and herb known to woman," said Elektra.

"Soup, canned vegetables and sauces, pastas."

"Oil, vinegar, soy sauce, et cetera," Elektra continued. "Chinese, Thai, Japanese seasonings and sauces. Three kinds of rice, and I've counted five kinds of dried beans."

"Five jars of marmalade, two jars of peanut butter—creamy and crunchy. One jar of almond butter."

"Do you want to look in the pantry too?" asked Elektra.

"Goodness—no!"

Elektra sat down again. "How about some kind of a hoisin and ketchup peanut butter non-gluten flour dill rosemary garbanzo dish, with maple syrup."

"Mmm, sounds yummy," said Susannah, giggling. "I was thinking of a black bean whole wheat cardamom Dijon pickled beet casserole, with butterscotch sauce." By now, both of them were laughing.

"This is a really nice griddle. Why don't I try some pancakes?" Susannah asked.

"Go for it!"

"I want to try pancakes with non-gluten flour since I'm trying to avoid wheat. Shall I just wing it, or do you want to Google a recipe for me?"

"Coming right up." Elektra pulled out a drawer at the kitchen desk and opened a laptop. "Here's one." She turned the laptop around so Susannah could read it.

"Yes, I think we've got all those ingredients." Elektra watched her prepare the mix and told her how to use the griddle.

"Do you like to cook, Elektra?"

"Yeah, I do, but I don't do it much. It's hard to do, like, for one person. My mom's a good cook, but we eat out a lot when they're home. She just doesn't seem interested in cooking anymore."

"Well, I can understand that. After you've cooked for your family for years, it can get kind of old." Elektra didn't mention that they'd had a cook for most of her life.

Like Drew, Susannah was amazed at how much Elektra could eat. But she needed to eat a lot—she was thinner than Susannah remembered.

"Well, I think you've found a good recipe," Elektra told her. "I'll print it out for you. I'm afraid I'm going to have to crash for a while, Susannah. I used up all my energy just having breakfast. Feel free to wander around the house, if you'd like to. Be sure to see the ballroom on the third floor. I taught Drew how to do the tango up there. He's so well coordinated and musical, he could do it in about five seconds. It was really fun."

After her tour of the house, Susannah settled herself in the living room with her laptop and worked on a short story she was writing. Three hours later, Elektra came down from her nap and they had lunch. Then Elektra showed Susannah her bedroom. "What a beautiful room, with the sun pouring in. You must love to study in here. Speaking of studying, am I keeping you from your homework?"

"You're really tactful, Susannah. Thanks for the reminder. I am behind a little, because I've missed a few days of school. I'll spend some time with my books, if that's OK."

"Of course. Grandparents are always in favor of homework being done! I'll go down and read some of my magazines. I get too many to keep up with; they're running my life!"

About an hour later, Susannah appeared with a cup of coffee for Elektra. "Thanks! It's nice having a grandmother around. You look younger than I imagine grandmothers look. I always think of them in frumpy shoes with their boobs down around their waistbands, but nice, of course. They make jam and pies and things like that."

"Well, I make jam, but rarely pies—too many calories!"

She was about to leave when Elektra asked her, "Did Drew tell you how crazy I am?"

"No, he didn't. Do you think you're crazy?"

"I get a little weird sometimes."

"Does it worry you?" asked Susannah, perching on the edge of an armchair near the window.

Elektra doodled on her notebook. "Yeah, I guess it does. Most of the time I can keep it together, but sometimes I lose it, and I guess

I'm a little afraid that I might *really* lose it sometime and never get back to normal." She looked up at Susannah.

"I see." Susannah thought for a moment and then said, "What do you think you should do about the situation?"

Elektra had been expecting advice. "Ummm. I haven't thought about it too much. But I guess I'd better start."

"Yes," said Susannah. "The head-in-the-sand position doesn't have much to recommend it. Paul says you're really well organized and efficient. Maybe it's time to turn your attention to this problem." She got up and walked to the door.

"I think Drew told me your folks are coming home tomorrow. There's not much fresh stuff in the fridge. Are you up for a trip to the grocery store?"

"That's a good idea. I should get out of the house, anyway. There's a really nice little supermarket just a few blocks from here."

"I thought I'd make a meatloaf and some baked potatoes, on the chance that Drew can come for dinner. If he can't, you'll have lots of leftovers."

Elektra's phone rang while they were in the grocery store. "Hi, Handsome! Perfect timing. Susannah and I were wondering if you could come for dinner tonight . . . Great! I'll see you about five."

It was a private joy to Susannah to see Elektra's face light up while she talked to Drew.

*****

Elektra was watching Susannah make the meatloaf and taking notes on the kitchen laptop. "Hamburger, grated carrots, minced garlic and onion, bread crumbs or crackers crunched up, celery, egg, dash of milk, salt, and pepper. Is that it?"

"Yes, that's it. This is an old Emory family comfort food recipe. I think my son and grandsons would eat it every night if it was put in front of them. Sylvianne has her own French version. You know she's half French, don't you?"

"No, I didn't know that. She's kind of Parisian-looking, now that you mention it. She's really elegant, and nice too."

"She is indeed—Alex is a lucky man. You've traveled in France, Elektra?"

"Yeah, we had a summer home there for a few years, so I learned to speak French pretty well."

"I went to France in college and fell in love with the language, and I've been back many times over the years, especially after Alex married Sylvianne. There've been lots of trips with the boys, so they would know the French side of the family." She put the meatloaf in the fridge. "There you go. Put the potatoes in an hour before the meatloaf—don't forget to poke the skin first—and then bake the meatloaf at 350 degrees for about thirty minutes."

Susannah had been watching Elektra carefully, though unobtrusively, through the day. Her color was returning, she didn't seem spacey, she'd done some homework, and had a long nap. Susannah thought it was safe to leave her for an hour, until Drew arrived. She'd probably be OK even if Drew wasn't due, though not nearly so happy. "I think I'm going to pack up my little bag and trot off to see what Will's doing, Elektra. Will you be OK for a while?"

"Oh yeah, I'm fine. I'm almost back to my usual self, just super tired. I really appreciate your coming over, Susannah. It's been fun hanging out with you."

"I've enjoyed it too, Elektra. I always jump at the chance to be around young people. You make me feel so alive!"

At the door, Elektra said, "I hope you're coming to the play in a couple of weeks. I think it's going to be pretty good."

"The whole clan will be there—don't worry. Take care of yourself, Elektra." Susannah gave her a hug.

Elektra poured herself some orange juice and curled up on the couch under an afghan. She was thinking about what Susannah said about the "head in the sand" position. She didn't think her parents would be much help, and figured maybe she could find some kind of counselor or therapist or something. She lay there, sipping orange juice, thinking about what to do.

A little after five the doorbell rang. She opened the door, hands on hips, and said, *"Tu ne m'as pas dit que tu parle Francais. Méchant!* 'You didn't tell me you speak French. Naughty!'"

"Uh, *tu . . . n'as pas . . . demandé.* 'You didn't ask.' Ha—so there!"

She threw her arms around him and gave him a bear hug. "Guess what, Handsome, you get meatloaf and baked potatoes for dinner!"

"You sure know how to make a guy happy. Meatloaf and Elektra—sounds like the title of a play, doesn't it?"

Later, when they were eating their dinner, Drew said, "Elektra, what are you going to tell your parents about what happened?"

"Oh, I don't know. Like I said, Drew, they've got their own problems. I sort of think I need to handle this on my own. Susannah gave me a little kick in the butt—nicely, of course. She didn't sympathize and shit like that, she just asked me what I was going to do for myself. So I've been thinking about it."

"Well, I think it's not just about you. It's a family thing, and it isn't necessarily something you can do by yourself."

She looked at him with eyebrows raised and her intense expression. "Since when are you an expert on bipolar disorder?"

It was the closest thing to a fight they'd had. He backed off. "OK, *chacun pour soi!*" Every man for himself.

*****

The next night, Drew rang the doorbell at Elektra's house about five thirty. A tall, gaunt man opened the door. Drew said, "Are you Elektra's father?"

"I am," he answered.

"I'm Andrew Emory, Elektra's boyfriend. I'd like to talk with you a few minutes, if that's OK."

"Of course, come in, Andrew. Ariston Stephanopolis," he said, extending his hand. "I guess you know that Elektra's recovered enough from the flu to go to the rehearsal tonight. We can go in the library." They went down the hall and into the wood-paneled room, filled with books, a highly polished wood desk, Oriental rugs, and comfortable chairs. Elektra's father invited Drew to sit down.

"This feels like a scene out of Jane Austen. Have you come to ask for my daughter's hand, Andrew?" he asked, smiling at the young man.

"No, but I really care about your daughter, and I think you should know what's been going on with her. A few days ago, my brother was in a bad car accident. He's going to be fine, but for a while there, we didn't know that. Elektra started acting strange— skipping school, missing rehearsals, not answering the phone." Drew got up and paced up and down the room.

"The night before last she called me about midnight and asked me to come over, said she was scared. When I got here, she was a mess, every light in the house was on, but she hadn't turned on the heat. She was wandering around barefoot in pink pajamas, and she looked like hell. She'd been crying. I got her to eat something and get in bed. Then I accidentally discovered about twenty bottles of pills in her medicine cabinet. So she hasn't been taking her meds. Did you know that?" He removed a plastic bag from his jacket pocket and dumped the contents out on the desk.

Ariston Stephanopolis looked increasingly concerned as Drew talked. He said, "Her mother calls the pharmacy every month to make sure she's picked up her prescription, but it looks like that isn't enough."

"No, it's not," Drew said curtly. "She cried a lot while I was here, and she told me about Elena. Since I met her, she's been talking about Elena, how she's been with your family for twenty-five years, how she takes care of Elektra: cooks for her, even taught her to cook, does the laundry, manages the house, saved her teddy bear when her mother threw out all the toys in the playroom after her sister's death." Drew stopped pacing and stood in front of Elektra's father. "Somehow she was never around when I came over. So I asked Elektra where Elena was, why she wasn't here to take care of her, and finally she broke down and told me that she'd made up Elena because she was so lonely. She's making up this person, talking to her, telling me about her—because she's lonely!"

Elektra's father was clearly shocked. He sagged in his chair, hands over his eyes. He looked up at Drew, finally, and said slowly, "Andrew, Elena was the name of Elektra's sister. And those pink pajamas—their brother gave the girls pink pajamas the Christmas before Elena died. He got the wrong sizes, way too big. Elektra wears them when she gets depressed."

It was Drew's turn to be shocked. Then he resumed his pacing. "Well, she seems back to how she's been most of the time I've known her, which is only about a month. But when I asked her if she was going to tell her parents about this . . . meltdown, she said no, she didn't want to bother you. I asked her what she would have done if I hadn't been around, and she couldn't answer." Drew dropped down into an armchair. "I told her she had to tell you, but she said she'd work on it herself, like, find a shrink or something. She'll probably be mad if she finds out I've told you, but I don't care.

I'm so worried about her. How are you going to feel if you lose another daughter? I can't fuckin' deal with this! She needs her family!" He was on his feet again, almost shouting.

They heard a knock and the door opened. Elektra was home early from the dress rehearsal. "Drew! What are you doing here?"

He strode out of the room, brushing her hand with his as he went by. "Call me."

When she found out why he'd come, Elektra was angry. She did not call.

12 TIME OUT

Ten days after the accident, a memorial service was held for Ron at his family's church. Paul felt self-conscious with his casts and stitches, sweatpants and sweatshirt. He couldn't wear regular clothes, and he couldn't use crutches yet. His whole family came with him. It was a small church, and the winter sun streamed in through colored windows on the hundred or so people in attendance. Ron's tennis racket and guitar lay on a table at the front of the church, along with his senior yearbook photo. There were remembrances of Ron from his family and friends, and the minister did her best, but it was a somber occasion, Ron's death being an event out of which no one could make any sense.

After the first few days of shock about the accident had worn off at their high school, things returned to normal for most of the students who knew Paul and Ron. Grades, basketball, college decisions, who was hot and who was not; these topics were back as the focus of attention. Paul was able to attend the play he was supposed to star in; his understudy did a great job, and everyone was impressed with how professional the production looked, which was due to Elektra's expertise and tireless work. Paul was disappointed. He had looked forward to this play, knowing he probably wouldn't do drama in college. Drew and Elektra avoided each other.

One day Drew came home from school and plopped down in a chair with a bag of chips and a Coke in Paul's makeshift bedroom. "I don't think I can stand to hear any more bitchin' about 'Dad won't let me drive the Beamer to school' or 'Mr. Hanson gave me a C just 'cause I didn't get my history paper in on time,' yada yada. Freakin' idiots haven't got a clue how lucky they are!"

"Yeah, I've been thinking a lot about what used to matter to me and whether it still does or not. I didn't even know what mattered to me. I mean, I didn't think about it. Like I enjoyed being popular with girls, but I never really thought 'I like being popular with girls. That matters to me.' Now I know it matters to me, and I may not be popular with girls anymore. I may look like Frankenstein."

"Jeez, Paul, you know better than that. You know that jerk, Jim Story? Everybody says he's all handsome. The girls I know can't stand him; he's so conceited. He acts like he should be on the cover of *Esquire*—every issue." They both laughed. Drew went on, "And remember who got voted most popular in last year's senior class? Tim Sheldon. Nobody would call him handsome; he's just hella nice."

Drew ate a few more chips and continued, "I'm sure I'd be worried too, if I were you. I'm not trying to pretend it's no big deal. But I think doctors can do amazing things these days, and you'll probably end up with some bad-ass scar that girls go all crazy over."

The doorbell rang and Drew went to answer it. He came back with Georgina, who had Paul's knapsack full of his books and assignments. They were in several classes together, so she was lending him her notes and keeping him posted on what was happening at school.

"Hey, George, thanks a lot for doing this for me. I really appreciate it."

"No problem, Paul," she said. "Glad I can help. You want me to explain the assignments?"

"Yeah, sure," he sighed. "Guess I'd better start getting caught up." Drew left for a run, after which he was going to hit the books. He had a test the next day.

Georgina looked around the room, trying to figure out where to put the books that Paul would need. "I think you're going to need some kind of table that's easy to move around with one arm," she said. "Like those tables on wheels they have in hospitals. Have you got a laptop?"

"Yeah, I've got one, but I don't know how I'm going to type, with one hand in a cast," he said, looking perplexed.

"Slowly," she said, and smiled shyly. He laughed and said he'd figure out something.

"My dad can't really type," she said. "He calls what he does 'hunt and peck,' but it's surprising how fast he is. You'll probably be really fast by the time you get your cast off. Here's a copy of my notes from all the classes we're in together."

After Georgina left, Paul began reading her class notes. He was impressed with her thoroughness, and the little comments and questions to herself that she included in parentheses. He had been dimly aware that she was a good student, but he could see now that she was very sharp. He was lucky to have her notes. He wondered if she always took notes like this, or if she had made a special effort for him.

*****

The next afternoon Susannah came over to be with Paul, since both his parents had to be away and weren't comfortable with his being home alone with such limited mobility. He could get to the bathroom and he had a cell phone, but they were still nervous about his being on his own. There was pain when he got out of bed to move around, but he didn't want to take pain pills. She knew he would prefer to make his own way, so she meditated in the living room and then got out her laptop to work on her writing. About three o'clock she knocked on his door and asked if he'd like something to eat.

Fifteen minutes later Drew came in from school, followed by Susannah with grilled cheese sandwiches and tomato soup—the ultimate comfort food in their family—and also chocolate cake and milk, enough for both of them. Paul ate a few bites of sandwich and asked her, "Grams, what do you do when you meditate?"

"Do you mean what happens when I'm sitting with my eyes closed, or do I actually do something, or what is meditation about? I just want to make sure I know what you're asking. And I'm curious *why* you're asking."

"Well, I know it's something you've been doing a long time, and it means a lot to you, so I was just wondering what it was all about."

She sat down on the edge of his bed and smiled at him. "You're right. It does mean a lot to me, so I'll try not to get too carried away and bore you with too much talk! The reason I do it is because I cope better with life when I meditate. I don't get angry or depressed, or hyper as much as I used to, and I get along better with people, and I can be more helpful to them." She smoothed the blanket as she talked.

"As to what I do when I meditate, it's kind of like a time-out. I stop my outer life, and I just sit there and pay attention. You notice all kinds of things when you pay attention. You have lots of thoughts and that's OK. Your mind doesn't turn off; it has thoughts because that's what your mind is for. But you don't pay attention to the thoughts. You just watch them, and they go by, if you don't get attached to them.

"I'll be right back, I forgot the ketchup," Susannah said, leaving for the kitchen. "Here you go." She handed the ketchup bottle to Paul and sat down again on the bed. "So, when you're meditating, you may also notice things in your body, like you have a pain behind your eyes, or between your shoulder blades, or a tightness in your throat. It varies from person to person and with time. Sometimes those places in your body that you notice are holding something emotional. Like if your throat is tight, maybe you've been wanting to say something really important to someone, but you've been holding back." She stood and picked up an empty soup bowl.

"So you practice paying attention, that's what you're doing. You're not trying to stop thoughts or feelings or images from arising; you just watch them come and go and don't get attached to them. And after a while, maybe you notice that there aren't as many thoughts or feelings or images. Maybe you notice quiet or stillness. Or maybe not—I never do, though some of my meditation friends do." She piled the silverware and empty dishes on a tray, while she talked.

"It's not what happens while you're meditating that matters. It's what happens in the rest of your life. It's funny—just practicing being aware with your eyes closed can make a big difference in your life."

"Why is that? That's what I don't get," Drew said, taking the last bite of cake. He found that he was very interested in this subject and wondered why.

"This is where it gets a little tricky," said Susannah. "Different people, and spiritual traditions, have different explanations of what happens when you meditate, though there is some common ground.

I'll tell you what I believe, but you'll have to decide if it makes sense to you or not," she said, pausing to choose her words.

"When you practice long enough, your definition of who you are changes. You're down to the basics—I AM. Not I'm Paul or a guy or an American or a brother or handsome or smart, just I AM—I'm conscious. All the other stuff comes and goes. So when you realize this I AM, you're not limited so much by all the definitions that you usually use. And the other thing you realize is that you're a part of everything else—you're not separate. Philosophically, it's called nondualism." She picked up the tray, ready to take it to the kitchen.

"OK, I'll stop talking. I'm sure I've overloaded you! If you want to give it a try, I'd be really interested to know how it goes. This might be a good time, Paul, because you can't do a lot of the stuff you would ordinarily be doing. You wouldn't be giving up a lot to spend time meditating. Does what I said make any sense, boys?"

"Yeah, it seems pretty straightforward, Grams, but kind of weird too," Paul replied.

She laughed and said, "Yes, it's kind of weird until you do it a lot, and then it seems very natural. Let me know how it goes. Want anything else to eat?"

13 REHEARSING

Every couple of days Georgina came by to deliver assignments to Paul, pick up his homework, and turn it in for him. Often his other friends were there too, and she would usually sit quietly listening, or go into the kitchen and work on her own homework. One day Pam Peterson, a junior, was there, telling Paul excitedly about a play that she was writing for her Honors English class. It was to be a one-act play, starring Paul, as a character who had been in an accident. So the stitches and crutches would be perfect! She was very enthusiastic—and very pretty and determined. Paul was flattered, though he was a little dubious about whether he could be in a play and still catch up with all his homework—while hobbling around on crutches. Pam swept all his doubts away; she would help him with his homework and carry things for him, and he was such a good actor, and she would have wonderful things to put on her college applications, et cetera.

Paul's parents were dubious too, but didn't make a fuss. They would see if he could manage, or if he would get too tired, in which case they hoped he'd drop the project. "It would be a good idea for you to tell Pam she should have an understudy for you," Sylvianne told Paul. "You may not be able to follow through with this." Pam made light of the possibility that Paul wouldn't be able to finish the project, but she did pick another good-looking guy to be the understudy.

Pam left the script with Paul, who read it and gave it to Georgina, asking her opinion. She chose her words carefully.

"Overall, I think the idea is pretty good, but I think it needs some work. Like when Steve talks to Liz about how he feels about the accident, that doesn't sound real to me. What do you think?"

"Yeah, I agree," he said. They talked about some other places that seemed awkward or didn't seem to flow properly. "Do you think she'd mind if we suggested some changes?"

"I don't think she'd mind if *you* suggested changes," Georgina said. So they talked about the script and discussed changes in the dialogue and action they thought would make the play better. The next time Pam came over, Georgina left and Paul had the job of managing the playwright's ego. She didn't object much; she was so excited that a play she had written would be directed by her, star her and one of the most popular guys in the school, and they even had a love scene!

About three weeks after the accident, Paul went back to school. He could get into and out of the truck and a wheelchair, and his friends were more than happy to carry his books or push his chair. He was managing to keep up with his substantive classes, and because he had taken a heavy schedule since he was a freshman, he had enough credits that he could drop a couple of lightweight classes and still graduate. They had checked with the colleges where he had been accepted, and there appeared to be no problems related to his accident. But he still had a lot of work to do at the same time he was recovering from serious injuries.

Since Paul returned to school, Georgina had stopped visiting. At the end of their history class one day, he asked her if she'd be willing to help him learn his lines for Pam's play. She thought a moment and then said she could help him two afternoons a week, and asked where they should meet.

"Would you mind coming over to my house, George? My folks want me to come straight home from school for the next couple of weeks; they're worried I'll get too tired. I think I'm fine, but I'm trying to humor them. You could ride home with Drew and me."

"Sure, that's fine," she said. "I'll take the bus home, like I did when I was bringing your homework. When do you want to start?"

"How about tomorrow? I've only got three weeks to learn all the lines. It's a good thing it's not a long play."

They agreed on the dates when they would practice and where they would meet after school the next day.

Susannah had volunteered to make dinner for her grandsons the next night, since their parents had to go to a meeting right after work. She was always looking for reasons to spend time with the boys. She was in the kitchen, listening to Paul and Georgina, who were in the living room. Paul had already begun memorizing his lines, and Georgina was reading Pam's lines, as well as the bit parts of the two other characters.

Susannah overheard Paul say, "Come on, George, you have to read the lines like you really mean them. It's hard for me to get into the spirit of the thing if you're not. Have you ever been in a play?"

"No, I haven't," she replied. "It, like, scares me to death to even think about it!"

"You shouldn't be scared—it's fun. It's like playing—duh, that's why they call them plays!" They both laughed.

"Remember what fun it was to dress up in Halloween costumes and pretend you were a witch or a princess or something? Just think of it like that. You're pretending you're Liz."

"OK, I'll try." She shut her eyes, took a deep breath, and then resumed reading her lines. As she read, she put more expression into the dialogue and even moved around as called for by the stage directions.

"Hey," Paul said, encouraging her, "now you're getting into it— see, you can do it! Don't even pretend to be Liz, just *be* Liz." She nodded and they continued.

When they reached the part where Liz was supposed to receive her first kiss, Georgina said briskly, "I think we can skip this part. I'm sure you don't need any practice for that. Let's start again from the beginning."

Paul kept on with his lines, but he was smiling inwardly. Maybe she'd never been kissed.

Georgina left after they had rehearsed for an hour. Paul went into the kitchen, just as Drew arrived home after his jazz band rehearsal. "How's the play practice going?" he asked Paul.

"It's going fine. George's helping me learn my lines." Paul sat down in the breakfast nook. "She's never been in a play, so I was pushing her to, you know, get into it, and she finally warmed up and got with the program. She's really pretty good when she lets herself go. She wouldn't do the part where we're supposed to kiss though; she seemed embarrassed. I think she's never been kissed."

"Well, it wouldn't surprise me," said Drew. "I'm sure she's never had a boyfriend. She doesn't even try to look nice. In fact, sometimes I wonder if she tries to *not* look nice. She's not really ugly, you know, she just sort of disappears into the woodwork." Drew got the milk out of the fridge and poured himself a glass. "I've been hanging out with her brother since we were in the eighth grade, so I've been around her for a long time. She can be really funny sometimes, and she's hella smart. Maybe she doesn't like guys."

Susannah said, "Maybe she's just painfully shy, or insecure. You guys must have felt that way at one time or another, so you know what it's like. Also, maybe there's some kind of face-saving thinking going on, like 'If I don't try to attract boys, then I won't be rejected.'"

Paul and Drew considered that thought. Drew said, "I guess I can see how someone might think that way, but it's pretty twisted."

"Yeah," Paul put in. "But everyone's twisted some way. I'm pretty weird about this scar." He looked at his brother. "And don't tell me not to worry! I know I shouldn't worry, but I still do."

"So imagine what it might be like for Georgina, or any girl," said Susannah. "There's this tremendous pressure in the culture to be attractive and sexy, and at the same time people want to be loved for who they are, not what they look like, so it's a tough place to be." Susannah wiped her hands on her apron. "Until it's somehow demonstrated to you that you're attractive and lovable, you may think you aren't, and you can't talk yourself out of the feeling, even though you may know in your head it's probably not true."

A week later Georgina got a call from her best friend, Judy. "I thought we were best friends. How come I hear by random gossip that you're dating Paul Emory?"

Georgina smiled to herself but said to Judy, "I'm not going out with him. I'm just helping him a couple of hours a week to learn his lines for Pam's play. It's no big deal."

"Well, the whole school is buzzing! You've been seen getting into his car and driving off with him after school."

"I can't help what random gossip is going around," she said, emphasizing again that it was nothing. But after their conversation, she hugged to herself the idea that people thought she and Paul were dating. As ridiculous as that notion was, it was nice they thought it could really happen.

*****

Random gossip had also been hot and heavy about Drew and Elektra's apparent breakup. It had been noticed that he wasn't taking her home after school; she was riding the bus again. And they didn't talk between classes. It was said that he'd decided that he liked Shaunee better; it was also said that he still wanted to be with Elektra, but she'd rejected him.

They were both miserable but didn't know how to settle their differences. Drew thought he'd been right to talk to her father, and she felt he had interfered. After Drew's visit, there were a lot of tears and intense conversations in the mansion on Lake Washington, visits to a family counselor were scheduled and made, and the three of them began to untangle the emotional mess they'd fallen into after Elena's death. Elektra's father could understand her point of view about Drew's coming to talk to him, but felt she discounted the stress Drew was facing.

"Elektra, I think you are being very foolish about this. Here is a fine young man who loves you and is worried sick about you—with good reason. He does the only thing he can think of—and the right thing. He goes to your parents. He's seventeen years old, Elektra! He can't be expected to take on a hallucinating bipolar girl running around in old pajamas! I think he was remarkably mature to do what he did, and exercised excellent judgment in coming to me. You really *are* crazy if you don't make up with him."

That was the most blunt her father had ever been with her. She thought a lot about what he had said and about what she would have done had Drew been the one melting down. She acknowledged that she couldn't have handled it herself.

She called him. "Hi, Handsome. I need you to bring me some of that *quatre épices* of your mother's. I want to make some pumpkin cookies. When can you come over?"

There was a long pause. "How about tomorrow night?"

"How about tonight?"

"I'll be there in twenty minutes. And you'd better be wearing that dress!"

14 THE PERFORMANCE

The week before Pam's play was to be performed in the school's small black-box theater, the rehearsal schedule heated up. They were practicing every afternoon, and Georgina's services weren't needed anymore. Pam was very excited. She had made flyers and posted them around the school, advertised through Facebook, and arranged for one of the students to make a video, which she could use for her college applications. She was really strung out; by the night of the dress rehearsal, she had a cough and runny nose.

Everyone was telling her to go home and rest, so she finally did. Paul asked their drama teacher, Ms. Dawson, "What are we going to do if Pam doesn't get better? She'll be really upset if we have to cancel."

"We'll just have to wait and see how she is tomorrow. Meanwhile, if you know an actress with a photographic memory, take her the script!"

Drew had arranged to meet Paul and Elektra, who was helping out with the rather simple technical aspects of the play. As they walked to the pickup, Elektra said, "I'm having a good time with this, trying to think up easy changes that will make the play seem more professional. But the whole thing is looking a little iffy right now. It'd be a real bummer if we have to cancel."

Pam stayed home from school the next day and then arrived at the theater thirty minutes before the play was supposed to start. The cast had a conference with Ms. Dawson. Pam had a fever and a cough, could barely talk, and had tears in her eyes at the prospect of canceling her big project.

The theater was filling up rapidly. Paul looked out at the crowd and saw Georgina with two of her friends. An idea hit him: she knew the play by heart because of all the times she'd been through it with him. He told the rest of the cast that maybe she'd be willing to stand in for Pam. For a moment, Pam was thunderstruck. The idea that this nondescript nobody could take her place was unreal. Then she thought about all the time Paul and Georgina had spent together and she was jealous. Ms. Dawson was looking at her, putting two and two together. "Well, Pam, what do you think? Isn't something better than nothing?"

Paul and Pam and Ms. Dawson hurried down to the seating area and motioned for Georgina to come talk to them. She climbed over several students to the aisle, looking puzzled. Pam explained the situation, overcame her jealousy, and begged Georgina to stand in for her. She was very persuasive, with her feverish face, gravelly voice, and plays on Georgina's sympathy.

Paul joined in. "George, you know *all* the lines, not just Pam's. You can play Liz one more time. You won't be able to see the audience because of the house lights, and it will be just like we're practicing in my living room. Come on, will you do it for Pam and me?" He looked at her beseechingly.

By now all the seats were filled and students were sitting on the floor and leaning against the walls. A more-than-full house. Ms. Dawson fervently hoped that the principal and the fire department didn't show up. The theater was buzzing; people had figured out what was happening. There was an even bigger buzz when Pam sat down in the front row with her parents and Paul and Georgina went up the stage stairs and disappeared behind the curtain.

Georgina felt as she had when her little brother had been hit with a baseball bat. There was nothing to do but react, do what needed to be done, and think later. As the curtain was about to go up, Paul said, "Break a leg, George—then there'll be two of us! You can do this—I know you can!"

The show went on. Pam had made no secret of the plot, and the "love scene." It was part of her advertising strategy. So there was a lot of anticipation in the audience. Georgina didn't think; she just *became* Liz, as she and Paul had practiced so many times. When he kissed her, it was perfect! It was a little awkward; they bumped noses, but she didn't break away quickly, and there was a fractional hesitation before she went on with her lines, as if she were a little dazed. It was so clear to everyone, including Paul, what she was feeling. So romantic!

There was much shouting, whistling, clapping, and stamping of feet from the enthusiastic audience. Paul limped to the front of the stage, his arm around Georgina's waist, propelling her to take her bows. Pam and the other cast members joined them onstage, to receive applause and flowers from the playgoers.

Pam was jealous of Georgina, but at the same time very happy that her play had been successfully produced and recorded. She thanked Georgina and Paul and the rest of the cast before being dragged home by her parents to take the next dose of antibiotics. The thespians were going to Elektra's for the cast party, so Paul offered to take Georgina. She told her friends she had a ride home, and she and Paul waited for Drew to pick them up in front of the school.

"That was really fun—you did a great job, George! Now see, it wasn't so bad, was it? If you were an underclassman, you'd be recruited by Ms. Dawson for the next play. Too bad you didn't do this before your senior year. You're a natural!" Paul sat down on a nearby bench to rest his leg. "And that kiss was perfect. Pam could never get it right; she couldn't even remember the first time she'd been kissed, so she kept doing her movie-star-kiss routine."

Georgina was glad that Drew drove up just then, and also glad that it was dark so Paul couldn't see her blush.

"Hey, it's the next Selena Gomez," said Drew, getting out of the car. "The Hollywood scouts will be after you, George! Nice job! Oh, my folks send their congratulations. They thought you both were really outta sight."

Elektra came running up to join the group. "Hey, Georgina—fantastic job! That was really awesome! I'm Elektra, the stage manager. I'm glad you're coming to the party."

*****

The cast was impressed with Elektra's house, and they especially loved the ballroom. As a part of her anti-loneliness campaign, Elektra had decided to host a party, and this seemed like the perfect occasion. She knew everyone, and it wasn't too many people. She and her mom had a good time picking out furnishings for the room, though there was a little difference in styles to overcome. Elektra's parents were very pleased that she had made this effort.

It was a noisy, happy party, with lots of reliving of little things that had gone wrong and reminiscing about other productions; all of the cast but Georgina had been in other plays. Soon they were into charades and improv. Georgina watched from the sidelines, amazed at their fearlessness and creativity.

Elektra came and sat down beside her. "How did it feel up there? You sure pulled it off. Pretty impressive."

"I don't know how I did it," Georgina said. "I did know all the lines, but that's the easy part. Getting up in front of people would normally scare me to death. But it happened so fast, and Paul asked me to do it, and Pam would have been so disappointed if it was canceled, and I didn't have time to think about it; otherwise, I would've been outta there in a minute! I don't know if it was fun or not; it'll probably take me a couple of weeks to figure that out. I can't even say I'm glad it's over. It's like a dream, almost like it didn't happen."

Paul sank into the sofa beside her. "Hey, actress, are you ready to go home yet? If not, I'll just go to sleep right here. I'm totally dead."

"I'm ready—I'm tired too," she said. "I'll see if I can tear Drew away from the pizza."

The three of them drove to Georgina's house, and Paul insisted on walking her to the door, in spite of her protests. As he limped beside her, he said, "Thanks again, George. It was really brave of you to do this acting thing tonight. I hope you enjoyed it as much as I did." He kissed her on the cheek.

15 JAZZ LESSONS

The jazz band had just learned that they would indeed be invited to the Essentially Ellington Competition at Lincoln Center, and the band and members' parents were in full fund-raising mode. Susannah, Will, Will's son Derek and his wife Bridget had joined the Emorys in the high school auditorium for a concert to raise money for the trip. The concert ended with Shaunee singing Peggy Lee's classic, *Fever*, which brought the audience to their feet for cheers and applause. After the concert, there was a bake sale in the foyer; Drew's family stood around, munching cookies, talking about the performance and waiting for him to bring Shaunee, so they could congratulate her in person.

While they were waiting, Will and Paul were talking about Will's yoga class. "Isn't that kind of a girly thing?" Paul asked.

Will laughed and said, "Careful, your ignorance is showing! I'll have you know yoga is a very demanding spiritual practice that's been around for thousands of years. Why don't you come with me sometime and decide for yourself if it's girly?"

"Tell you what, Will. If you'll come camping with us, we'll go to yoga with you."

"Ha!" Susannah gloated. "He got you! You can't wiggle out of a camping trip. You're just going to have to confront your warped ideas of camping and try it out."

Will laughed again and said, "OK, I give up. After years of resisting the idea of sleeping in the dirt with bugs and eating food with ashes in it, I guess I'll just have to endure it."

"Man, talk about ignorance showing!" Paul joshed him. "You won't believe how cushy camping can be. The Emorys don't travel light when it comes to car camping. We'll break you in on car camping, and then later Drew can get you into backpacking. Where shall we go?"

"What about Lake Kachess?" Susannah suggested. "It's close, it's got a lake and trails, and we could take our bikes. And it's on the other side of the mountains, so it'll be warmer. Why don't we look at early June?"

Just then Drew arrived with Shaunee. She was a little overwhelmed to meet all of Drew's family at once, but was very happy to hear how much they enjoyed the concert and her singing. "How can you *do* that?" Bridget asked her. "I'd be so scared to be in front of so many people!"

"Oh, it's fun!" Shaunee replied with a big smile—she had a lovely smile. "Guess I'm just a show-off, but I don't get nervous, usually. As soon as we start, I'm fine. We're such a group, we're so together, we're playing for each other as much as the audience."

"You could be the next Ernestine Anderson, Shaunee," Derek told her enthusiastically. "Are you planning a performing career?"

"Oh, I don't know . . ." Her elation seemed to disappear. "I'd like to go to Cornish, but that's kind of a long shot, and without training, you have to be awfully good and awfully lucky to make it. Even *with* training, you have to be really good and lucky. So I'll just have to see how it goes."

The family walked back to their cars. Derek and Bridget walked with Susannah and Alex. "So this is the young lady that Drew got all banged up over?" Derek asked. "She's a knockout—and really talented. Did everything work out OK for her?"

"We think so," Susannah replied. "She got a job at a day-care center after school, and from what we've heard from Drew, she and her grandmother were eligible for some state programs for low-income folks, and that's helped a lot. But they just recently learned that her grandmother has cancer, so I don't know about college. Drew's urging her to apply for scholarships at Cornish and the U, but she doesn't think she could swing it, even with a scholarship."

"You're all coming over for dessert, aren't you?" asked Alex. "Sylvianne's made her famous apple tart."

*****

The six adults sat in the Emory living room with their coffee and apple tart, talking about the concert and Shaunee's situation. Derek said, "You know, I had an idea during the concert as I was watching Shaunee. Our band director's having a hard time with his seventh and eighth graders right now. They're acting out more than they usually do at that age. I was wondering if Shaunee and maybe two or three band members could come do a concert for them. Maybe they could even work out a two- or three-week teaching block on jazz, with the teens doing the teaching. It would blow the middle schoolers away to be taught by kids near their own age who are really, really good." Derek was getting more and more enthusiastic as he talked.

Drew and Paul arrived, carrying wedges of apple tart. Derek told them his idea, and Drew was immediately supportive. "I'll talk to Shaunee tomorrow and to Mr. Williams, the jazz band teacher. You know, I think I heard him telling a story once about playing in schools when he was performing with his own band. They got some kind of funding from the arts commission or something. Do you think they'd get paid, Derek?"

"They *ought* to get paid!" said Derek. "They're certainly professional-level players, and this would take some effort on their part. Talk to Mr. Williams about that—how much would be appropriate, and so on. Also, this would look great on their college applications."

"Hey, thanks, Derek. This is a great idea! I'll call you tomorrow after school and let you know what Shaunee and Mr. Williams think. Now I've got to study for a test. G'night everybody."

After he and Paul left to study, Derek said, "I had another idea, but I thought I should wait until we see if this one works out. If it does, there are lots of other schools in the area that would like to have this kind of a program. It would be a way for the kids to earn some money. Not all of the schools could afford it, but I'd love to underwrite something like this. I wouldn't want them to know; we could just give the high school an anonymous grant to be used to support this program. Shaunee could be the coordinator, if she's got the talent for that kind of thing." He waved his hand. "All that could be worked out."

*****

Drew called Derek back to tell him that Shaunee, Mr. Williams, and the band members were enthusiastic about Derek's idea. They agreed that it would be good for Mr. Williams and Derek's school's band director, Dan O'Donnell to talk, get a feel for the level of accomplishment of the middle schoolers, and what their teacher would like to have as an outcome of the "jazz block."

The appropriate conversations were held, Shaunee volunteered to be the coordinator, and several jazz band members agreed to participate on different days, so it would take less of their time and the younger students would be exposed to more instruments. The jazz class was scheduled for late May, after the Essentially Ellington Competition.

Drew and Shaunee met for coffee on a Saturday afternoon to go over the plan for the two-week class, before presenting it to the teachers. Shaunee explained what she'd come up with. "So I'll start by talking about the history of jazz, and give them a list of books on various jazz artists, and each student will have to do a short paper on a famous musician. I'll have a list for them to choose from. There's tons of stuff online too. And they'll have to listen to at least three pieces performed by their artists. That's one piece."

Drew nodded. "Sounds good so far."

"Another piece will be jazz styles, like what's Dixieland, bebop, fusion, big band; what musical influences formed jazz—that kind of thing," said Shaunee. "I thought we could demonstrate all the different styles, maybe play one theme or piece in each style, so they could hear the difference. And then we need to talk about improvisation; how do you think we should do that?"

"We just pick a piece and play it once, and then we play it again differently," said Drew. "We can do that easy, it just might be a little hard for them to hear and remember the difference. We don't know their skill level. Maybe we could do a real different tempo the second time; we'll talk about it and think of something. But back to the history, why don't we start out with a bang, instead of a history lesson? The history's important, but why don't we put that after they've heard the different styles?"

"Cool—that's an improvement," said Shaunee, taking another sip of coffee. "Now, another part would be for the kids to play. The teachers are putting together some sheet music for the different instruments. The kids will be practicing three tunes. My idea is to have a concert and invite the parents. We could play with the kids, and do some tunes on our own. I thought this would be a good lesson in marketing. Each kid would have to invite at least three people, they'd have to do up a flyer for publicity, arrange for someone to take donations at the door, and so on. We could even have an open mike part of the concert, for anyone brave enough to get up and solo. They need to know that's how you get gigs."

"Totally! Great idea! This will be a life lesson as well as a music lesson. I'm pumped!"

"Me too, Drew. I'm really getting into this. I'm surprising myself about how much fun I'm having. If it works out, maybe we could do it again."

*****

The Starbucks coffee shop near the high school was always crowded with students. They came before and after school, at lunchtime, even during classes; it was a favorite place to hang out. Shaunee's friend Charlene got up to leave just as Elektra picked up her triple grande mocha and looked around for a place to sit. She hesitated for a moment and then walked over to Shaunee's table. "Mind if I sit here? It's the only seat left."

"No problem. Make yourself at home." *So this is the girl Drew's so crazy about,* she thought as Elektra sat down. *A little on the thin side, but definitely dramatic.*

"I guess we've never formally met. I'm Elektra," she said, and then thought, *So this is the girl Drew's been helping. I hope I'm not competing with her. She looks like a Victoria's Secret model.*

"I know who you are," said Shaunee.

"I know who you are too."

Everyone was watching this little drama play out. Speculations were rising like the steam off their lattes and Chai teas. Both girls were aware of the glances and whispers.

Elektra leaned toward Shaunee and said, "Shall I pull a knife on you or are you gonna turn the table over on me?" They both burst out laughing.

"So, where'd you come from, girl?" said Shaunee, arms crossed on the table.

"I transferred in from Holy Names this year. My favorite drama teacher wasn't coming back this year, and I decided I'd done the girls' school thing long enough." She leaned back in her chair. "Why miss 50 percent of the population? So here I am. The drama program is really good; otherwise, I would have gone somewhere else."

"Speaking of the other 50 percent, I'd say you really scored there."

"Yeah, I got lucky, didn't I? Knock on wood." She knocked on her wooden chair and smiled at Shaunee, savoring this acknowledgment of Drew's desirability and their relationship.

"You got lucky, all right. And you better appreciate him because there's a line of girls a mile long waiting to take your place!"

"Are you in the line?" asked Elektra, grinning wickedly, as she lifted her coffee to her lips.

Shaunee laughed and said, "Not now, but I might push my way to the head of the line if you don't treat him right."

"You don't need to worry. He's the best thing that's happened to me since . . . I can't remember when. I just hope I don't screw up and blow it."

Shaunee took in Elektra's direct gaze, the slightly worried expression, the little trace of tension that had come into her voice.

"Well, I don't think you need to worry either. He's so into you, it's pitiful!" She smiled, and Elektra smiled back.

"So, what's Drew told you about me?" Shaunee was a little bit nervous that Drew might have told his girlfriend about her brush with prostitution.

"He said that you had a problem, and he was helping you with it. That's all. Except he's always 'Shaunee said this, Shaunee did that, you should have heard Shaunee's take on "Over the Rainbow,"' stuff like that. I have to be careful not to get jealous."

Shaunee just smiled. "Want to walk back with me? It's time for band practice."

16 THE PROM DRESS

The date of Paul's twelve-week check-up appointment with the plastic surgeon to discuss further surgery was fast approaching. He was trying not to be anxious about his appearance, but was, though he didn't talk about it to anyone. He told his folks they didn't need to accompany him. They acquiesced, unhappily. They were practicing the letting go that has to come as a firstborn goes off into the world, and they were finding it difficult. Unbeknownst to them, Paul had asked Georgina to go with him. He didn't know why she was the person he wanted with him, but she was willing to go.

They got on the bus together after school on the day of the appointment. He was walking well enough now that he didn't need to be driven all the time. She noticed that he was kind of quiet, not chitchatting as he usually did, and she guessed he was anxious.

They got off at Dr. Thomas's office building and took the elevator up to his office. He was pleased with the healing that had occurred. "Well, Paul, it appears that you don't have any permanent injury to your eye or eyelid, just the disfigurement of the scar. In a few months it will be far less noticeable than it is now—to you and to other people. That would be the time to decide if there's anything further we can do for cosmetic purposes."

As they walked out of the medical center and into the sunny spring afternoon, Paul asked "How about a frappuccino?"

"Sure, sounds good," she replied. They walked down Madison to the nearest coffee shop, and Paul ordered drinks for both of them.

She could tell he was preoccupied. After a few sips of his drink, he said, "What would you do if you were me? About more surgery, I mean."

"I don't think it looks that bad, Paul, really," she said. "It probably looks worse to you than to other people. People like you for who you are, and they're not going to stop liking you because you have a scar. Your friends won't even notice, after a while. You won't either. And if you do notice it, it'll remind you to be glad you're alive."

"Yeah, here we are drinking frappuccinos on a sunny afternoon, and Ron's dead." He swished his drink around with the straw.

"Do you feel guilty or something?" she asked.

"No, not guilty . . . well, maybe. Grams tried to talk me out of that. I know it wasn't my fault. But I feel . . . something."

She sat back in her chair. "It's pretty sad. I didn't know him, but I'd feel sad if I were you. He was your friend." She was quiet for a while, and then went on, "You know my mom died of breast cancer?" She looked up at him, eyebrows raised. He nodded and she continued. "When Mom died, it was like getting whacked with a two-by-four. You suddenly realize life is tough. I mean, we know people die, but the first time someone dies that you know, it's a shock. The reality of the person not being there anymore is right in your face. Big-time loss."

"Yeah, that's kind of what I've been feeling," he acknowledged. Then he changed the subject. "Are you going to the prom?"

She blushed and shook her head. "Why not?" he asked.

"Nobody's asked me, and I'm too shy to ask someone."

"Why don't you come with us?" he said. "A bunch of us are going together, not, you know, with specific dates. Let's see: Maria, Sam, Penny, Beth, Rick, Suzie, maybe some others. You know Maria and Beth, don't you?"

"We've been in the same classes since grade school, so, yeah, I know them, but we're not, like, friends or anything."

"Come on, George, come with us. I'll pick you up. I'm picking up Maria, Sam, and Penny, so there's room for you too. We're going to Penny's afterwards for fondue. You only get one chance to go to your senior prom. You should do it."

After a pause, she said, "OK," as if resigned to a necessary task. "I probably should go. Wouldn't want to regret it when I'm old, if I didn't go."

"Yes!" he said enthusiastically, pumping his fist. "Talked you into it! You'll have a really good time; I know you will."

Just then, Susannah walked into the coffee shop. She often frequented the little bookstore next door, and had just been in to buy a book that had been recommended to her.

"Hi, you two—what a surprise!"

While Paul and Susannah were talking, Georgina was half listening and half thinking about the Dress Issue. She didn't have anything to wear to the prom, and panic was building as she thought about shopping for a dress. She couldn't imagine shopping with her friend Judy, whose wardrobe consisted of five pairs of black jeans and an assortment of rock band T-shirts. She mulled over various possibilities as the conversation continued between Paul and his grandmother. Then it was time for Paul and Georgina to catch the bus. As they were leaving, she said to Paul, "I'll be right back; I have to ask your grandmother something."

She hurried back into the coffee shop. "Ms. Emory, would you do me a favor? Would you go dress shopping with me? Paul invited me to go with him and his friends to the prom, and I don't have anything to wear. I could use some help picking something out. I'd ask my best friend, but she's about as useless as I am when it comes to clothes." Susannah knew that Georgina had lost her mom. She felt a pang in her heart that Georgina's mom wasn't here to watch this big event and to help her daughter into womanhood.

"What fun! I'd be delighted to go shopping with you, Georgina. What are you thinking: long formal, cocktail dress, vintage?" Georgina looked bewildered. "Maybe you haven't had time to think about it yet. Something you might consider is just browsing through the fashion magazines to see what styles you like, what's in, and so on. It's always interesting to see what they're doing with makeup and hairdos."

They agreed that Susannah would pick Georgina up the following Saturday, and they would check out the consignment shops. Georgina knew all about them and was determined not to spend a fortune on a dress she would rarely wear. The next day she stopped at Bartell's and looked at *Elle*, *Cosmo*, *Teen Vogue*, and *Vanity Fair*. She saw some hairstyles that she liked and got a few ideas for dresses. She also read an article about teenage girls' poor posture—evidence, the author suggested, of self-consciousness about developing breasts and, if they were tall, being taller than boys their age. She decided that since she wasn't going to get any shorter or less buxom, she might as well stand up straight.

*****

Susannah picked Georgina up at nine thirty on Saturday morning, and they drove to a big consignment shop in Kirkland that had lots of prom dresses. "Georgina, I encourage you to try on lots of things; you may be surprised at how something looks so much better when you have it on than when it's on the hanger. Besides, you don't get to do this very often, so we might as well have a good time! Let's plan to spend two hours, and then I'll treat you to lunch, and we can go somewhere else if you haven't found anything."

"OK, sounds like a plan," Georgina said happily, as she started through the racks. She picked out four dresses and the clerk, whose name was Sally, took her and the dresses to a dressing room. Susannah continued looking.

Of the first four, only one was a possibility, so Sally took the others away, and Susannah gave Georgina four more, while Sally searched too. Of the second four, again only one was a possibility. Sally came back with another four, two of which were short. No luck. Three more shorts and four more longs came and went. Only one from that batch that they all liked. After two hours, they had two long dresses and two short dresses that they all liked, but Georgina couldn't make up her mind.

"OK, time for lunch!" said Susannah. "I have an idea. Why don't we call Paul and ask him to come help you choose. If he's not busy, he could meet us here in an hour. That will give us time to talk about the pros and cons of the final four, and maybe you can narrow it further. If not, he can help. What do you think?"

"I don't know . . . wouldn't he think it's a drag?" Georgina asked.

"Well, I'll flatter him and tell him we need the masculine opinion, and it won't take more than thirty minutes, and I'll buy him a frappuccino and a brownie at Starbucks." Susannah called him; he was free and amenable to the food bribe. She gave him the address, and he agreed to meet them in an hour at the shop. They found a restaurant nearby and ordered lunch.

After eating, Georgina was ready to tackle the final decision. They went back to the shop and met Paul, standing at the door. His casts had come off a few days earlier, and he was limping. "This is a little weird," he said, with an easy grin. "It's the kind of thing you could use for your college application essay. You know, you're supposed to talk about something out of the ordinary, so they'll remember you. How many guys go prom dress shopping?"

There were lots of girls shopping with their moms or with friends, since it was prom season, but Paul was the only male. The other shoppers looked with interest at this attractive guy, dressed in flip-flops, cutoffs, and a muscle T-shirt. What was he doing here?

Susannah sat down in a chair, and Paul lounged against the wall while Georgina went into the dressing room to try on the first dress. It was long, a pale metallic blue stretchy fabric, and very formfitting, with spaghetti straps. Susannah was watching his face in the mirror behind Georgina, and watching her check his reaction. Susannah could imagine what was going through his mind.

She guessed right on the thoughts, if not the verbiage: *"Sweet Jesus! Why has she been hiding that gorgeous body? Shit, every guy at the dance is going to have one thing on his mind if she wears that!"* He noticed that she was biting her fingernail and quickly said, "That's really nice. Turn around, let's see the back." Georgina pirouetted. In one glance his eyes took in the womanly bosom, the curves of her backside and thigh. "OK, got it; let's see the next one."

Georgina went back into the dressing room and appeared five minutes later in a long white sleeveless dress with a slit up the front seam that ended above the knee. It had two three-by-eight-inch cutouts just above the waist on either side, covered with a see-through fabric and surrounded by lace—demurely sexy. "That one's nice too." He nodded approvingly. She went back to the dressing room.

Susannah made Paul sit down and rest his leg, and she stood. She noticed with amusement the intense interest from the other shoppers in this little drama. "This will make a good story to tell your friends," she teased him. "You're a good sport to do this."

"Yeah, it's really tough, looking at girls in pretty dresses," he joked.

Georgina reappeared in a short, glittery hot-pink number, strapless, with an irregular hem. Her ponytail was a mess, with all the dress changes. She pulled the rubber band off, and her long, heavy golden hair fell down her back. Unconsciously tucking a strand behind her ear, she turned around so that he could see the back of the dress. He considered, and then said, "It looks nice on you, but I don't think that's the one."

"Only one more. Thanks, both of you, for being so patient," Georgina said.

"This is not difficult *at all*, George; not to worry," he assured her. As she was changing again, he wondered why she never wore her hair down. It was really sexy.

She was back in five minutes in a short pale-green chiffon with a halter top that tied behind the neck in a bow, a fitted bodice with silver beading, and a swishy skirt that stopped above her knees and showed off her shapely legs.

"Nice. OK, now what? Do we have a powwow, or do I just choose, or what?" Paul asked.

Susannah gave Georgina a look that said, "It's up to you."

Georgina said, "We liked all four, and they all have pros and cons, so why don't you just decide?"

"OK, it's the last one. I liked the others too, but I liked the green one the best. Are you sure you like it, George? Hey, you know what? I'm going to stop calling you George. It just really doesn't fit you. How about Gina?"

Her expression changed from anxious to quietly happy. "I like that. And yeah, I like the green one a lot." She had a big smile on her face as she went back to change into her jeans.

*****

Sylvianne made sure she got photos of Paul in his tux before he left to pick up his friends for the dance. She made him promise to take pictures on his cell phone of everyone in the group. She knew Susannah would love looking at them. Paul made all the prom-goers pose on their doorsteps as he picked them up, because he figured he'd forget to take photos later on.

Georgina looked like a movie starlet in her green dress, silver flats and earrings, with her hair streaked and partially piled on top of her head, the rest flowing in waves down her back. "Wow!" Paul exclaimed, "You look really great!" He took her photo and another of her with her dad. "She'll be home by two, Mr. Gregson. We're going to Penny Hayworth's house for fondue after the dance."

"Have a good time, kids," Georgina's dad said, waving them off with a restrained smile. His little girl was growing up, and her mom wasn't there to see it.

The girls all oohed and aahed at each others' dresses and complimented the guys on how handsome they looked. Georgina was very excited. She couldn't quite believe that she was going to the prom, and with people she'd always admired from afar. She was feeling shy, but told herself to think about the other people instead of thinking about herself so much.

Paul had to take several breaks, because his leg was still weak. But they danced till they dropped and had a wonderful time. A million cell phone pictures were taken that evening and would begin appearing on Facebook before dawn. About eleven thirty they collapsed into their cars and drove to Broadmoor to Penny's. Her family was well-to-do and lived in a mansion in a gated community. Her folks had left a big spread of hors d'oeuvres, two pots ready to make cheese fondue and another pot for chocolate fondue, as well as assorted beverages. They had discreetly absented themselves, but Penny knew they would be back around two in the morning. The gate would keep out party crashers.

Some of the kids had brought liquor, smuggling it into the house under jackets or in big handbags. They made the obligatory attempts to hide it from Penny, but she knew what was going on and pretended not to. Some of the girls figured they could get away with drinking because they were staying the night. Paul noticed Georgina watching what was happening. She seemed a little wary, but not disapproving. The two of them helped Penny make the fondue, which disappeared very quickly, as did the rest of the food.

Some of the kids found a stack of games in the family room and started a raucous round of Uno. Others started a game of Risk, and then some began pairing off and disappearing into the many dark rooms of the big house. Georgina began to feel a little uncomfortable. She didn't want to be paired off with anyone but Paul, and didn't expect that to happen, so she wasn't sure quite what to do. Someone handed her a glass of Coke, and she continued with the Risk game.

A few minutes later Paul finished his round of Uno, came over, and told everyone Gina was conceding defeat because he wanted to show her something in the living room. There was much laughter and joking, and Georgina blushed as he led her away.

They went into the dimly lit living room, and he settled them on a sofa. "I don't really have anything to show you, Gina; I just wanted to check out your drink." He took a drink of her Coke and put it on the coffee table. "It's got rum in it. I'll bet you didn't notice."

"Oh, so that's what rum and Coke tastes like—it's good!" she said. "But I'm glad I didn't drink very much of it. I don't want to miss any of this evening. Thanks so much for talking me into coming, Paul. I've really had a good time." She screwed up all her courage and put her head on his shoulder. Then she shut her eyes to savor this moment and make it last as long as possible.

Paul looked at her bare arms and shoulders, her bare feet resting on the coffee table. He noted, not for the first time that evening, the bow (that could be untied) behind her neck. He put his arm around her shoulders and buried his face in her hair, which had come partially unpinned and was very alluring. "Mmm, you smell good!" They both laughed.

"Paul?"

"Mmm-hmm," he said, not really interested in talking.

"Why did you like this dress best?"

He thought a moment. "Well, the pink one and the white one were OK. They looked nice on you, but they just weren't really fantastic. The blue one . . ." He paused. "That was a really nice dress, but it was kind of . . . suggestive . . . or something . . . and I didn't think that's what you'd want. Some girls do, but I didn't think you would."

"Oh—thanks for saving me from a mistake. But did you choose this dress just because it was the only one left?"

'No, no! I really like it. It's a really good color for you, and green happens to be my favorite color. It shows off your figure too, even though it's not tight. The way it's made, or something, you know. And short skirts are great for girls with nice legs. But . . . I probably shouldn't tell you this. It's the tie around your neck with the bow that was the clincher. It's really sexy. It makes a guy think about untying it—not that I would, of course."

She gave him a big smile, and then put her head back on his shoulder. "Now I know a little something about what guys think. Thanks."

He was playing with a long ringlet that had fallen out of her coiffure, and lay across her collarbone. He really wanted to kiss her. Her proximity, bare shoulders, disheveled hair, and all this talk of sexy dresses was getting to him.

She was willing him to kiss her with all her being. And he finally did, turning her face to his and giving her a lingering kiss. As she kissed him back, she felt her mind turn off and her body turn on. Sometime later, she drew back a little and said, "I've never been drunk, but this must be what it feels like. I feel light-headed, I couldn't walk if you paid me, I can't think, and I just feel so happy."

"This is way better than drunk, Gina—believe me!" He kissed her shoulder, her neck, her mouth. Sometime later they were half lying on the couch, wrapped in each other's arms, when they heard a discreet cough behind them. "Sorry to break this up, you two, but it's one forty-five." Penny's mom was making the rounds.

They all got themselves together, into the car, and Paul took Rick and Sam home first. Gina and Paul kissed again under her dim porch light. "Thank you for such a wonderful night, Paul," she said, her face radiant.

"You're welcome," he said, smiling at her. "It was pretty special, wasn't it?"

*****

Sunday afternoon, Sylvianne stopped at Susannah and Will's to show them the prom photos Paul had taken. "I knew you'd be dying to see these, Susannah. I was too. Paul put them on a memory stick for me, so we can make prints." They sat in front of the computer screen and looked at the photos.

"How can they only be eighteen?" said Will. "They all look like twentysomethings! Man, Georgina is gorgeous—nice job on the dress shopping, Honey."

"She and Paul deserve all the credit," Susannah said. "I was just happy to be involved around the edges. We're so lucky with these kids. Lots of kids wouldn't even consider shopping with their grandmothers."

"Give yourself some credit, Susannah," said Sylvianne. "You're not just any grandmother. You enjoy life, you're fun to be around. How many women in their seventies row and take dancing lessons and have husbands who do yoga classes three times a week? I think Gina knows a good grandmother when she sees one."

17 THE CONCERT

Shaunee was in a panic. She'd just learned that her grandmother's cancer surgery was the same day in early May as the concert marking the finale of the jazz block she was coordinating—how could she not be there to make sure everything went off according to plan? And how could she not be with her grandmother at the hospital? There was no one else to be with her, and Shaunee knew her grandmother was scared. Neither of them had much experience with doctors and hospitals.

The jazz band was practicing one of the numbers they planned to do for the concert, and Shaunee missed her entrance. "Sorry, could we start again?" she asked. Mr. Williams nodded; she didn't miss her entrance this time, but he could tell something was up. After practice, he walked out of the band room with her and asked if she was OK. "Yeah, I'm fine, just a lot going on, you know," she said, giving him a quick glance and a little smile.

"Well, let me know if there's something you need help with," he said, going out the door to the parking lot as she continued down the hall to her locker.

Lester Thomas was their first chair trombone and had had a crush on Shaunee since grade school. He was leaving the band room behind Shaunee and Mr. Williams and heard this exchange. He caught up and walked down the hall with her. "Hey, you OK?"

"Not you too! Can't a girl miss an entrance once without everybody freakin' out?"

"Nobody's freakin' out, Shaunee. You just never miss your cue, so . . . what're we supposed to think?"

He set down his trombone case and leaned against the locker next to hers. "So what's happenin', girl?"

She looked up at him—way up. He was about six four and skinny as a rail. "Oh, all right! My grandma's surgery is the same day as the middle school concert, and I can't figure out what to do. I know I'm not going to get either of those dates changed."

He knew about Mrs. Brown's surgery, since his mom was a pillar of the church they both went to, and his mom knew everything about everybody. She was also in charge of the Guild, the group that organized support services for members of the congregation. "What time is the surgery?"

"It's at one o'clock, and I know the concert's in the evening, but I can't leave her alone at the hospital. She's really scared about this operation."

"Hmm, yeah, I see why you're worried. But there's still two weeks to figure somethin' out. Want a ride home?"

*****

About a week later, Shaunee fell into step—two to his one—with Lester on the way out of the cafeteria. "Hey, Mister Magic, thanks!"

"What you talkin' about, girl?"

"You know what I'm talkin' about. Your mom's got a whole string of people arranged to stay with Grandma after she wakes up from the surgery, bring her home the next day, and bring casseroles till hell freezes over!"

He laughed. "Yeah, that sounds like my mom, all right. And I'm bringing you from the hospital to the concert and back again so you can be with your grandma as much as possible, and still do the concert thing. So. You gonna miss any more entrances?"

"No, guess I haven't got any excuses now. Thanks again, Les." She gave him a big hug, right there in the hall, unleashing untold amounts of speculation from those who saw it and those who very soon heard about it.

*****

Shaunee sat in the surgery prep waiting area beside her grandmother's gurney. Lester's mom sat in the other chair, cheerfully filling the time with light chatter, trying to help the other two relax. "This is a simple surgery, you know; they do it all the time, and the follow-up treatment isn't so bad. You'll be up and around in no time, Pearl. And Shaunee, you know the Guild will take care of meals and trips to the doctor's office until your grandmother is back on her feet. You don't have to worry about any of that."

"Yes, I know, Mrs. Thomas, and Grandma and I really appreciate your help. It's a big relief, knowing we're not totally on our own."

"Shaunee, I'm feeling pretty hopeful about how all this will go," said her grandmother. "But since I found out about the cancer, I been worrying even more about your future, once I'm gone. Now don't go getting all upset. I hope it will be a long time from now. But what if it's not? We got to think about that." She took Shaunee's hand and patted it. "We'll talk about this more after the operation, when I'm feeling better. But I want you to know that Mrs. Thomas and Pastor DuBois have agreed to be your guardians if something happens to me. We're going to do all the paperwork as soon as I'm up and around. You know Albert Wilkins from the church, you used to play with his daughter, Alia?" Shaunee nodded. "He's a lawyer and he's going to take care of everything for us. So the best thing you can do for me is not worry. The Lord's brought us a whole lot of help, and don't you forget where that help came from!"

"I won't forget, Grandma. I just want this to be over and you to be all well again."

The nurse appeared to wheel Mrs. Brown to the OR. "They're ready for you, Mrs. Brown. All set?" she asked with a reassuring smile.

"As set as I'll ever be," she said. "Now Shaunee, you have a good time at your show tonight; you hear me, girl? You let those folks hear some fine jazz. Your grandpa's watching, so you sing good!"

"I will, Grandma, I will. And I'll be back here right after the show to see you. Les is bringing me back." She squeezed her grandmother's hand tightly and tried not to cry. By the time the surgery would be over and Mrs. Brown was not too groggy to talk, it would be time for the final preparations for the performance. Mrs.

Thomas would stay at the hospital and call Les's cell phone to give Shaunee an update as soon as there was anything to report.

Les was waiting for her at the appointed place. "The car's just a block away. You have any lunch?"

"No, I forgot about it."

"OK, let's stop somewhere on the way to the school and get a sandwich. I'm starving!"

"You're always starving; you've been starving since the first grade! Why don't you eat more?" she said.

"You been asking me that since the first grade." They bantered back and forth as they sat in the grocery store deli, eating their sandwiches. She was glad to have an old friend to talk to. He was glad he could be there for her and was trying to figure out how to let her know he'd like to be more than a childhood friend.

"Ohmigod! I forgot about my clothes! Les, can you drive me home so I can get my clothes for tonight? I'm sorry, I should have thought about that this morning. Shit! I told the kids I'd be there at three thirty to start setting up. Now I'll be late!"

"No problem. I'll call the school and tell them you'll be a little late. They can start setting up chairs and music stands without you. You got 'em all trained and everything. They know what to do. Let's go—I can finish my drink in the car."

"Thanks for being so patient, Les. I'm kind of a nutcase right now."

"You been a nutcase since the first grade, girl," he said, laughing. She punched him on the arm as they walked out to the car. As she was getting in, she noticed the black Mercedes creeping by. James gave her a wave and a leering smile. She pretended not to have seen him.

About six o'clock, Les told her he'd got a call from his mom. The surgery was over, and Shaunee's grandmother was doing fine.

*****

The middle school kids got a standing ovation from the big crowd in their school's multipurpose room. Their band director asked the audience to be seated so he could give his thank-yous. "First, I want to thank Derek Bailey, who came up with the idea to have this jazz block after hearing the fine musicians from Eisenhower High School who are with us tonight. Then I want to thank their band director for backing the project and encouraging his students to participate. Huge thanks to the musicians from Eisenhower High School. These are among the very best high school jazz musicians in the *country*, right here in our town. Next week they're going to the Essentially Ellington Competition at Lincoln Center—only the best of the best get invited to that event. We are so lucky to have them, and my students know they've had the chance of a lifetime to learn from and play with these outstanding musicians." He was interrupted by applause.

"But the really special thanks go to Shaunee Brown, who coordinated the whole thing, worked out the problems, came up with creative approaches, and never failed to be upbeat and inspirational to our students. She made this whole project work, and these kids will never forget this experience. And to top it off, she's a fantastic singer!" Everyone, including her classmates, gave Shaunee a standing ovation, as a boy and a girl came forward with armloads of flowers for her.

When everyone had quieted down, the girl gave her little speech. "Shaunee was really cool with us. She didn't put up with any messing around, she made us work, but she also made us *want* to work, to get better. And she is so much fun—and beautiful!" She handed the flowers to Shaunee and gave her a big hug.

The boy said, "We learned so much from Shaunee and Drew and the other guys who came and taught us. We learned stuff about jazz and where it came from and, like, how to play it. But what we really learned was how hard you have to work to be really good at something. So thanks, Shaunee and all the rest of you." He gave her his flowers and an awkward hug, to another round of applause.

Shaunee was mobbed after the concert. Everyone wanted to thank her, tell her how much they liked her singing, encourage her to perform more, and let them know when she did. Did she have a website? Drew and Les were watching all this adulation.

For the performance Shaunee had worn a simple black cocktail dress, sleeveless with a V neck and high waist, and glittery earrings and heels. They watched her as she walked down the hall toward them, talking to the last of her well-wishers, her arms full of flowers and her face glowing.

"She looks terrific in that dress, doesn't she?" said Drew.

"Man, I'm going to have to play the 'A Train' backwards to get my mind off that dress!" Les let out a big sigh and gazed at the ceiling, while Drew laughed.

"Thanks for waiting so long, guys. I'm ready to go now, Les. I can take all these flowers to Grandma; isn't that great?" Drew held the flowers while Les helped her with her coat.

They walked out together. "Awesome job, Shaunee! See you tomorrow," Drew said as he got in his old pickup.

"You want to put those flowers in the back?" Les asked her, unlocking the car.

"No, I want to hold them; they smell so good." She got in awkwardly, the bouquets practically filling the front seat. "Guess I'll have to go without my seat belt," she said, as he stood there, waiting to shut her door for her.

"Not allowed." Les pulled her seat belt out and leaned in, trying to figure out how to get it under the flowers and across her lap. She giggled as he fumbled for the seat belt latch. "You're not helping a bit!" he said. He tried to sound annoyed, but she could see he was smiling. It was all he could do to keep from kissing her. So she kissed him.

They were lost in their own thoughts on the way to the hospital. Shaunee relived the evening, all the successes and the little things that had gone wrong, things she'd like to do the next time, if there were a next time. And Les, what about Les?

He couldn't think of anything but that kiss. What did it mean? Was she interested? Was she just being nice? Should he do something, or just wait and see what happened? If he should make the next move, what was it?

He drove into the hospital garage and parked, unlocking her seat belt as well as his. They struggled with the flowers, laughing, and finally found the way to the elevators. Shaunee was surprised to see Pastor DuBois there, along with Les's mom, when they arrived at her grandmother's room.

"Look at all the flowers I brought you, Grandma! Aren't they great? And they smell so good!"

"They're real nice, Shaunee, real nice. Looks like the audience liked your performance." She lay propped up on her pillows, weakly trying to smile. Mrs. Thomas was already out the door to ask for some vases. "Sit down right here by me, and tell me all about it."

Shaunee chattered happily about the evening, with Les joining in occasionally. "So it went really well, Grandma, and I'm hoping we can do it again sometime at another school.

"Now tell me about you, Grandma. You look pretty tired. Les gave me Mrs. Thomas's message that the surgery had gone fine, so when do you get to come home?" Mrs. Thomas was filling vases with the flowers, and all three of the adults seemed totally absorbed in what she was doing. No one responded to Shaunee's question.

"What's wrong? Something's wrong, isn't it? What's going on, Grandma?"

"We got some bad news, Shaunee. It could be worse, but it's bad enough," said Mrs. Brown. "The cancer's spread. They can treat it, but I've got from six months to a couple of years." She took Shaunee's hand in hers. "It depends how the treatment goes. I know you have a million questions, and so do I, and I don't know many answers yet. We'll find out in due time. But I do know this, Shaunee. You're going to be fine. There're plenty of people ready to take care of you and help you out when you need help. Pastor DuBois and Mrs. Thomas and I have already started talking. So don't you worry."

18 POSSIBILITIES

Derek arranged a meeting between the two band teachers not long after the concert to discuss the possibilities for repeating the program at his and other schools. He told them he knew of a funding source that could support the program, assuming the schools it was offered to could also come up with some matching funds. Shaunee's band director thought she would be an excellent coordinator. Derek also made discreet inquiries about Shaunee's chances for college scholarships.

Drew had filled Derek in on Mrs. Brown's situation. After she had recuperated sufficiently, and her life and Shaunee's had settled down a bit, Derek invited Shaunee and her grandmother and Drew to meet him at a crêperie in Madison Park for a Saturday lunch. As they waited for Drew to pick them up, Shaunee's grandmother fidgeted with her purse and said, "Why am I invited to this lunch? What kind of a place are we going to, anyway?"

"I'm not sure why you're invited, Grandma, but you are, so just have a good time! It's a French place; they make crêpes."

"What's a crêpe?"

"I think it's kind of like a pancake."

"Pancakes for lunch? Must be kind of like the IHOP."

A knock at the door, and Drew was there to be introduced. "I'm glad to finally meet you in person, Mrs. Brown. You're a big inspiration to Shaunee, and she's a big inspiration to the band."

"So this is the young man who helped you find all those programs on the computer? Well, we owe you many thanks, young man, many thanks."

"I was glad to do it, Mrs. Brown." They smiled, liking each other instantly.

At the restaurant, Shaunee made the introductions. "Grandma, this is Derek Bailey; it was his idea to do the whole jazz block project. Derek, this is my grandmother, Pearl Brown."

They were shown to a table and given menus by their French waiter. Mrs. Brown looked around at the blue-and-white décor, the marble-topped tables, and watched the others remove the big white napkins from their water glasses and place them in their laps; she followed suit.

"I recommend the apple cider, Mrs. Brown; it's a specialty of the region where crêpes come from," suggested Derek.

"OK, I'll have some of that. What else do you recommend?"

"Oh, it's all good. Seafood, spinach and cream sauce, or ham and cheese if you like something basic."

She chose the basic. After they'd placed their orders, Derek began, "So, Shaunee, Mrs. Brown, I have a possibility I'd like to discuss with you. I'd like to know if Shaunee's planning to go to college, and if I could somehow support her to do that. What do you think?"

Shaunee was speechless. She thought maybe they would talk about continuing the middle school program, perhaps with other schools, which she was very enthusiastic about, but Derek's question was completely out of the blue for her. "Ohmigod, I don't know what to say . . . except . . . I don't know what to say!" Drew and Derek laughed. "I'd like to go to college, but I haven't really considered it. Drew's been encouraging me to try for scholarships, but I just didn't think I'd have a chance." Conversation paused when their drinks arrived.

"My grades are OK; they could be better. I don't work very hard at school now. But I think I could handle the studies in college; I'd really work hard if I had a chance to go. I just never thought I'd have a chance."

"I think you could get a scholarship, Shaunee. Your credentials are really strong: all these years with one of the best high school jazz bands in the country, a jazz musician for a grandfather, your experience with the middle school jazz workshop, lots of talent.

What college wouldn't want you? But no scholarship covers everything, even if they give you a job in addition to a scholarship. So I'm willing and able to provide you with a loan to cover whatever isn't covered by scholarships and a job."

Mrs. Brown's lively brown eyes went back and forth between Shaunee and Derek.

Shaunee was again speechless; tears began to run down her cheeks. She wiped them away with her napkin. "I don't know what to say . . . this is so . . . generous!" She continued dabbing at her eyes.

Derek said, "Since this is such a new possibility for you, why don't you think about it for a while, and do some research, and then decide if you want to pursue it. I asked your band director if he thought you'd have a chance for scholarships, and he said definitely yes. So why don't you look online for some colleges that have good programs—he'll advise you—and get their scholarship application materials and see what's available?"

"It's really nice of you to be so encouraging, Derek," she replied. "This is pretty overwhelming. But I totally want to try. I'll start the research tonight! And I'll talk to my band teacher on Monday."

By this time Mrs. Brown had polished off her 7 percent alcohol hard cider. "Why are you doing this, Mr. Bailey?" she asked, looking at him intently.

"Before I answer, may I order some more cider for you?"

"Sure, this is better apple cider than I ever got from Safeway!"

Derek signaled the waiter for two more ciders. "Mrs. Brown, my parents died in a car accident the week after I finished college. I inherited some money from them, and I like to use it to help deserving people. I'd like to help Shaunee. We can talk about the amount and the terms later on; I just want you to know that this resource is available. Do you have any misgivings about what I'm suggesting?"

"Are you married, Mr. Bailey?"

"Grandma!" Shaunee looked horrified.

"Yes, I am, Mrs. Brown. And I have a little girl." He pulled out his wallet to show her a photo. "I've been teaching grade school and coaching soccer for several years."

Conversation paused again when their crêpes arrived, and they began eating.

Pearl Brown took up the conversation. "This is a mighty fine pancake, I must say! Now, Mr. Bailey, I've had a hard life. Not much money, my husband traveled a lot, and now he's gone for good. My daughter's . . . a sad case, I guess you'd say. So I don't have a lot of experience with . . . good fortune. Nothing like your offer has ever turned up in my life. The most important thing to me is Shaunee. I want what's best for her, even if it's coming in a package that looks . . ."

"Kind of suspect?" Derek finished for her. "I can understand your reservations, Mrs. Brown. You're right to be careful. Let's just let this offer stand until you and Shaunee can think about it from all angles. And then if you want to proceed, we can. How's that?"

"That's fair, Mr. Bailey. I appreciate that you haven't taken offense at what I've said. That says a lot about you."

Sunday evening Shaunee called Derek to tell him that her grandmother had thought things through, talked to some friends, and had no worries about his offer. She had asked Shaunee to extend her heartfelt thanks and to tell him that she would ask the Lord's blessing on him and his family every day as long as she lived.

"I'm glad it's worked out, Shaunee. Also, I wanted to tell you that I like to keep a low profile with these projects of mine, so let's keep it among us. No one else needs to know about the loan."

"I won't say a word, you can trust me, Derek," said Shaunee. "This is so awesome!"

"Yeah, I have to say I really enjoy doing stuff like this. I'm lucky to have these resources, and to be able to do good things with them. So thanks for giving me this opportunity, Shaunee."

*****

By the last week in May, the Emory family had returned from the Essentially Ellington Competition in New York, in which Drew's band had come in second in the nation. Drew was disappointed that he didn't get to solo. He lost a lot of practice time because of his hand injury. But he knew he was lucky just to be there—and there was always next year. Sunday morning, Sylvianne was reading the paper when her husband came into the kitchen, yawning. He poured himself a cup of coffee and stood looking out the window, trying to wake up. "Alex, look at this. The *Seattle Times* has been running a series on teenage prostitution, and how the Seattle police have been cracking down—I'm sure you've seen it."

He nodded. "Yeah, but I haven't read much of it; it's such a heavy subject, and there're so many—heavy subjects, I mean—that I just kind of skim over them. What do they call that? Compassion fatigue or something, when you hear so much bad stuff you just shut it out?"

Engrossed in the article, she didn't answer him. "The last article in the series was about the pimps and traffickers. Apparently, the police and county prosecutor are really going after these guys. Finally—it's about time! They've arrested a bunch of them. Anyway, this article is more of a human-interest story about one of the men they arrested. His name is James Walker, age eighteen. Is that the same James that was giving Drew and Shaunee a bad time?" Sylvianne refilled her coffee cup and sat down in the breakfast nook with the section of the paper she was reading.

"I don't know, Honey. I'm not sure I ever heard his last name." He got the milk out of the refrigerator and the cereal from the cupboard and yawned again.

"Well, this kid was taken from his parents when he was about seven, because he'd been abused and neglected, and then went through a series of foster homes, dropped out of school. Has a history of violent behavior. Which isn't hard to understand, given that background."

"How did they get all this information? Isn't that kind of stuff supposed to be confidential?"

Sylvianne looked up at her husband as he sat down opposite her with his bowl of cereal. "Apparently, the reporter convinced him to tell her about his life. Or maybe his lawyer thought he'd get more lenient treatment if there were sympathy for how he got into this business. Anyway, he was eighteen when he was arrested, so he's going to be tried as an adult."

"If it is the James who assaulted Drew, I hope they lock him up, so he won't be a threat to Drew and Shaunee." Alex paused, spoon over his cereal bowl. "In my head I can feel sorry for him, for a kid with that kind of background. But emotionally it's hard, when I think of how bad it could have been for Drew. The kid's background's no excuse for taking advantage of other people or hurting them."

Drew appeared in the kitchen, rubbing his eyes and heading for the coffeepot. "Morning, Parental Units," he said, sleepily. "Hey, Mom, I was thinking, why don't we get one of those espresso machines so I can make lattes without messing around with a pan to heat the milk? What do you think?"

His parents just looked at each other, amazed at the workings of the world.

19 DESERT SCHOOL

Paul had agreed to be the lead staff person for the Desert School. In late May the program took about two hundred freshmen and sophomores to a campground in eastern Washington and taught them kayaking, beginning climbing, desert biology and geology. The students did all the planning, shopping, food prep and teaching, with a few adults along to keep parents from too much worrying. It was a very popular program with a waiting list, and the underclassmen were in awe of the upperclassmen, who clearly had it together. It was an honor to be chosen for staff.

Drew and Vicky followed Cathy through the aisles of Costco, loading items onto the big carts and pushing them through the store. Cathy had a clipboard on which she marked off the items as they picked them up. She knew just what aisles to go down and in what order so that she didn't have to backtrack.

Vicky said to Drew as they were loading up ten gigantic boxes of Cheerios. "Wow, Cathy is amazing! I've never got through Costco so fast in my life. And my family never spent more than two hundred bucks. We're going to spend several thousand!" They moved smartly down the aisles, finished by picking up pancake flour and rice and then went on to the checkout counters. Cathy paid with the program's debit card.

"Tell me again why I volunteered for this," Paul asked his brother, as they schlepped heavy boxes of food from the Costco loading dock into the thirty-foot truck, which they would later finish filling with climbing gear and other Desert School equipment.

"Glory, Bro. Glory. You just wanted to impress all those girls with your organizational skills." Drew grinned at his brother as he pushed another box of groceries into the truck.

"Right here." Cathy pointed. "Can you snug it in closer, Drew?" Cathy was in charge of the food. She'd called Paul fifteen minutes ago and asked where he was with the truck. She'd been standing on the loading dock for *two* minutes.

"Yes, ma'am, anything you say!" answered Drew, pushing the box further into the truck and saluting.

They finished loading the truck just as the boys' father came out of the store with the few items he'd picked up for their family. For insurance purposes, an adult needed to drive the truck, and he'd volunteered to be a chaperone. Vicky and Cathy drove away in Cathy's car and Alex, Paul, and Drew drove the truck home.

The next morning the student leads were at the school parking lot an hour before the campers arrived. They had a quick conference and then scattered to their various duties. Hui came running back to get the keys to the kayak storage place from Paul. "Give them to Pedro when you're done. He'll need to get into the climbing gear locker. Thanks, Hui."

Cathy hurried up, a furious look on her face. "I don't believe it! I told those guys exactly what kind of water bottles I wanted, and they didn't get the right kind!" Paul reminded Cathy that water was water, and a cent or two more per bottle wasn't going to break the bank, so she should relax. She stomped off, her ponytail swishing back and forth—the control freak without control.

Two hours later they had about five tons of luggage and gear in the truck, the kayak trailer was ready to go, and only two campers were missing. Paul had just told a lanky young man that, as everyone had been warned, he couldn't go unless he provided the permission slip from his parents; the boy was frantically trying to reach his parents on his cell phone to have them fax the form to the campground office. A silver SUV pulled into the lot, the doors flying open before it came to a full stop. Out jumped the missing campers, dragging sleeping bags, duffle bags, and boxes of doughnuts.

"Is this a bribe?" asked Paul as he took a doughnut out of the offered box.

"Yeah, sorry we're late. My mom just had to stop at Krispy Kreme."

Paul tried to keep a serious look on his face as he waved a thank-you/good-bye to the doughnut mom. "OK, let's hit the road!"

*****

Vicky was a junior and in charge of the orientation. The campers and staff were all assembled in the dining hall to get their cabin and activity assignments. Vicky stood in front of them with her clipboard (just like Cathy's) and ran through the list, nervously tucking her long dark hair behind her ear. The rules were strict. No alcohol, no drugs, no guys in the girls' cabins or vice versa. Cabin curfew was ten thirty, lights out at eleven. Everyone had to participate in all the activities, since they were getting out of school to attend. Kids had been sent home in earlier years because they'd broken the rules, and the staff made sure that the campers knew that. "So, that's it. Any questions?" No one dared to ask a question. "Well, if you have any, come see me, or any of the other staff. They're the ones in the green staff shirts. You're going to have a great time! OK, let's have lunch."

The big room was immediately filled with chatter and good-natured shoving as the campers shuffled into lines to serve themselves potato salad, hummus, carrot sticks, sandwiches of peanut butter and jam, cold cuts, cheese, and tuna fish. Cookies for dessert.

The afternoon was open for getting settled, exploring the campground, hanging out, and, for the dinner cooks, getting everything prepared. Angie and Hui supervised the dinner crews, Sam and Natalie supervised the lunch crews, and Cathy and Pedro supervised the breakfast crews. This event had been going on for so many years, they had it down to a science, as each year's staff passed along their meticulous notes and wisdom to the next year's staff.

Paul and Drew walked out to the climbing rock to look things over. The brown buttes and rocky ground studded with tumbleweed, sagebrush, and other desert flora were such a contrast to western Washington. The only green was the trees and plants of the wetland in the center of the campground, and the lawn, which had been planted next to the dining hall to make a field for games.

They waved to their dad, who already had his tent up and was helping Julie Sorenson set up hers about a hundred feet away. The chaperones could stay in the cabins with the kids, or stay in their own tents.

After dinner there was an introduction to the next day's activities. They explained the rudiments of kayaking and climbing, and some general dos and don'ts. The campers would be divided into groups, with some kayaking while others climbed, and other groups studied biology or geology. Each group would rotate through all the activities.

"So, how's it going?" asked Paul. It was around ten at night, and the staff was assembled around one of the tables in the cafeteria.

"Dude, were we such airheads?" asked Hui. Everyone laughed. "I can't believe it. I told these girls to boil water for spaghetti, and they managed to boil it dry and burn it! We had to start all over using Saturday night's pasta."

Cathy said, "It's OK: we can ask one of the chaperones to go to town tomorrow and get some more for Saturday night."

"I've already had two kids ask me if they could skip the climbing class," reported Angie. "You'll have to give your famous 'conquer fear' lecture, Drew."

"No problem. I've got that one down."

Pedro reported that he'd also had a couple of requests to skip kayaking. "Why do they come when they know what we're going to do and they don't want to do it? I don't get it."

"Well, if there's only one thing you don't want to do, might as well try to get out of it so you can at least do the other fun stuff," said Natalie.

"OK, we've all been through this before, we can handle it. Good job, everyone. Sleep well," Paul told them, standing up.

*****

The next morning a freshman boy, Josh, appeared at breakfast with half his face bright red and puffy and an eye swollen shut. "What happened, Josh? Does it hurt?" Paul asked him, pulling him out of the breakfast line. He pointed out Angie to the guy standing next to Josh and asked him to go get her.

"I don't know what it is; it's never happened to me before. But it doesn't hurt, so I'm fine."

Angie hurried up, took one look at Josh and said, "Shall I ask Dad to drive him in to the hospital? That looks serious."

"Yeah, would you get him right away—I don't want to mess around with this. We'll meet him in the parking lot." Angie left to find her dad, who was one of the chaperones.

"Really, it doesn't hurt! Jeez, I don't need to go to the *hospital*. I really don't want to miss my climbing session," Josh complained.

"We can put you in another group so you won't miss the climbing, Josh," Paul told him. "But we can't just let this go untreated. Your parents would freak if we didn't try to check it out. It only takes an hour to drive to town, and a doctor can probably see you pretty quick, so you won't miss much. Sorry, but this is potentially too serious to ignore. It's probably just an allergic reaction to a spider bite or something, but we have to make sure it's not something worse."

Paul and Josh arrived at the parking lot at the same time as Angie's dad. Paul gave him the group debit card and PIN number to pay the doctor, and asked him to pick up five boxes of spaghetti at the Safeway on the way back. Then he went back to the dining hall to eat breakfast. He saw Pedro and Cathy sitting together, laughing about something, and took his tray over to join them. "I hope that's our only ER run this year! We had two last year, didn't we?" he asked, sitting down.

"Yeah, a sprained ankle and heat exhaustion," answered Pedro. "We kept telling them to drink a lot and wear hats, but some people just won't listen. It was wicked hot last year, though." They finished breakfast and split up to teach their classes. Paul watched Pedro and Cathy walk out together, wondering if there was something going on between the two of them. He hoped so, since as far as he knew, Cathy had never had a boyfriend, and he liked Pedro.

*****

Drew was in charge of the climbing lessons. Paul walked out to the climbing area where the first group was being shown how belaying works.

"OK, do I have a volunteer to show you how to put the harness on?" Drew asked. A pretty redhead raised her hand and stepped forward. She was wearing a tank top and short shorts that showed off her noteworthy legs.

"I'll volunteer," she said, tossing her long hair over her shoulder.

"You're Anita, right?"

She nodded.

"OK, thanks, Anita. Here's your helmet." He waited while she fastened the strap. Then he showed her how to put her legs through the leg loops. She put one hand on his shoulder as she stepped through one loop and then the other.

"Shorts are probably not the best thing for climbing," he told the assembled students, "but you can get by."

He pulled the harness up so that the leg loops were tight enough around her thighs and the waist band was right at her waist, reached around her and pulled the end of the waist strap through its buckle and cinched it tight, explaining all the while why it was important for the harness to be snug. Hands on her shoulders, he turned her around and showed the group how to tighten the back leg straps that go across the climber's bottom so that the harness doesn't slide down and become loose. The guys were really focusing on how the leg straps went over that nice bottom.

"You're all buckled in, Anita. Are you ready to go up and belay down?"

It's one thing to have a handsome guy help you into some weird gear; it's another thing to dangle fifty feet from a rock. Now Anita looked a little less eager, but she nodded.

"All right, everyone, we'll get five more climbers into their harnesses and then we'll send up a party. But first I'm going to belay Pedro, who's already up at the top of the rock." He pointed up to Pedro, already in his harness, who waved back. "I want you to see how safe this is. There is no way you can fall—absolutely no way. I want you to understand how it works, so you won't be scared."

Drew continued with his lecture and demonstration, belaying Pedro down the rock. The students looked amazed, and some still a little dubious. But they followed instructions, and soon the first group had climbed up and belayed down. They were excited and comparing notes as they took off their harnesses for the next group.

"Dude, when it was my turn, and I looked down, I almost upchucked my breakfast. But it was really cool!"

"Yeah, I can hardly wait to do it again. This is awesome!"

As the next group was getting into their harnesses, one girl said to Drew, "I really don't think I can do this. I'm, like, scared to death of heights. I always have been. I asked Angie if I could skip this part, but she said I couldn't." She looked imploringly at Drew.

"What's your name?"

"Gloria."

"Look, Gloria. I've taught other kids to do this who had a fear of heights. I'm sure you can do it too. It's OK to be afraid. I'm not saying you shouldn't be afraid. Healthy fear is a good thing when you're climbing. But it's also really awesome to conquer a fear, especially where there's really no danger. Do you really think you could fall?"

"No," she said, the strain showing on her face as she twisted the strap on her helmet back and forth. "I've watched everyone, and I understand how it works, from your explanation, and I know I couldn't fall. But I'm still really scared."

"Tell you what. Let's take it a step at a time. You climb up with your group, and then we'll talk about it some more when you get up there. If you absolutely can't do it, it's fine, but I know you can and you'll be so glad when you do. It's a high you won't ever forget! OK?"

"OK, I'll try."

Angie and Pedro were at the top of the rock, double-checking everyone's harness and coaching them in how to start down the rock face and communicate with the belayer at the bottom.

When it was time for Gloria's group to belay down, Pedro and Drew changed places. Drew had a great success rate with scared climbers. He was chatting with Gloria as the rest of the group descended, one by one. "I used to have this bad dream. I had it lots of times. This gnarly monster was chasing me, and I'd run and it was hella scary. Then one time I stopped running, and I turned around and guess what? No monster. So what do you make of that?"

"You're telling me if I do this, I won't be afraid of heights anymore, right?"

"Well, I can't promise, but I'll bet there's a good chance that'll happen. Are you ready?"

They stepped to the edge of the rock, and he fastened the rope to her harness. "You can do this, Gloria! Don't look down; just keep looking up at me, OK? All right, grab the rope right here, now just hang on and walk down the rock. OK, that's it, good, good, look at me! Don't look down! Way to go, see, you're doing it. Nice and slow, there you go, no problem. And if your feet slip, no sweat, you'll just hang there nice and safe and they'll belay you down—oops, don't panic! You're OK, aren't you? Talk to me!"

A scared little voice said shakily, "Yeah, I'm all right. Tell them I want to come down really slow, OK?"

"Sure, no problem, Gloria. Nice and slow, Pedro!" he shouted down to the belayer.

By now, everyone was cheering for Gloria. When she reached the bottom, she was surrounded by fellow campers giving her hugs and high fives. She looked dazed but had a wobbly grin.

*****

At the end of the day there were lots of sunburns, a few cuts and scrapes, and a lot of happy campers, proud of their new climbing and kayaking skills. There was some killer volleyball after dinner, dancing to a car CD player, and some couples forming and enjoying the full moon. By the time the staff had all their kids corralled and the lights were out, Paul was tired but pleased with how the day had gone. He was just about to climb into his bunk when he noticed a light in the kitchen. Now what? "I'll be right back," he said to the boy in the nearest bunk. "Looks like someone's raiding the cookie jar."

Sure enough, he caught a couple of boys sneaking into the kitchen to get some ice cream bars and cookies to tide them over until breakfast. By the time he escorted them back to their cabin, minus the ice cream, it was eleven thirty. It was a quiet, beautiful night. He wished Gina were here. He was fantasizing about what he'd like to be doing with her, when he noticed a man and a woman out by the chaperone tents. The man had his arm around the woman, and she seemed to be staggering. What the hell!

He walked down the little trail; it was bright enough to see in the moonlight. It was his father and Mrs. Sorenson! As he got closer, he could see that his father looked like he'd got dressed in a hurry— shoes but no socks, his belt was unbuckled, and his V neck T-shirt was on backward. She was wearing lounge pants and one of those skimpy tight tops with little tiny straps, and she had a wine bottle in one hand.

"Paul, is that you?" Alex asked in a low voice.

"Yeah, it's me, Dad. What's going on?"

"Give me a hand, will you? Julie drank a whole bottle of wine and decided to come visit me. I'd just climbed into my sleeping bag. I managed to talk her into going back to her tent, and we'd just started back when she threw up. She's going to have one hell of a headache tomorrow."

As Paul was trying to get her other arm around his neck and his arm around her waist, she mumbled, "Damn husband . . . him and his new girlfriend . . . boobs like watermelons!"

Father and son looked at each other over her head. "Watermelons," said Alex, trying not to laugh. Paul couldn't help it—he laughed. "I know this isn't funny; I feel sorry for her, but the whole thing is wicked ridiculous! What should we do after we get her into her tent?"

"Can you get her daughter without too much hullabaloo? Just tell her that her mom's sick. I'll stay with Julie while you get her daughter."

"OK, I'll be back in about ten minutes. Uh, Dad, you might want to buckle your belt and put your shirt on frontwards before Stephanie gets here." He grinned at his dad.

"Gee, thanks for the advice, Son! Here, take this bottle and hide it somewhere so the kids don't see it tomorrow."

Paul made his way back to the kitchen, stopping on the way to put the empty wine bottle under the seat of the truck. In the kitchen he found his roster of who was in which cabin, then found Stephanie's. Angie was the staff person for that cabin. He quietly opened the door and saw that she was still awake, reading in her bunk with one of those little lights that fasten onto your book. "Hey," he whispered, "can you wake Stephanie Sorenson up? Her mom's sick, and I think she should stay with her tonight. I'll wait for her on the front porch."

Angie brought a worried Stephanie to Paul in about five minutes. She had her shoes and her sleeping bag and pillow. Paul whispered, "Your mom's going to be fine, Stephanie, don't worry. I think it's just like a twenty-four-hour flu or something, but I don't think she should be alone. Thanks, Angie."

"How did you know she was sick?" Stephanie asked Paul in a low voice, as he led her along the path toward Julie's tent.

"Uh, she told my dad, and he came and got me. He's waiting with her until you get there."

Julie Sorenson had the family's car-camping tent, big enough to sleep six. Paul waited outside while Stephanie dragged her sleeping bag and pillow into the tent. He could hear her talking quietly with Alex, who emerged after a few minutes.

Father and son walked about halfway back to Alex's tent. "I told Stephanie what really happened," Alex said. "But I told her you and I wouldn't tell anyone, so neither she nor her mom needs to be embarrassed. Since we have another woman chaperone, it's no problem if Julie leaves tomorrow, and Stephanie can go with her, depending on how she's doing. I feel sorry for both of them. They're probably both going to be miserable."

"Yeah, tough situation. But nice save, Dad. I couldn't believe my eyes when I first saw you! Are you going to tell Mom?"

"You bet! I hope the story doesn't get out, but I want her to hear it from me first, if it does. I know she trusts me, but I wouldn't want her to get blindsided by some wild tale. I know she's going to think it's funny. Except she'll feel sorry for Julie."

"I'm wiped out—time for bed. G'night, Dad."

*****

An hour before breakfast the next day, Paul and Alex were helping Stephanie and her mom load their car, which was parked right next to the truck. Jean Carpenter, the other female chaperone, bustled past them to the truck, opened the cab door, and pulled out the empty wine bottle. She thrust it in Paul's face and said, "I saw you, young man, trying to hide the evidence. And you set yourself up as a leader! What have you got to say for yourself?" she demanded.

"Now wait a minute, Jean, this isn't what it looks like. You're jumping to conclusions," Alex said in an even tone.

"So what is it, if it's not what it looks like?"

"Frankly, it's a private matter. You'll just have to trust me when I say that Paul hasn't done anything wrong."

"Well, I'd expect you'd cover up for him, you're his father, after all. I just don't think it's fair that someone in a leadership position thinks he can get away with things."

"I resent your charge that I'd cover up something wrong that my son had done. I've raised my kids to be accountable for their actions, and if they make mistakes, they have to take the consequences." Alex was a little steamed.

Julie was, of course, listening to all this. She turned from tucking her knapsack in the back end and said to Jean, "As Alex said, Jean, this is none of your business. But since you seem intent on making it your business, let's get things straight. Last night I had a bottle of wine and a little crisis, and Alex and Paul were gentlemen enough to take care of me so that I didn't hurt myself or embarrass my daughter completely." She picked up her sleeping bag and slammed it into the car.

"So in your ignorance, you come rampaging out here first thing in the morning to lynch one of the nicest and most popular young men in the high school. Give me that bottle!" She grabbed the bottle from Jean, who flinched; Julie threw it in the back of her car.

Hands on hips, Julie continued, "If one word of this gets out, you'll be personally responsible for my daughter's further embarrassment, you judgmental harpy!" Jean flinched again, as though she'd been slapped. "And all the kids in the school will be glad you're not their mother! You can go now; I want to talk with Alex and Paul."

Jean left.

"Way to go, Mom!" said Stephanie, giving Julie a hug.

"Julie ten, Jean zero," said Alex.

"Thanks for sticking up for me, Mrs. Sorenson," said Paul. "I'm sorry you . . . I mean that she . . . Well, anyway, thanks."

"You're welcome, Paul. Nice job on the parenting, Alex. You've got a fine boy there."

"Mom, are you sure you're OK to drive all the way home alone?" Stephanie asked.

"Yes, Honey, I'll be fine. I need some time alone to sort myself out, and I don't want you to miss your climbing and kayaking. I'm sorry, Steph," she said, hugging her daughter.

"We'll figure it out, Mom; don't worry."

On the way back to the dining hall, Paul said, "Jeez, Dad, Mrs. Sorenson is something else! I couldn't have thought all that up that fast if you paid me."

"Yeah, it was pretty amazing, all right. She should write for *Saturday Night Live*."

As they approached the dining hall, Alex said, "You know that old saying 'Hell hath no fury like a woman scorned'?" Paul shook his head. "Well, I think you've just seen an example of what that saying is about. Looks like Julie's pretty angry about her husband's affair, or whatever it is. Jean just happened to be in the wrong place at the wrong time, and got the brunt of all that bad energy. Not that she didn't deserve it."

*****

It was their last day. The morning went well, and it was a noisy crowd for lunch. Paul sat at a table of campers, rather than with the staff, so he could get acquainted and get some feedback on how they felt about the Desert School experience. They'd have formal evaluations for everyone to fill out, but he liked to talk with people too. "So, how's it going? You guys having a good time?"

As they were chatting, Anita, the long-legged redhead, sat down beside Paul. "Hi, Paul. This is really, like, awesome. I'm having a really good time."

"Glad to hear it. What do you like the best?"

"The staff is really fantastic. You guys are so . . . competent, and everyone is really nice."

"Thanks," he said, smiling. "We really care about the program, so we try hard to do a good job. Nice to know it's appreciated." Paul noticed that the other girls at the table were giggling and glancing at Anita, who seemed oblivious. "Well, nice to talk to all of you. Thanks for the input. See you this afternoon. I've got to get ready for my kayak class." Paul got up to take his tray to the kitchen.

"Oh, I'll walk down with you. I'm in that class this afternoon." Anita got up and followed him with her tray.

The class was assembling on the shore of the little lake where they taught kayaking as Paul and Anita walked up. He thought the girls were a little more giggly than usual, but didn't pay much attention. He gave his talk on technique and demonstrated how to hold the paddle, fielded questions, and then they all got in their kayaks. Paul was busy teaching his novices when he noticed that Anita had paddled off across the lake by herself, against instructions. He signaled to Hui that he was going after her.

"Hey, Anita, wait for me," he called. She kept going. He didn't believe she couldn't hear him. In a few strokes, he caught up with her and grabbed her kayak. "Hey, remember, everyone is supposed to stay together? It's not safe for you to go off alone."

"I just wanted to look at the ducks in those reeds over there; they look really cute. Besides, nothing bad's going to happen to me. I could roll this thing, no problem. My mom taught me how to kayak, like, ages ago. We're liberated women," she said, adjusting her sunglasses.

"Well, I'm glad you're liberated, but that doesn't mean you can ignore the rules. C'mon, let's go back," he said, a little gruffly.

"Sure, anything you say," she said, giving him a big smile. She turned her kayak deftly, and they began paddling back.

Then, not wanting to seem like the enforcer, he suggested, "Why don't you help teach the class, since you already know a lot about it?"

"Oh no, I'm sure I couldn't do it as well as you do. You're an awesome teacher." He smiled politely at the compliment. He was beginning to get the drift of what was going on.

After they got the kayaks onto the trailer and strapped down for the trip home, Paul and Cathy walked up to the dining hall together. "Well, how's your cute redhead?" she teased him.

"She's not my redhead," he huffed.

"Well, she'd like to be. She's got a ten-dollar bet with her best friend that she'll get you to kiss her before the trip is over. Everyone knows; everyone's watching."

"What? You've got to be kidding!"

She poked him in the ribs and laughed. "Must be nice having all these cute girls chasing you."

"It's a pain in the butt! I mean, it's flattering and all, but I'm not interested. I don't want to hurt her feelings or make her feel rejected or anything, but . . ."

"But there's Gina," she finished for him.

"Yeah, what would she think of all this?"

"She thinks it's funny. She's already got about five cell phone calls giving her a blow-by-blow account of what's happening. She told Angie that you're not her property and you can kiss whoever you want. But I don't think she's taking calls anymore."

"God! Now what do I do?"

"Don't ask me, Romeo. I think it's hilarious!"

Paul went back to the bunkhouse to get some dry pants, and then he took a pad and pencil and sat in the truck cab to write a note to Anita.

"Hey, Anita, heard about your bet. I'm flattered, 'cause you're a really nice-looking girl. But I also feel a little weird, like I'm being used. The girl I <u>really</u> want to kiss isn't here, but I'll see her tomorrow night, so I'll just have to wait till then. P. "

He folded up his note and slipped it to Cathy at dinner. "Hey, Cath, do me a favor and get this to Anita as soon as you can, OK?"

"OK, Romeo, anything for a friend."

Cathy delivered his note when Anita was returning her tray to the kitchen after dinner. She opened it immediately, read it, turned bright red, stuffed it in her pocket, and rushed out of the dining hall.

"Dude, what did you tell her?" asked Pedro with a grin on his face. "Did you tell her you wouldn't kiss her if she were the last girl in the world, or did you ask her to sleep with you, or what?"

"I told her my girlfriend had an IQ of two hundred, looked like Jennifer Lawrence, only prettier, and that she had a black belt in karate and didn't like anyone messing with her man. How's that?"

"No shit!"

"I'm kidding, Pedro," Paul said, laughing. "I tried to be nice but honest, so I hope I didn't make her feel bad."

"Well, it was kind of a dumb thing for her to do," said Cathy. "The gossip is that she got expelled from Lakeside for breaking some rules or something. She's into pushing the limits, I guess."

Word flew around the campground that Anita had paid her friend ten dollars. There were whispers and giggles and lots of speculative looks at Paul and Anita, but Paul just acted like nothing had happened, and pretty soon it was all forgotten.

*****

Alex, Paul, and Drew were quiet on the ride back to Seattle. It was hot, and they had worked hard packing everything up, making sure the campground was left in good condition, and getting the campers off with all their stuff. After stopping in Ellensburg for root beer floats, they got back in the truck for the last leg of the drive.

"Well, guys, what did you learn at Desert School this year?"

There was silence for a while. Then Drew said, "You know Dad, I really like teaching people stuff. I think that's what I learned. People say I'm good at it, and it's fun. I was thinking maybe I might go into some kind of teaching thing. You know, like Outward Bound, or Peace Corps or recreation programs, or something like that."

"Good insight, Drew. And I agree, I think you're a natural teacher. There's a lot to learn about doing it well, but some people have a gift to start with, and I think you're one of them."

They rode along in silence for a few more miles, and then Paul said, "I learned a whole lot about how people screw each other up. I was thinking about how Mrs. Sorenson's husband did something bad to her, and then she did something that was potentially bad for herself and her daughter. Then there was Anita. Who knows why she pulled that stunt, but she probably didn't think about how it would make me feel. She was just thinking about herself and what she wanted. And the bottle episode. If Mrs. Sorenson hadn't said what she did, Mrs. Carpenter could have made a big stink that would've been bad for me and for the program. People just act without thinking, and it causes a lot of trouble. Why can't they get what they want without causing other people grief?"

20 THE CAMPING TRIP

It was just the four of them. Elektra was steadfastly resisting camping, and Gina could only join them on the second day of their trip. They were lucky enough to have a good stretch of warm June weather. Susannah knew the drill, having gone on innumerable camping trips with Alex and his dad, and later with Alex's family. She had volunteered to be in charge of the food shopping and meal prep, while the guys got the gear together and packed the cars. Besides bags of food, there were two large coolers, sleeping bags, tents, folding chairs, Dutch oven, stove, lanterns, air mattresses, firewood and charcoal, the camping box, which held all the cooking paraphernalia, and assorted other "necessities." Also, the guys wanted to bring their double kayak.

"You weren't kidding when you said the Emorys don't travel light!" Will observed. "Does everybody camp with this much stuff?"

"This is nothing. Some people take it *all* with them—campers, TVs, boats, generators—you name it. Wait'll you see what some people bring along," Drew said.

It was about eleven in the morning by the time they got under way, and about half past noon by the time they arrived at the campground. Since the Emorys had camped here so many times in years past, they had their favorite spots. One of them was available, close but not too close to the restrooms, off the main road, with good screening between them and the adjacent camping spaces. And it was big enough for two cars and two tents.

"Let's set up the kitchen first, so we can make some lunch," Susannah said. Once that's done, Will can rig the hammock, and we can start in on the tents." In a couple of hours, everything was in its place. Will and Susannah had the "castle," the six-person tent that had been in the family for twenty years, and an eight-inch-thick double air mattress. The boys had a two-person backpacking tent and less cushy mattresses, but they were used to them.

Susannah and Will headed off on their bikes for a tour of the campground, and Paul and Drew drove their car down to the boat launch to take the kayak off and put it in the water. They began untying the lines holding it onto the car-top carrier, having pulled up beside a truck with a trailer from which a twenty-foot ski boat was being launched by a very attractive girl in a very skimpy bikini. She was pretty hard to miss as she pushed the boat off and waded around the end of the trailer to pull the boat up on the shore by its bowline. She was also being watched by the boat's owner, a guy about their age who was the size of a Seahawks lineman. He had four inches and fifty pounds on both of them. He chugged a beer and said to them with a self-satisfied smirk, "That's a mighty fine piece of ass, ain't it?"

Paul didn't respond to the question, he just asked, "Is she your girlfriend?"

"Yeah, till I go to the UW this fall. I got a football scholarship. I expect I'll find plenty of women there," he bragged.

"Well, she's a nice-looking chick," Drew responded. "Later, dude." He and Paul carried the kayak down to the water while Mr. Football drove his truck to the parking lot.

"What a jerk," Paul remarked. "He's probably used to being the big fish in a little pond. He's in for a shock when he gets to the U. He'd better be good, or he'll get eaten alive!" They grinned at each other as if they thought that wouldn't be a bad outcome.

The brothers paddled for a couple of hours. Ms. Bikini got up from her beach towel and walked down to the boat as Drew and Paul pulled it up on the beach. "Hi," she said. "I've never been in a kayak. Is it hard to paddle?"

"You get the hang of it pretty quickly," said Paul. "Want to try it out?"

"Totally!" she replied. "Tell me what to do."

Paul helped her into the front seat and showed her how to hold the paddle. Then he got in the backseat and pushed them off, leaving

Drew watching from the beach. With very little instruction, she was paddling well. She wanted to know how it turned, how fast it could go, and if he'd ever flipped.

"Where are you guys from?" she asked.

"Seattle. My brother Drew and I brought our grandparents for a couple of nights of camping. I'm Paul."

"I'm Rosalie. I'm up here with my family and a friend," she told him. "We're camping for a few days. Some of my other friends are coming tonight, and we're going to have a party up at the group campsite. It's not open to the public yet, and it's far enough away from the main campground that we can have fun without a bunch of adults breathing down our necks. You and your brother should come."

"Thanks for the invitation, maybe we'll do that. I'll see what's up with everybody else." By then they were back to the shore. Rosalie thanked Paul for the kayak lesson and walked back to her beach towel where the ski boat owner sat with a sour look on his face.

The brothers arrived back at the campsite about five, ready for beer and munchies. Paul and Drew built up the fire so they could barbecue the chicken, once they had a good bed of coals. Will was cutting up tomatoes, cucumber, bell pepper, and green onions for a Greek salad. "Hey, Will," said Paul, "this is where we kick the ashes in your chicken, so you can have the full camping experience. Ashes really add a special flavor."

"I'll pass on the ashes, thank you very much," said Will, punching Paul's shoulder.

"This is super good, Grams!" said Drew, as they were finishing up their dinner. He and Paul were mopping up their BBQ sauce with chunks of French bread. They polished off all the chicken, salad, and loaf of bread, and then put the rest of the food in the car; the garbage went in the Dumpster so bears wouldn't be tempted to visit them. Paul and Drew regaled Will with camping stories as they took an after-dinner walk along the stream to the trailhead.

"Oh, hey," Paul said, "that girl I took for a kayak ride invited us to a party tonight, Drew. You want to go?"

"Sure, why not?"

"You guys go have a good time," Susannah said. "I'm going to bed. Will, it's the guy's job to make sure there's a water bottle for drinks in the night, a flashlight for midnight trips to the toilet, and to warm up the sleeping bags for his partner. Could you please get right on that?"

"Hey, guys, is she putting me on?"

"Oh, no, absolutely not! Cross my heart. Whatever the cook says goes, otherwise she might not cook," Paul said with a straight face.

"OK, guess I'd better get right on it, then, or else plan to cook!" Will headed for their tent, grabbing Susannah around the waist and pulling her with him as he went.

*****

The brothers located the group campsite partly from memory and partly from the sound of a party going on. They arrived to find about a dozen people drinking beer and dancing around a campfire to the music from a boom box. Rosalie greeted them, handed them each a beer, and made some cursory introductions. Drew was snapped up by a couple of girls who invited him to join the dancing, and Rosalie sat down on a picnic table bench, indicating a space next to her for Paul to sit. He nodded at Mr. Football, who cast them an annoyed glance every now and then.

"The big guy over there," Paul said to Rosalie, "I think you said his name was Dwayne? He told us you were his girlfriend when we were at the boat ramp this afternoon."

"Oh yeah, he'd say that, all right. He wants people to think he's got a hot girlfriend; makes him think he's something special. I don't call him on it, because I like to use his boat. So we have a little understanding. He's OK, not an Einstein, but OK. So, where do you and your brother go to school?"

"I just graduated, and I'm going to the UW in the fall. Drew'll be a senior at Eisenhower in Seattle. Where do you go to school?"

"I'll be a senior at Soap Lake High School. One more year—I can hardly wait to get out of that place! I'm going to college too, but I don't know where. Wherever I can get a scholarship. I pay attention to the grades. They're my ticket out of the little town in the middle of nowhere!"

Rosalie was very pretty. She had long black hair, which she frequently pushed back behind one ear. Her tight, low-rise jeans and snug T-shirt showed off her nice curves. She finished her beer, started another while they talked, and then they got up to dance with several others of the party. She was definitely coming on to him. He was flattered and attracted to her, but he couldn't help thinking about Gina, who was arriving in the morning to spend the day with him.

Rosalie was really into the dancing. Finally, she got tired and pulled Paul down beside her on the bench again. "God, I love dancing," she announced, taking another drink of beer. "Don't you?"

"Yeah, but I'm wasted!" Paul replied, grinning at her.

She leaned across him, her long hair brushing his arm, and ran her finger down the scar next to his eye. "Where'd this come from?" she asked.

"Car accident earlier this year. Messed me up pretty much, but I was lucky. I'm mostly back to normal now. One leg is a little weak, but it'll be fine in time.

"Hey, thanks for inviting us tonight. I'm going to turn in. Like I said, I'm wasted! Maybe we'll see you tomorrow."

"OK," she said, smiling at him. "Glad you could come. I'm *sure* I'll see you tomorrow."

About midnight, Paul and Drew crawled into their tent and pulled on their preferred camping sleepwear: sweatpants and hooded sweatshirts. "Hey, Bro, that chick was after you!" Drew teased his brother.

"Yeah, she's OK. Not really my type, but nice enough."

"When is Gina supposed to get here?" Drew asked Paul.

"She was hoping to arrive around nine or nine thirty, so she could be here most of the day. She has to babysit at seven thirty, so she'll have to leave here by five."

As Paul dropped off to sleep, he considered how he felt about Gina. She was smart and funny and inexperienced with boys; he felt protective of her. He realized that she was turning up in his thoughts more and more. Why was she the one he wanted with him when he went for his appointment with the plastic surgeon? The more he knew her, the better looking she became. Or maybe she looked the same and he had never noticed. He certainly had missed what an attractive body she had, until the prom dress episode. But they were going in different directions at the end of the summer, and he wondered if it was wise to get too involved.

*****

Georgina was inwardly excited about the prospect of a day with Paul, but her dad couldn't tell. She gathered up her swimsuit, food, and other necessary stuff for a day at the beach and seemed her usual quiet self as she put everything in the car, waved good-bye to her father, and left town about eight in the morning.

Gina had had a crush on Paul since they were freshmen; he was aware of her, since they'd had many classes together through high school, and their younger brothers were friends, but they ran in different circles. Paul was a big man on campus, and Gina considered herself a smart but nondescript nobody.

But that had all changed. When he invited her to join the group going to the prom together, a friendship had turned into what almost felt like a romance.

The attentions of a popular and handsome young man had made Gina blossom. She no longer slumped, she took more care with her clothes and appearance, and she was more outgoing than she'd ever been. She glowed. She was happy. She was ready to be a friend to everyone.

Gina was mature enough to know that it would all be over at the end of the summer. She was going to college in New England, and Paul would be at the University of Washington. She knew they were too young to think about anything permanent and that it would be very difficult to sustain a relationship over time and distance. So she relived every moment they had been together, cherished the memories, and vowed to make the most of every hour they had left. She had no qualms about getting involved, even for a short time. She was already madly in love.

Gina arrived just as they were getting ready to take the cinnamon rolls out of the Dutch oven. Paul sat her down beside him at the picnic table for a second breakfast.

"Wow, these are fantastic, Ms. Emory!" Gina exclaimed, echoed by the others. "I wish I could have seen you making them. It must be quite a production."

"Well, it's a little bit of work, but I don't see why she isn't making these for me every week at home," Will said.

"Dream on!" Susannah said, poking Will in the ribs. "I only do this for camping trips." To Gina, she said, "Yes, it *is* a lot of work.

And after all that, I forgot to put in the cinnamon! And this isn't the first time; can you believe it? Too much multitasking."

"I won't tell them how many pans you've cooked dry while you're multitasking, Honey," Will said, kissing her cheek.

After they had consumed every crumb of the non-cinnamon rolls and the rest of their breakfast, they cleaned up the remains of the meal and went their separate ways. Susannah and Will went exploring on their bikes, and the young people headed for the beach. They spread out their blankets, iPods, cooler filled with drinks, books, sunscreen, Frisbee, kayak paddles, and other sunning paraphernalia about twenty yards from Rosalie and one of her friends, who were already at work on their suntans, sitting on beach towels with books, magazines, and headphones strewn about. She waved and the brothers waved back.

Rosalie's presence faded to the edge of their awareness as Drew and Gina became absorbed in a game of Frisbee; Paul kibitzed from the sidelines, not wanting to overstress his healing leg.

Before Paul had time to tell Gina about the party the previous evening, Rosalie and her friend sauntered by on their way to Dwayne's boat, carrying towels and water skis. "That was fun last night; thanks for coming," she said to the guys, with a brazen look at Paul. "Want to go water-skiing?" she asked. Drew accepted immediately, while Paul declined, so Drew and the girls walked down the shore to the boat.

Paul and Gina went for a kayak ride, during which he told her about the party the previous evening. He didn't mention that Rosalie was coming on pretty strong, but Gina figured it out. Faced with some serious competition (Gina thought Rosalie looked like Penelope Cruz) and unsure of how Paul felt about her, a cloud of doubt appeared to darken the day she had been looking forward to.

She and Paul settled themselves side by side on a blanket with their books. Gina was on her tummy, book propped up on a rock. After a while, Paul asked, "Do you have sunscreen on?"

"I have it on my front, but not my back," she answered.

"Do you want me to put some on your back for you?" he asked chivalrously. "You'd better have some, or else move into the shade, or cover up."

She handed him her sunscreen. "Yes, please. Thanks."

He took his time. How often did a guy have license to rub good-smelling cream on a beautiful back and neck and arms? He looked longingly at the backs of her shapely legs.

Her eyes were closed as she rested her cheek on her overlapped hands. "Paul?"

"Yo, Gina."

"What did your parents tell you about sex?"

He dropped the lid of the sunscreen, and then fished it out of the sand. "Do you mean, like, how it works, or what not to do, or what?"

"Not the mechanics, everyone learns that in school. No, I mean did they give you a lecture on abstinence, or the importance of marriage or avoiding STDs, or what?"

Paul settled down on his back, his head propped on a folded beach towel, and remembered the Big Conversation with his dad. "It was my dad, but he told me he and Mom had talked about what they wanted to say to us when the time came, so it was really coming from both of them. They said it was a big deal, and you shouldn't treat it lightly. It wasn't just entertainment or to make you feel good, like drugs or alcohol." Paul stopped to fiddle with his sunglasses and recollect what his dad had said.

"Dad said you should like and respect the people you're doing it with, and not just use them, or do it because you feel sorry for them. And he said it wasn't just a physical thing, that really good sex has to do with your maturity, you know, like your self-confidence and your willingness to make someone else feel good. I read this book he recommended, at least a lot of it. It's written by a guy who counsels people who're having marital problems or sexual problems. That blew my mind! What an eye-opener—especially for a thirteen-year-old! It made me feel really grown up that he'd recommend a book like that for a kid my age. And it wasn't just that book. They had several books about sex, and they told Drew and me where they were, so we could read them whenever. They got a lot of use." They both laughed.

He thought for a moment, rolled over on his side, facing her, and then went on, "I was really relieved to read some of that stuff. You know how in grade school boys and girls can't stand each other? Then all of a sudden when I was about twelve, I started noticing girls and what they looked like. I thought I was turning into a perv or something. So it was good to read all that stuff's normal." He dragged a little branch through the sand, making stick figures, and then wiping them out.

"So what did he say about avoiding pregnancy?"

"Oh yeah, he talked about protection, because a pregnancy really opens up a huge can of worms if you're not married. There's the whole abortion thing, and what if the girl doesn't believe in abortion and the kid gets adopted, and some adopted kids feel like they've been abandoned. Well, you know about all the problems. And he said not to trust that a girl was using birth control; you gotta use a condom no matter what. What did your parents tell you?"

"I was only eleven when we discovered my mom had cancer. When she realized she wasn't going to be around when I was a teenager, she knew she'd have to do her best talking to a kid. She explained the mechanics and basically said, 'It's fine if it's with someone you love.' And my dad was just lost. The only thing he said to me—I was fourteen—was 'Just be careful, go with nice boys, and don't get pregnant.'"

They lay there side by side, lost in their own thoughts. Then Gina said, "My parents said so little that there's really nothing to disagree with. Do you agree with what your parents said?"

"Yeah, pretty much, I think. I'm not sure why they think it's a big deal. I'd like to know more about that. I should probably read that book again—I think a lot of it went right over my head. But basically, I thought it was good advice."

*****

Drew, Rosalie, and her friend Natalie put their towels, hats, and sunscreen in the boat, arranged the ski ropes and gas tanks, and got ready to leave. Rosalie kept looking back at Paul and Gina. She said with a smile, "He's sure enjoying putting sunscreen on her back. Not that I blame him; she's really cute. That's been kinda fun to watch."

Hmm, Drew thought to himself, but he didn't say anything.

Rosalie remarked, "I wonder why she's wearing that frumpy swimming suit. She has a great figure."

What's with this chick? Drew thought. "I wonder why you're wearing hardly *any* swimming suit," he commented mildly.

"If you've got it, flaunt it—that's my philosophy."

*****

When Drew returned from water skiing, he, Paul and Gina gathered up their stuff and walked back to the campsite, where lunch was waiting for them. As they sat around the table, Drew recounted his conversation with Rosalie, leaving out the bit about the sunscreen. He didn't think Gina would be hurt by the remark about her swimming suit. She wasn't; she just laughed and said, "It *is* frumpy. I've had it for four years, and the elastic is coming out of the seat!"

Drew told Gina about the previous day's encounter with the football player. "Makes you wonder what goes on in a girl's head, to hang out with a guy who talks like that about her. Just from talking with her in the boat, I can tell she doesn't have a totally empty head. But she's really bought into the idea that she has to look like a sex worker to attract guys."

In between bites of carrots and hummus, Drew asked, "Where does this stuff come from, where do girls get the idea they have to look like Madonna or something, for guys to like them?"

"What do you think?" Will asked them, putting more cheese and crackers on his plate.

Paul put down his sandwich and said, "Advertising, for sure. Ads for everything use sex. If you buy this product, you'll be sexy, or someone sexy will like you."

"But what's the big deal about sexy?" Will persisted. They all pondered the question.

"Isn't there a relationship between sex and love, at least some of the time?" asked Gina. "I mean, I know people who don't love each other have sex, but usually it's something you do with someone you care about. So people think sex means love, and everyone wants to be loved."

"I think you've hit the nail on the head," Will said. "Now whether the relationship between love and sex is really strong intrinsically, or because we've been conditioned to think the two go together, is another question. We could talk about that a long time." Will rested his arms on the table.

"But I think there's another aspect to this question. Sexuality used to be considered a sacred thing. Not only was it about fertility, regeneration, and so on, it was also about transcendence, a way of reaching the Divine. If that's the case, then no wonder sex is a big deal. But organized religion has made sexuality into something that has to be condemned, controlled, proscribed—whatever. I think the current emphasis on sex is a perversion, whether it's wrapping women in burkas or stripping them down to bikinis." He reached for the last cookie.

"It's kind of like drugs. Drug use in indigenous societies is sacred, and now it's been perverted in our culture into recreation. I'd even go so far as to say that many religious practices are perversions—self-flagellation, fasting, looking at a cave wall for ten years.

"Oops! Sorry. Guess I kind of got on my horse about this! Must be tough having a professor for a grandfather," he said, sheepishly. Will got up and started putting food away. "You guys can hike without me this afternoon. I'm going to snooze in the hammock since I got my exercise on the bike this morning."

"I'll keep him company," Susannah decided. "I'm at a good place in my book."

*****

Drew's day pack already had his emergency stuff and a water bottle in it, and Gina added her bag of home-made cookies. The three young people left for the trailhead, not far from their campsite. They crossed a log bridge over the swiftly flowing creek and started up the trail, which rose and fell among the Doug fir and huckleberry brush along the western side of the lake. In some places it was quite steep, falling almost straight down to the rocky shore below.

They had not gone half a mile when stumbling down the trail toward them came a little boy about six years old, crying and calling for help. Paul was in front, and he knelt down and put his arm around the boy as he reached them. "What's up, buddy? Can we help you?"

He said through his tears, pointing up the trail, "My grandpa fell down the hill. I'm going to find my mama."

Drew's training kicked into gear. He too knelt down to the boy's level, and said, "Hey, it's gonna be all right. Show us where your grandpa is, and we'll help him." Gina reassured the child, and asked his name, which was Esteban. She gave him a cookie out of Drew's pack, took his hand, and they started back up the trail.

Drew led them at a fast pace, warning them to be careful of their footing. They were keeping watch for where the man might have fallen, not sure they would be able to see him from the trail.

About a hundred yards from where they met Esteban, they found a pack and could see that the downhill trailside bushes had been broken and crushed. It was very steep. They peered over the edge and could see, about thirty feet down, a crumpled shape at the water's edge.

"Dude, it's almost a vertical drop! He's probably unconscious. At least he didn't roll into the water. I've got enough line for us to get down, but we'd never get him back up. Paul, you shouldn't be trying to go down there with your weak leg. You've only been out of the walking cast a few weeks. I'm thinking that we could maybe get him out in a boat. Gina, are you willing to try to get down there with me while Paul takes Esteban and goes back to find someone with a boat?"

"I'm willing, Drew, but I don't know anything about search and rescue. Do you think I'll be able to help?"

"Sure," Drew answered. "I can tell you what to do, and when Paul gets back, we'll have more help."

To Esteban, he said, "This is Paul, and he'll go back to the campground with you and find your mama, and Gina and I will help your grandpa." To Paul, he said, "I've got a basic emergency kit besides the climbing line, but you should contact the rangers and tell them what's happened. I don't think our cell phones will work from here, but they might in the campground. Tell the ranger we're about half a mile from the trailhead. And don't hurry so fast that you trip! We probably can't hope for a stretcher, but bring a beach towel or blanket or something like that in the boat. Ask the ranger to call an ambulance."

Paul left immediately with the little boy. Gina and Drew began looking for something secure to which they could tie the line. The closest trees were so big that they would use up too much rope trying to get around them. Up the trail fifteen feet was a cedar with a diameter of about eight inches and what appeared to be firm roots. Drew tied the rope around the tree.

He went down first and then shouted up to Gina that the line was a little short and she'd have to drop the last four feet. Gina joined him within a few minutes, following his instructions on how to climb down the rope. The old man was barely breathing; he was very pale, unconscious, and bleeding from a gash on his head. His pulse was very weak and irregular. They also noticed that one arm was in an unnatural position and assumed it was broken.

Drew was thinking out loud. "This gash on his head doesn't look too bad. Head wounds always bleed like crazy, so they look worse than they are. I've got a butterfly bandage in here that should take care of it. Then maybe we can splint that arm while he's still out." Gina searched around and found some relatively straight tree limbs that they could use for a splint. They slit the man's shirtsleeve with a pocketknife and found that the broken bone had not come through the skin. Drew cut up several long strips of duct tape, and they managed to get the arm splinted. Then Gina began checking to see if a boat could get close enough to take the injured man aboard.

They were on a rock ledge, about three feet above the waterline. It appeared the water was deep enough to allow a boat to come alongside the ledge, but it wasn't clear how they would get the man into the boat. "We'll have to deal with that when someone gets here," Drew said. "It couldn't be worse than trying to get him up this hill and then back down the trail. I wish we had something besides my parka to cover him with." There was nothing to do but wait.

They had been sitting there nervously watching the old man for about fifteen minutes when he moaned and opened his eyes. Drew knelt close to him, took his hand, and told him that help was on the way. "Can you tell us how you feel?" he asked.

Barely audible, the old man whispered, "Chest hurts, hurts bad, hard to breathe."

"Just relax, if you can," Drew replied, trying to sound encouraging. "Try to think of something good. Help will be here in just a few minutes."

"Tell my family," the man whispered weakly, "I'm sorry. Tell them . . . I love them." He closed his eyes, continuing to breathe shallowly.

Drew frowned and looked across at Gina. He tapped his heart, and she nodded, chewing on a fingernail. Drew watched the old man's breathing and kept checking his pulse.

After a few minutes: "Shit, shit, shit! No pulse! Got to do CPR, Gina. Do you know how to do this?" he asked as he began the chest compressions.

"I've had the training a couple of times, but I don't know if I can do it right."

"I'll go as long as I can," he replied, "and then you can spell me, and I'll coach you. Just watch what I'm doing."

Then they heard boat engines. Dwayne and his ski boat barreled into view, carrying Paul and Rosalie, followed by a Forest Service boat. Paul called out to them that they had found a doctor in the campground, and she was in the boat behind them. The ranger piloting that boat pulled alongside the ledge so that Drew and Gina could help the doctor out of the boat. She had her bag with her.

"Hi, guys, I'm Helena Hammond. How long have you been doing CPR?" she asked, kneeling to see if she could get a pulse. Gina told her what the old man had said, that he'd then stopped breathing and they found no pulse, so they had started CPR less than five minutes ago. The doctor looked grim and said, "I'm pretty sure he's had or is having a heart attack, and we need to get him to the ambulance *now*. I think I've got a pulse—good work! Looks like his heart has started again." She opened her bag, rummaged around, and came up with a vial and a syringe, explaining that she was administering an injection to try to reduce the heart damage.

By this time, Rosalie was kneeling beside the unconscious figure; tears were running down her face and she was holding his hand. "Grandpa, Grandpa, why weren't you careful? We'll get you to the hospital soon—don't worry." She gave Dr. Hammond an imploring look. "Can't we do something?"

Dr. Hammond asked the ranger to try to contact the ambulance driver and let him know what they would be dealing with and to get to the boat launch ASAP. "OK, folks, let's get him into the boat. We need a stretcher or something like it," said Dr. Hammond.

"We've got a beach towel and duct tape," Drew said. "If we had two poles that were long enough and strong enough, we could make a litter, but we haven't been able to find anything that would work. What if we just get him onto the towel, and then four of us hold the ends and we lower him into the boat that way?"

"How about a boogie board?" asked Dwayne. "I've got one in my boat that's probably not long enough, but it's flat and not too heavy. We could put it on the towel, and Grandpa on the board, and lower the whole thing into the boat."

"Go for it, guys," said Dr. Hammond tersely. "We don't have much time." They got everything set, and while Rosalie and Gina held Dwayne's boat close to the ledge, Paul, Dwayne, the ranger, and Drew lowered the injured man carefully into the boat. Then they helped Dr. Hammond into Dwayne's boat, along with Rosalie; Gina and Paul got in the ranger's boat.

Drew told them to go ahead, that he'd hike back after collecting his gear. He made his way along the shore until he found a place where he could climb back laterally to the rope; then he hoisted himself back up to the trailside. Going up was a lot more work than coming down. It took Drew about ten minutes, totally focused on the climb. Reaching the trail, he gathered up his pack, unfastened the climbing rope, coiled it, and started back down the trail with the older gentleman's pack.

He moved as quickly as he could down the rock-strewn trail, which was crisscrossed with fallen trees and roots. After only a couple of minutes, he looked out at the lake and saw both boats dead in the water. It looked like the ranger was talking on a radio or cell phone, shielding his eyes from the sun as he faced the boat ramp. In the other boat, Dr. Hammond was kneeling over Rosalie's grandfather. As nearly as he could tell, she was giving CPR.

Not good, he thought, increasing his speed to a lope as he reached the more heavily used flat part of the trail. He could hear the siren in the distance. Then he saw that the boats had begun moving again. By the time he had run through the campground and reached the boat launch, the ambulance had arrived and was surrounded by a crowd of people. The rangers were clearing a path so that the vehicle could get out quickly. Drew found Paul and Gina standing beside Dr. Hammond at the back of the ambulance. They were just closing the doors.

"How's he doing?" Drew asked, out of breath.

"Not well," answered Dr. Hammond. "They'll try the defibrillator, but I'd be surprised if he makes it. Oh, I'm sorry for being so blunt. You're not his family, are you? I didn't think you were."

"No, we aren't family. We just found him on the trail and tried to help," Paul said.

"Well, you did a good job—the best that could be done, given the circumstances. You've been well trained."

*****

It was four o'clock by the time everyone was back at the campsite. Susannah and Will got a blow-by-blow description of the rescue attempt. The young people were strung out, tired and hungry. Susannah got out milk and the rest of the previous day's cake, and they ate and talked.

"Hello. Are you the folks that helped rescue the elderly gentleman?" A different ranger walked into their campsite, hat in hand.

"Yes, it was these young people," answered Susannah. "My grandsons and their friend."

"Well, I'm afraid I've got some bad news for you. I was at the gate when the gentleman's grandchildren drove out a few minutes ago. The young woman was crying, and she told me that her grandfather had a heart attack and they couldn't revive him. Sorry to bring you this news." He was turning his hat in his hands as he spoke. He nodded his head, turned, and left.

The occupants of campsite 312 sat silently at their picnic table. A happy camping trip had turned into something none of them would have imagined.

"I'll go see if Rosalie's friends are still around to help her family pack up, whenever they're ready to go," said Drew.

"I have to go," Gina said anxiously. "I'd like to stay and help, if there was anything I could do, but I'm expected for a babysitting job and my dad needs the car back."

"It's OK, Gina," Paul assured her. "I wish you didn't have to drive back alone after this bad news, but I need to stay and help break camp here tomorrow."

"I'll be all right," she told him. She said her good-byes to Susannah and Will, and Paul walked her to her car. He held her close, kissed her, and promised to call her the next evening.

The family had a late dinner and sat around the campfire afterward. Poking the fire with a stick, Paul said, "I feel guilty all over again! Just like I did when Ron died. I know it's not logical, but why are we alive when that guy is dead?"

No one answered immediately. Then Susannah said, "I don't think that question has a good answer, Paul. Whatever we might say is going to sound trite; it won't make us feel better. We just question and grieve until each of us finds a way to live with the reality of death." As they lay in bed that evening, each was immersed in his own thoughts. Drew, Susannah, and Will were remembering the anguish they felt in the hospital waiting room until they heard that Paul would not die from the car accident. Paul relived the memorial service for his friend Ron.

After breakfast the next morning, they began rolling up sleeping bags, putting clothes into packs, deflating the air mattresses, dismantling the tents, and doing all the other thousand tasks involved in breaking camp. They finished tying the kayak down and stuffed the few remaining items into the cars.

Paul and Drew were quiet as they drove down the Forest Service road toward the highway. Finally, Paul said, "You just never know what's going to happen! Two days ago we were planning a really fun trip, and we *had* a really fun trip, but now it all looks totally different. It's like parallel realities. How does that work, anyway?"

"I dunno, Bro. I dunno," Drew replied. "I guess stuff like this is going to be happening to us our whole lives. I mean stuff that doesn't seem to make sense. And then we've gotta make sense out of it somehow."

21 EXERCISES

They had a deal. Paul and Drew would go to yoga (which the boys thought was a little "girly") with Will, if he would go camping with them. Will's first car-camping trip was as cushy as promised, and now it was time for the brothers to attend yoga. They settled the date for a Sunday morning.

Will had suggested the boys eat a light breakfast, wear loose clothing, and show up at a quarter to ten so they could get all their props together and find a good spot. Sunday morning was a popular time at the studio he attended, and the room filled up early. He promised them pancakes at the IHOP afterward.

Drew appeared at the yoga studio at the appointed time to meet Will. Paul had declined at the last minute in favor of helping Georgina build a sandbox at the low-income day-care facility where she volunteered. Drew and Will went in, took off their shoes and socks, and picked up a mat, blanket, strap, and hard foam block. Drew was interested in their two dozen or so classmates, mostly women, but six or so men. Ages ranged from eighteen to eighty, and attire ranged from mismatched shirts and shorts to totally coordinated expensive yoga wear. Will introduced him to the instructor, Melinda, who promised to give Drew a little more explanation about the poses than she would normally give to the regulars.

They started out with *pranayama*—breathing exercises. Melinda explained that different methods of breathing affect the body's health and life force. In addition to deepening the yoga practice, learning ways to calm or invigorate the body through breathing would greatly benefit one's life in general.

She guided them through the steps of an elaborate exercise in which the participants alternate breathing through one nostril and then the other. Drew dutifully followed instructions, but it was all he could do to keep from bursting into laughter. Will was grinning beside him, imagining what Drew was thinking.

Then they went on to sun salutations. Melinda instructed them to stand in *Tadasana*, or Mountain Pose, with hands in a prayer position at the heart. "Bring the arms out to the sides and straight up beside your ears, with a slight backward curve in your back. Swan dive down, hinging at the hips. Lift up to a flat back, bend forward again; move into a low lunge, then into Downward Facing Dog Pose. Come forward to Plank Pose."

Drew was beginning to sweat. Melinda went on. "Drop your knees, chest, and chin; come forward to a low Cobra, back to Downward Facing Dog. Step to a low lunge, then forward bend into *Uttanasana*. Bring the arms out to the sides and up, reversing the swan dive to *Urdhva Hastasana*. Come to *Tadasana* with the hands in a prayer position at the heart. Now we'll repeat the entire sequence with the left leg."

They did a total of six sun salutations, and Drew was breathing hard and aware of his inflexibility and weak spots. Melinda led them through Triangle Pose, Warrior Pose, and shoulder stands, working her way through the class to correct pose positions and offer suggestions. By the time they had completed that session's routine and were resting in Corpse Pose, Drew was exhausted. They put away their props and walked to Will's car, talking about their experience.

"Dude, the chick in front of me was holding that Warrior Pose with no sweat, and my legs were shaking! And did you see her do that shoulder stand? Her legs just glided up into the air like . . . I don't know what. She made it look so easy. No wonder you're in such good shape, Will," Drew said. "This is a crazy workout!"

"You did pretty well with the girly stuff," Will told him. "You deserve a good breakfast."

As they worked their way through pancakes, eggs, and sausages, Drew asked Will where yoga came from. Will explained that it originated as a spiritual practice in what's now India. It could be done as purification before meditation, or it could be used as a means of transcendence in itself. Drew was used to his grandfather slipping into professorial mode.

"I don't know if I was transcending, but I sure wasn't thinking about anything else when I was trying to do that Warrior Pose. And then in that Corpse Pose, it was so relaxing after such a workout. My head was totally empty." He took another bite of pancake.

"You know what else? What amazed me," said Drew, "was that most of the exercises we do for soccer or aikido all seem to come from yoga. I had no idea we were doing yoga poses when we were doing all those stretches. But I gotta say, Will, that breathing stuff was weird!"

*****

With Elektra gone to a summer drama program at Yale and then to Europe with her family, Drew had more time on his hands than if she had been in town. He talked Will into an introductory backpacking trip. They would just go for one night, and Drew chose a scenic trail with a waterfall and not too much elevation gain. The Emorys had accumulated an enormous amount of outdoor equipment over the years, so Will would have the benefit of the latest gear, and Drew promised him gourmet camping meals.

A few days before they were to leave, Drew e-mailed Will a list of things he should bring, and a list of what Drew was bringing. He brought over a pack for Will the next day, so he could put everything in and see how much it weighed. He also brought a sleeping bag and pad, a camp stove and fuel, some nesting pans, a big lightweight water bottle, and a telescoping hiking stick. "I'll carry the tent and the food and the other heavier stuff," Drew told him.

The night before they were to leave, Will spread everything out on the living room floor and checked it off his list and Drew's list. He looked doubtfully at all the gear. "I'll never get all this stuff into that pack!" he told Susannah.

"You don't have to get it all inside," she said. "You can have things hanging off the outside. The sleeping bag and mat can be strapped on, so you have more room in the pack, and the water bottle goes in that little sleeve on the side. Besides, you don't need all those clothes, and Drew is taking a first aid kit, so you don't need one too." For years Susannah had watched her son Alex prepare for backpacking trips, so she knew all about it. And now the equipment was even more lightweight and high-tech.

They put everything in the pack, and Will was surprised to find there was room to spare. He put on the pack, fastened the bellyband, adjusted the straps, and decided he could probably manage. He took it off and set it by the door, ready for their early-morning departure. Susannah presented him with a little one-shot plastic bottle of Kahlua, and one of bourbon. "You and Drew will really enjoy these in the evening," she assured him. "They'll make your feet feel better."

*****

While Will and Susannah were packing, Drew was on his way to a party of college kids who lived in a rental house north of the university. He was going with Nikki, a jazz band friend, who had just graduated. She had picked him up, along with Sonja, another recent grad. Nikki had agreed to be the designated driver and to limit herself to a little pot for the evening. Her older brother, Neil, lived at the party house and had invited her.

Drew's parents had never outright forbidden their sons to do anything, but they had used a pretty persuasive combination of information and reasoning and picking their shots over the years, trying to keep their boys out of trouble. Hearing from other kids how their parents tried to control their offspring, Drew and Paul appreciated their folks. Sylvianne and Alex gritted their teeth when Drew went rock climbing or dangling from a rope in snow crevasses; they just told him to be careful and have fun. But he knew they would not want him to be going to a party with an older crowd where there were likely to be illegal substances.

They arrived about nine at a seedy looking house whose front yard hadn't been mowed in recent history. They were greeted by a guy in dirty jeans, a T-shirt and a man bun. "Hey, dude, you came with Nikki? She's really cool. I'm Jim, one of Neil's roommates; glad to meetcha. Booze is in the kitchen. I'm into martinis, just finished my third. I like 'em with olives," he babbled, waving toward the kitchen.

Drew wandered through the dilapidated house, wondering how anyone could study there, looking for Neil, and every now and then looking around for his friends, who had agreed to keep track of each other during the evening, just in case. With his looks and laid-back manner, Drew appeared much older than his seventeen years, and he was feeling a little smug to be passing for a college guy. It was kind of fun being where he wasn't supposed to be. The party was in full swing and crowded, but the vibe seemed to be pretty low-key. It wasn't quite what he expected, though; the guys looked more like a skate-park crowd than what he thought college guys would look like.

"Hey there, lookin' for someone?" asked a heavily made-up girl stuffed into tight jeans and a low-cut top.

"No one in particular," he answered, smiling at her uneasily.

"Well, I'm pretty particular, and you look pretty good to me," she told him, with a drunken leer. She had a cigarette in one hand and a beer tankard in the other.

Just then he felt an arm around his waist. "This one's taken," said Nikki to Ms. Makeup, smiling sweetly and pulling Drew away, into the crowd.

"Thanks for the rescue, Nikki," Drew said, laughing. "I was getting ready to tell her that I was looking for my boyfriend. Have you seen Neil?"

"Yeah," she said, "he's out in the back yard; he's saved you some mushrooms." They went through the crowded kitchen and out to the backyard, where they found Neil and some plastic lawn furniture and settled in. Two years older, Neil had been in the Outdoor Program when Drew and Paul had joined, and Drew felt he could be trusted.

*****

Because time seemed to stop and start after he ate the mushrooms, he had no idea how long they'd been there. Suddenly a gaseous, dark-red cloud appeared before him; it felt bad. He heard a male voice saying, "Come on, Nikki. I know you've got the hots for me—let's go upstairs." The owner of the voice grabbed her arm and tried to pull her out of the chair.

"Beat it, asshole!" she told him, jerking her arm away. He got more aggressive, trying again to pull her out of the chair.

The dark cloud in front of Drew got more lurid and swirled more wildly. He stood up, surprised to find himself a little woozy, but he drawled to the drunk, "Hey, dude, Nikki's with me. Why don't you just get yourself another drink and chill?" Faced with what looked like a light heavyweight boxer, the guy backed off, muttering something about coming back with friends.

"Let's get out of here," said Nikki. "Three hours of this is enough." Sonja had found someone she liked, who promised to drive her home, so Nikki took Drew's hand and they slipped out the back gate and walked down the alley toward the car. "You OK?" she asked him.

"Yeah, cool," he answered. "This stuff is really cool. Can't talk—too much to watch."

"I'm going to take you to my house until this stuff wears off," she told him, opening the car door and shoving him in.

*****

Drew arrived a few minutes late the next morning at his grandparents' condo, but he was ready to start packing. Into the car went Will's pack and walking stick and the muffins and sandwiches Susannah had made, then the gear and supplies that Drew brought. Will noticed that Drew seemed a little clumsy—he kept dropping things. Finally, the car was loaded, and they headed for the Cascades. The trailhead was only a ninety-minute drive, and there were a half-dozen cars in the lot when they parked. As they were putting on their packs, a couple of girls about Drew's age were also getting into their packs and preparing for the hike. Will and Drew started up the trail at an easy pace.

While they walked, Drew outlined his plan. "I figure we'll hike for a couple of hours, have lunch, and then hike for another couple of hours. That will get us near the waterfall, and there's a meadow nearby where there're lots of campsites."

Will was impressed with the sizable stream that ran alongside the trail. It was very cold and clear, with pools here and there big enough for a person to submerge his whole body. As they hiked up the trail and the day got warmer, he looked forward to putting his feet in the water. "Hey, Drew, have you ever heard of *misogi*?" he asked.

"Nope," said Drew.

"It's a Shinto purification ritual. You probably know that Shinto's Japanese, but you may not know that it's a very ancient religion. Nobody pays much attention to Shinto, compared to the much more popular Zen Buddhism, but when you get down to basics, all the great religions are about healing and enlightenment, they just come at it differently. Anyway, *misogi* is a ritual in which you purify yourself by dunking yourself in a stream or river or under a waterfall."

They followed the trail upward, with Will continuing his explanation of *misogi*. "Doing this immersion ritual is supposed to generate energy, a sense of renewal, lots of good things—through contact with nature. In Shinto, nature is the ultimate reality. The idea is that there's nothing more authentic than standing under a waterfall or in a stream and being immersed in nature. You don't know where your physical existence ends and the flow of the water begins. For a moment, you're one with nature, you're in pure experience."

"That's kind of interesting," Drew said, thoughtfully. "I felt like I was in pure experience when I was doing that Warrior Pose—at least I wasn't thinking about anything else! Maybe that's not the same kind of thing."

"Well, it's getting close," Will said. "The Sufis have whirling dervishes. Tantric yoga uses sex. People have come up with lots of different ways to get out of themselves and their limitations, or transcend themselves, to come into contact with the Divine. All the great religions have practices designed to help the person realize that contact, or connection."

"I bet I know where this is going, Will," Drew said. "You want us to do this *misogi* thing."

"Sure, why not?" Will said, grinning. "Didn't you say we're going by a waterfall? We can dunk ourselves in the waterfall or the river tomorrow morning and see what happens. You're supposed to meditate for a while before and after," Will added.

"Oh brother! Grams is teaching us meditation. You've got us doing yoga and jumping into ice-cold rivers. When do we get to try the sex thing? I could go for that kind of getting out of myself!"

They hiked and talked until it was time for lunch. Taking off their packs, they sat down on a log, just off the trail. "Drew, you can tell me to butt out, if you want, but, uh, you don't seem to be quite yourself this morning."

Drew looked surprised and said, before thinking, "I ate some mushrooms at a party last night. You won't tell Mom and Dad, will you?" asked Drew. "I don't plan to make a habit of this; I just wanted to try it, and I don't want them to worry."

"No, this discussion is just between us, if that's the way you'd like it. And don't forget I was young once too," said Will, grinning at Drew again. "I was in college in the sixties, and I experimented a little. Then when I was casting around for a PhD dissertation topic, I did some research on entheogenic drugs—drugs used for spiritual purposes, you know, peyote, cannabis, ayahuasca, certain types of mushrooms, and so on." Will dug around in his backpack and found an apple. "I was really into it, but my superiors decided that it wasn't an appropriate topic for my dissertation. Anyway, it was fascinating.

"Was this a spur-of-the-moment thing?"

Drew told Will that he'd done some online research about mushrooms and he knew they weren't addictive; he figured if he was with a sober friend who could look out for him, he'd be fine. "Man, it was something else! I felt like I was on another planet or something. And everything was so mellow, like I just faded into everything around me and everything faded into me. Except for this dirty red cloud at one point, the whole thing was positive. I wasn't scared at all." Drew glanced at Will now and then as he talked.

Will was listening carefully. "It sounds like you had a pretty good trip. But I have to confess to some worry. This is nothing to mess around with. Taking this kind of stuff at the wrong time in the wrong place—like when you're stressed or upset or with the wrong people—it can get really dicey. And I have a prejudice, Drew, which won't surprise you, since you know my background. I really don't like the idea of folks taking something meant to be used by specially prepared people for spiritual purposes, and turning it into a recreational drug. With that kind of thing going on, it's no wonder people have bad trips." Will stood up and stretched. "Are you going to tell any of your friends about this . . . experience?"

"Uh, I guess I haven't thought about it. It's not like I'd make a big deal out of it, or brag or anything."

"Well," his grandfather said, "I guess I'd recommend you not say much about it to anyone but maybe your brother. You don't know how someone else would react if they tried it, or whether they knew what they were doing going into it. The experience can vary a lot, depending on whom you're with. If people heard you say it was cool and you had no problems, they might try it but with very different results." Will put his candy wrapper back in his pack. "And I have to do my grandparent thing and remind you that it's illegal as hell! You get caught with this stuff in the wrong place at the wrong time, and it can screw up your whole life. I know you know that. Young people are going to try risky stuff—I did too. But it looks a lot different from my age than it does from yours. OK, I won't belabor the point. I know you've heard me."

*****

They were finishing their sandwiches and apples when the two girls they had seen in the trailhead parking lot caught up with them.

"That looks like a good idea," the lead hiker said. "I think we'll stop for lunch soon too."

"You're welcome to share our log," Drew offered hospitably. The girls looked at each other and seemed to communicate nonverbally. They both began unbuckling their packs.

"My name's Drew. This is Will."

Will volunteered, "He's my experienced trail guide, and I'm the tenderfoot. Never been backpacking before. Are you two old hands at this?"

"My name's Alicia, and this is my friend Kat. We've been hiking with our families since we were little, and in high school we got into orienteering. I'm sure you'll really enjoy backpacking," she told Will.

"How far are you going?" Drew asked.

"We're going to camp near the meadow, and then tomorrow we'll hike up to the pass, and then back out," replied Kat. "Where are you two going?"

Drew told the girls that they were also going to camp near the meadow, but they would have a lazy morning in camp, and start hiking out around eleven.

The two men got up and put on their packs. They started up the trail, with a farewell wave to the girls. After hiking and talking for another hour, they heard voices behind them. A group of five loud young men were coming up behind them. Will and Drew stood off the trail and let them pass, since the group was moving much more quickly.

"Not exactly a friendly bunch," remarked Will. "They didn't even say hi, or thanks for moving aside."

"They didn't look very well equipped either," Drew noted. "Pretty sketchy packs. I wouldn't want to get lost or hurt in *that* party. We can hope they'll camp somewhere far away."

Another hour's hiking brought them to the waterfall. The beautiful spot beckoned Will to stay for a while, but Drew thought they should go stake out their campsite first. They didn't know how many campers were already there, or how many more would come. So they continued for another five minutes and emerged from the trees into a valley with a meadow at about four thousand feet. There was one other party they could see, camped across the valley.

"Great: we have our pick of the spots! How about over there, away from the trail?" Drew pointed. "It'll get the last of the afternoon sun, and it's not far from the creek."

"Looks good to me—you're the boss," Will told Drew.

As they were unpacking their stuff and setting up the tent, Alicia and Kat hiked into the meadow, waved, and continued up the trail.

They laid out their sleeping bags and mats, applied another coat of bug repellent, and walked over to the stream. Two cans of beer went into the water to cool, while they took off their boots to soak their feet. "Well, I feel pretty good," Will said proudly. "I guess all that biking and yoga is paying off. I'll probably be too sore to move tomorrow, but I'm fine now."

"I'll bet you sleep really well tonight!" Drew said. "Tell me some more about this *misogi* thing, Will."

"OK, here's a little background. As I said, in Shinto, the emphasis is on the natural world, its power to heal, to strengthen, to enlighten. Nature itself is spiritual: plants, rocks, waterfalls, everything. The material world and the Divine are one. Most Westerners think of the Divine as invisible—what's behind nature or what made it. The visible and material, in Shinto, is more fundamental and real than the invisible and immaterial. *Misogi* is real experience, a purification that increases your awareness of nature as the Divine."

"I used to lie up in the tree house in our backyard, watching the clouds and the leaves and the cherry blossoms," Drew remembered. "I spent a lot of time in that tree house, when I was around four or five, I guess. Mom and Dad would read us stories about fairies. I used to think I saw fairies."

"That's possible," said Will. "I heard a piece on NPR a few years ago . . . or maybe I read it in the paper, about how in Iceland people still don't build in certain places because they are known to be places where gnomes or earth spirits live. They actually don't give building permits for those places, or they reroute roads around them. I thought that was really neat. You seem to be more open to this kind of stuff than a lot of people are, Drew. Why is that, do you think?"

Drew considered. "I don't know. I guess I'm just open to things. Just because people can't explain everything doesn't mean that things don't happen. I mean, maybe the old-time Japanese were onto something, and some people can still . . . experience it or whatever. But the people who can't experience it just deny that it happens. I'm up for the *misogi* thing. Even if nothing special happens, it'll make a good story."

*****

They took their beer and went back to their camping spot to start dinner, lugging a full two-gallon foldable plastic water container with them. While Will ran the water through the water purifier, Drew readied his little camping stove. He got out plates and sliced up cleverly packed tomatoes for each of them. While the pasta was cooking, he took a plastic container of frozen pesto sauce, which by now had thawed, out of his pack and also a bag of grated Parmesan. He strained the pasta, mixed in the sauce and cheese, and dinner was ready. They washed down their tomatoes and pasta with beer.

As they were cleaning up, they saw Alicia and Kat coming across the meadow. The two girls left the trail and walked toward their camp. Drew called out, "Hey, you just missed dinner, but we can give you some tea." The girls gave them anxious smiles, and asked if they could join them. "Sure, sure, no problem," said Drew. "Come sit down."

"A kind of weird thing happened, and we decided we didn't want to stay where we were," said Alicia. "We had chosen a camping spot near the stream, but not in view of the trail, and we were going to go skinny-dipping to cool off. The bugs aren't so bad up here, so we were down to our underwear when this old guy walks into our camp. He just stood there looking at us, about fifteen feet away. We started putting our clothes back on as quickly as we could, and Kat told him he was intruding, and asked him to leave. He didn't say a thing, just kept watching us."

Kat continued, "Then Alicia told him if he didn't leave, we were going to start yelling for help. We knew there was a party of guys up the trail and down the trail, and we told him someone would hear us. Then he just turned around and walked into the woods. It was really creepy! So, would you guys mind if we pitched our tent near you tonight?"

"No, we wouldn't mind," said Drew. "It sounds like that would be a good idea. Make yourselves at home."

"What did this guy look like?" asked Will.

"He was wearing a little knapsack," answered Alicia, "and a beat-up kind of Aussie hat, and his clothes looked dirty, like they hadn't been washed in a long time." She looked at Kat, who continued the description.

"He had a shaggy beard and looked like he was maybe in his seventies."

Drew attempted to reassure them. "Well, he was probably harmless, but he sure was out of line. I've hiked up here a lot, and so have my friends, and we've never heard of anyone having any problems. I'm sure you'll be fine here, anyway."

The girls had their tent pitched and their dinner ready in no time. The two parties shared their chocolate bars, cookies, and after-drinks, appreciated the moon and stars, and chatted until bedtime. Will folded first, announcing that the young people should talk as long as they wanted. He was sure he'd be dead to the world in five minutes. Kat crawled into their tent about thirty minutes later, and Drew and Alicia sat talking for another hour. They were both avid outdoors people. Alicia wanted to take the emergency medical technician training and do rescue missions. She was considering a fire-fighting job the next summer. Drew told her about carrying out the body of a hiker who'd fallen to his death, and she told him about bringing out a skier who'd got caught in an avalanche, but who had lived.

"Have you ever asked yourself why you like to do this stuff, or has anyone else asked you?" Alicia inquired.

"Hmm," Drew said. "No, I've never thought about it. I just like it. Why do you like to do it?"

She *had* thought about it. "Lots of reasons. It's exciting. It's different. Not that many girls get into it big-time. You get to help people. Also, it sort of makes me feel like I'm in control; you know what I mean? I feel like if I get into a tough spot, I'll have some ideas and some confidence to help me out. I won't get stuck in the 'helpless female' role."

Drew was thinking about the girls moving their camp to be close to helpful males, when she went on, "It's not like I think I can handle *everything*. You've always got to be asking yourself what's the best thing to do. Like that weird guy. We could have just stayed where we were and slept with our jackknives in hand or something. But how much fun would that be, just to prove something? I figured it was better to be safe than take a chance."

"Yeah, what's that saying? 'Discretion is the better part of valor.' Makes sense to me. And I agree with your reasons for liking the hiking and rescue stuff. I feel the same way. I'd add one more thing. I really get off on being in the mountains . . . or boating, or in the desert. Any kind of nature experience."

"Sounds like we've got a lot in common," Alicia replied. "Well, I think I'd better turn in. I'm tired. See you in the morning."

"Sleep well," he said. Drew thought Alicia had a really nice voice, not loud but distinct, or definite, or something. He couldn't put his finger on it, but he liked it. He went to bed.

*****

Will shook his shoulder the next morning about six and whispered, "Rise and shine; time to do our thing." Drew sleepily pulled his fleece over his sweatshirt, put on his shoes, and dragged his sleeping bag out of the tent behind him. During dinner the night before, they'd planned their *misogi* adventure. Drew followed Will to the stream where Will had scouted out a special place, with pools big enough for a person to completely submerge.

Will spoke quietly. "We'll meditate for ten minutes, then strip down and get into our pools. Face the sun, dip completely under, and stand up. Then repeat the dip two more times at your own pace. We won't talk, and we'll be paying attention to what happens

185

internally. For example, do you have a vision or an image, do your thoughts stop, or do they just intensify? If you have thoughts, what are they about? Do you have emotions? Just pay attention as best you can. There aren't any expectations—no way to do this right or wrong. Whatever happens is fine. When you're done, get dried off and into your bag, and meditate for ten minutes more." Drew nodded, and they settled into their first meditation.

About ten minutes later, Will touched Drew on the shoulder. The men took off their clothes and waded into the ice-cold water. Will had a calm look on his face and immersed himself immediately. Drew stood in the water with his eyes closed for a few seconds before following suit. He waited longer than Will between dips and stayed immersed a bit longer. The water part of the ritual took no longer than three minutes, and then they were wading back to the stream bank. Teeth chattering, they pulled on their clothes and got into their sleeping bags without saying a word.

Will meditated for another fifteen minutes and then got up quietly and walked back to their campsite, carrying his sleeping bag. Drew stayed about fifteen minutes longer. When he opened his eyes, he was looking at an old man with a scraggy beard, who was sitting across the stream and watching Drew intently.

The man said, "Powerful stuff."

"You ever done this?" Drew asked, returning his stare.

The man nodded. "And walking on hot coals, ten-hour meditation sits, shamanic journeying, drugs, other stuff. I've tried it all."

"What did you find out?"

"That people think I'm crazy. But you found out something, didn't you?"

"Yeah, I did. How did you know?"

The man didn't answer. He stood up and disappeared into the trees.

Drew got up to return to camp. Then he noticed Alicia, sitting half-hidden in the trees behind him. He bushwhacked through the huckleberry and salal to where she was sitting and sat down beside her.

"Did that guy scare you?" she asked. "I was ready to start yelling if he had come across the stream or tried anything."

"I was kind of startled when I opened my eyes and saw him there, but right away I felt like I didn't need to be afraid."

"I was awake when you and Will left. I'm terribly curious and when I saw you walking off with your sleeping bags, I couldn't resist following. That was pretty impressive to watch. I hope you don't mind that I watched—I didn't want to butt in. It seemed like some kind of religious thing."

"It's called *misogi*. It's a Shinto purification ritual that's s'posed to get you to God, or at least beyond yourself . . . or something. My grandad's a professor of comparative religion, and he talked me into trying this. Grams is big on meditation, so we get a big dose of this kind of stuff in our family. It's pretty interesting."

Alicia twisted a strand of her long hair around her finger, around and around, while Drew fiddled with his shoelaces. Finally, she said, "I think it's neat that you did this with your grandfather. A lot of guys wouldn't be caught dead with their grandfathers, let alone take them camping. And this ritual. It's kind of macho—it takes guts to get in that cold water. But at the same time, it's not macho—it's spiritual, or whatever." She looked at him approvingly, and smiled.

"Well, it sure makes a guy hungry." Drew laughed. "I'm ready for breakfast!"

They walked back to their tents, where Will and Kat were drinking hot chocolate and beginning breakfast. Will had retrieved the food bag from the tree where they'd hung it to keep it away from animals, and he'd figured out how to start the stove. He was frying bacon. Kat was mixing up pancake batter.

"Hey, Will, guess who showed up for *misogi* after you left? Mr. Shaggy Beard."

"What were you guys talking about?" Alicia asked. She looked shamefacedly at Will. "I was watching your ritual from a distance, but I was too far away to hear the conversation."

"You talked to this guy, Drew?" asked Will.

"Yeah, he's some dude. He told me he'd tried a lot of different spiritual practices: walking on hot coals, drugs, all kinds of stuff. Then he just left. Weird!"

The girls ate their pancakes with applesauce, cleaned up, and packed a small rucksack for their hike to the pass. "Maybe we'll see you before we all leave," said Alicia. "If not, it was fun camping with you!"

Will and Drew scrambled some eggs to eat with their bacon, and then went on to pancakes, finishing with oranges. Drew began telling Will about his *misogi* experience.

"Kind of an interesting thing happened when we were doing that *misogi*, Will. I sort of blanked out. I mean, I was aware of where I was, but there weren't any thoughts. It was just real quiet. I didn't even hear the water. Then after, when I was sitting in my bag, I started shaking. It wasn't the cold; it was something else. I had this sense of huge power, like a volcano, or lightning striking right next to me. It was so much power, it was scary, but at the same time, it wasn't scary. Or it was OK that it was scary. I'm not explaining this very well. It was pretty strange."

"Well, I'd call that getting beyond yourself, wouldn't you? Looks like *misogi* works! I'm not going to try to explain what I think that was all about, Drew. But I encourage you to remember it and think about it, and pay attention to whether you look at things differently after it than you did before. With all this spiritual stuff, it's not what happens while you're doing it, it's not the experience that matters. In fact, it's easy to get caught up in the flashy stuff, if you have that, and to kind of get a "spiritual ego," so to speak. What really matters is how your life changes as a result of the spiritual experience or practice."

Drew was quiet, taking in what Will had said. Then he continued, "I didn't want to bring it up in front of the girls, but that guy, Mr. Shaggy Beard, he seemed to know I experienced something. When I finished meditating and opened my eyes, there he was." Drew recounted his conversation with the stranger.

"Hmm," said Will thoughtfully. "This is really fascinating! Maybe this guy just fried his brains on drugs. Or maybe he's really got some kind of spiritual perception. When you read about people who've had 'enlightenment experiences,' they're all over the place. Some of them are pretty crazy, but some seem ordinary, except they all have some kind of *knowing*. They've had some kind of awakening or an experience that the rest of us could have, but haven't had."

"Why don't more of us have these . . . awakenings?"

"Oh, lots of reasons. We don't try. We don't know how to try. We don't believe in awakenings. It's too hard. But I think that's what life's all about—waking up to what's *really* real, not just what you think is real."

They had a lazy morning, making a lunch for the trip out, journaling, taking photos, reading, and then packing up.

As they hiked back down the trail, Drew said, "Will, do you ever think about why things happen like they do? I mean, just think,

Grams might not have remarried, or she could have married someone else, and then we wouldn't have known you. And then who would I talk to about mushrooms and *misogi* and gnomes and whirling dervishes and . . . volcano experiences . . . or whatever that was?"

"Yeah, sometimes I think about things like that too, Drew. Finding your grandmother was one of the most important things that ever happened to me. What if we'd been on different planes and never met, or what if she didn't like me? Sometimes everything seems so random, doesn't it? On the other hand, how could it be random? Some things just seem meant to be."

"Well, I couldn't give a very logical explanation, but random just doesn't cut it for me."

They hiked on down the trail, homeward bound.

22 FUTURE TENSE

Paul and Gina hadn't seen nearly as much of each other that summer as they wanted. They both had summer jobs with odd hours and only managed to get together every week or two. She had been nannying, and her employers had taken her with them for three weeks to Hawaii. And now she was leaving the following Monday for Dartmouth.

They lay side by side on their beach towels at Golden Gardens Park, soaking up the late August sun. "Paul, could I ask you a favor? I'm a little embarrassed . . . this is going to sound weird."

"Shoot—it's OK," he replied.

"Would you have sex with me? I've never done it, and I want the first time to be with someone I care about, and not just a, you know, a hookup. I know we're not really going together, and we're headed in different directions in a few days, and I'm not expecting any kind of commitment from you or anything like that." She had been playing with the corner of her beach towel, and she glanced up at him.

He was dumbfounded, totally at a loss for words.

"If you don't want to, it's fine. I know you weren't expecting me to say something like this . . ." She was blushing and looking out at the water.

"Jesus, Gina! Yeah, I'm surprised, but it's not like I don't want to. Don't think that. It's not like it hasn't crossed my mind about seven hundred times!"

She smiled a little, relieved to hear these sentiments.

He rolled onto his side, propped his head on his hand, and ran his other hand up and down her bare arm. He smiled at her and said, "I'm pretty flattered. You must think I'm quite the stud. Is that why I'm getting this offer?"

She knocked him over on his back and began tickling him. "Don't get too full of yourself!"

They laughed and wrestled, and he finally got hold of her wrists, so she had to quit. They looked at each other, both of them turned on by their nearness and what they were contemplating.

"The thing is, Gina, having sex really amps things up. We're already more than friends, and going all the way might change things. This might make separating a lot harder."

"I've thought about that a lot, Paul. This is how I see it. We could do this, and I'd have one of the most important experiences of my life with a guy I like and respect and who likes and respects me. I hope you'd enjoy it; I'm a little nervous, but I expect to enjoy it."

She stopped for a moment and then said, in a different tone, "You know, this doesn't sound like I intended; this sounds so . . . calculating. It sounds like I'm using you, like I'm trying to trap you." She had tears in her eyes now. "Forget it, Paul. I care about you too much to have you think I'd just use you. Just forget I ever brought this up." She turned away from him and hid her face in her hands.

People sitting nearby or walking past them would see two healthy young bodies, tan and lithe, his arm around her, the discreet tears, the trembling smile of one, and the reassuring smile of the other. Onlookers might imagine a little tiff, a misunderstanding, but would assume they'd get over it. They were so much in love, so beautiful to behold.

They had fish and chips at Ivar's on the way back to Paul's house. Drew was backpacking, and Paul's parents were away for the weekend. Gina left a message for her dad that she might stay with a friend that evening, so not to worry if she didn't come home. They smiled at each other over their fish and chips, but conversation was a little stilted.

Gina had been at the Emorys many times, but had never been in Paul's room. It was tidy, bed made, a heaping basket of clean clothes overflowing on the floor, photos on the wall, including one of their group at the prom. Books on the bedside table. It was dusk; the room was just dimly lit.

He put his arms around her and kissed her. She slid her arms around his neck and kissed him back. Then she pulled back and said, "Um, before we go any further, I want you to know I went to Planned Parenthood and got a diaphragm and some condoms." She rummaged around in her bag and pulled out a box of condoms. He pulled a box out of his nightstand drawer. They both laughed.

He pulled her close again. "Well, we're prepared, anyway. Uh, this is kind of awkward. Did you have something in mind, Gina? Something you wanted to do or me to do? You know, I haven't really done this all that much, so I'm almost as much of a novice as you are."

"That's OK with me." She smiled at him shyly. "I've read so many romantic novels, and seen so many sex scenes in movies. It seems like there's lots we could do. I just want us both to enjoy it. You said earlier that you'd thought about having sex with me. Just do what you thought you'd like to do. And I will too." She kissed him.

Five days later she was gone.

*****

Paul's lifeguarding job was down to weekends after Labor Day, and ended in mid-September. He was patiently going through his room, deciding which things he wanted to take with him to the dormitory at the U, which things he wasn't sure he was ready to part with, and which things he knew he could dispose of. His mom came in and sat on the bed, watching him. "Good for you; you'll be so glad you did this. It seems to get harder as you get older, or maybe you just have less time to think about it and more pressing things to do."

"It sure brings up a lot of memories. Mostly good stuff." She noticed the dried rose from the senior prom, tucked behind the prom photo.

He looked up from his desk drawers and smiled at her, then went back to his sorting. "Guess I'd better keep at this."

"Dad's making steaks tonight, with corn on the cob." This was one of his favorite meals.

"Great," he said, without his normal enthusiasm. "I'll look forward to that." Sylvianne left as he kept sorting. He put the hand-made thank-you card from the Desert School staff in the save pile, along with the program from Ron's memorial service and the programs from plays he'd been in. He gathered up all the photos of him and Gina, the program from Pam's play, and his dried-out prom boutonniere, slipped them into a big manila envelope, and put them in the bottom of a drawer.

Sylvianne went into the kitchen where Alex was preparing the steak marinade. She hugged him around the middle, tears in her eyes. "He's so sad; it's all I can do to keep from bursting into tears."

Alex put down the soy sauce and laced his arms around her. "I know, Honey. It's hard to watch. You want them to be happy every minute, but you know life isn't that way. I just keep telling myself that he and Gina had something wonderful together, and there will be other loves in their lives. You don't want to skip the good parts because you're afraid of the bad parts. Right?"

"Yes, I know, but it's still hard to watch."

"It'll be better once he moves into the dorm. Lots of new people, stimulation, challenges. He'll still miss her, but the distractions will make it less painful."

After dinner, Drew and Paul sat in the backyard, drinking beer and talking in the warm summer evening. "You getting excited about starting at the U?" Drew asked.

"Yeah, I'm looking forward to it . . . I know it'll be fun and stimulating, once I get there. But right now I'm more—I guess *aware* is the word—of what I'm leaving, what's over with. I guess high school graduation is—what do they call it—a rite of passage for Americans? So now I'm on to another phase of my life. It's hard to imagine that I won't see many of the friends I've had for years. Some I'll see now and then, some maybe never. So that's kind of weird."

"But the really good friends you'll see again, like Gina."

There was a long pause while Paul took another drink of beer. "Well, we've agreed not to try to get together for a while. We think it would be too hard. We know we can't keep something going long-distance, and we're too young to make a decision about staying together, so it's over."

"Jesus, Paul! I didn't know. I just figured you'd see each other at Christmas, and maybe things would, like, wind down over time, or something."

"We decided that would be prolonging the agony, so we're going 'cold turkey.'" He stopped for another drink. "I was kind of afraid something like this would happen. We slept together right before she left. We knew it might make it harder to break up, and dude, has it! I will *never* forget that night, no matter who I end up with in the long run! She was so . . . free, so . . . what's the word I want, so uninhibited. I just couldn't believe it. She said it was because she trusted me . . ." He paused, a faraway look in his eyes.

"I had no idea it would be this painful to break up. But when I ask myself if it was worth all the pain, I have to say yeah, totally."

They sat in silence for a time.

"Elektra and I have never gone all the way," said Drew, drawing figures in the condensation on his beer can. She's definitely into making out, kissing and touching, but at a certain point, it's like she turns off or something. She's had sex a few times, but she decided, as she puts it, 'it's not all it's cocked up to be.'" They both laughed.

"She does have a way with words, doesn't she?" said Paul.

"Yeah, she sure does. Anyhow, the way she described it, it sounded to me like she got fucked. Not raped, but none of these jerks was making love to her; they were just 'getting some.' She said she felt used. I want to make love with her, but she thinks when somebody says 'making love,' he means fucking. She doesn't get the difference. For someone who's so sophisticated in so many ways, she's kind of . . . out of it, or naive, or something, in other ways." They again sat without talking for a while.

"It's hard to know what to do, isn't it?" Paul said. "You know you're not going to have a long-term relationship or marry everyone you have sex with. Part of the reason for having sex before you settle down is to know if you'd be compatible in that way. But once you do it, things seem a lot more serious, and ending things seems harder. I guess that's why some people are so casual about sex. They don't want the emotional stuff that goes with it."

"I don't know, but I think it's pretty hard to have sex without the emotion, without the caring. People sure try hard to do it that way. Dude, just look at all the porn, and how sex is used to sell stuff. Still, even with all the casual sex in movies, everybody wants a happy ending with people caring about each other. Even if they start out just having sex, they fall in love or something." Drew looked up at the moon, which was becoming brighter as they sat talking.

"Elektra will be back next week. I can hardly believe it's been almost three months. Time's dragged and it's flown at the same time. We can hardly wait to see each other. A phone call or an e-mail every day or couple of days doesn't really do it. Anyhow, I don't know what will happen with Elektra. I don't know if she'll overcome her . . . whatever it is about sex, or not. I don't know if she'll trust me. But if she's willing, I'm going for it, even if that makes it harder when we . . . if we . . ."

Another silence. Then Paul said, "I've been thinking about this year a lot lately. Cleaning out my room brings back a lot of stuff. Ron's death and how close I came to dying, and how weird it is that I don't think about it as much anymore. Does that mean I really don't care about what happened, that it didn't affect me much? And all the people I knew or met who seemed to care about the wrong things. Like Jennifer who broke up with me because she found somebody richer. Or Mrs. Carpenter, that chaperone who was ready to lynch me for something I didn't do. Not to mention Gene and that whole transcript mess."

"Yeah, there was a lot of bad-ass stuff that happened this year. I've thought about it a lot too. Elektra scared the shit out of me when she had that bipolar . . . whatever it was. I had to tell her dad, even though I knew she didn't want me to. And that run-in with James, and what might have happened . . . At least Shaunee's got some good possibilities, even though her grandmother doesn't have long to live."

"Man, I've thought about all this a *lot*," said Paul. "And I finally decided you gotta do the things that matter, even if it's hard when you're doing them or when they're over." Paul looked at his brother in the dusky summer light.

"Yeah, Bro, I'm with you on that. You gotta do the things that matter. Even though, like Grams and Will said, you have to think about what they are your whole life."

OTHER BOOKS BY DIANN SHOPE

The Upper End Of In Between was published in late 2015. It's the story of Paul and Drew's grandmother, Susannah, and begins when they are babies. Here's a summary:

Widowed, introspective, attractive, and witty, Susannah Emory's problem is that she can't be content with an easy life. Living in Seattle at the upper end of middle age, she asks, "Now what?"

She loves to dance, she rows crew, she's a serious meditator—but there's a blank space in her life that she'd like to fill with a relationship. Filling that space will require dealing with modern dating and sexual mores, ageism, and her own insecurities.

Maybe it will be Peter, a jack-of-all-trades who lives on a houseboat. Maybe it will be Marty, a cardiologist who loves art and music. Maybe it will be Will, a former priest who's a popular professor at the university.

To paraphrase Bette Davis: "Aging is not for sissies." This is a novel about love in later life, about how difficult it is to overcome old ways of thinking and being and to live more fully. And also about the rare satisfaction of learning that one has wisdom to share and that others are helped by hearing it.

Diann's third novel, *Living Arrangements*, is expected in 2017; here's a synopsis:

How many people in their early seventies would buy a house and move in with people they've only known for about a year? How would they decide on the house, what color to paint the kitchen, who gets which bedroom, what to eat? How do these seniors manage yoga, sex, love, service, and companionship along with physical decline, grief, and loss? It's their *Living Arrangements*.

ABOUT THE AUTHOR

Diann Shope has lived in Seattle for forty-nine years with her husband, having moved here shortly after they married. They grow pears, raspberries, blueberries, and grapes in addition to the usual flora of an urban lot. Her husband is a marine surveyor, and when he's not surveying, he tends the house and garden and makes grape juice and wine. Diann makes a lot of jam. They're lucky to have their two sons living in Seattle with their families—who eat a lot of jam. Diann and her husband have traveled in Romania, France, Ireland, Greece, Finland, and Scotland. And they're active in supporting Waldorf Education. Diann got her degrees in international relations from Lewis and Clark College in Portland, Oregon, and the University of Denver.